MORE THAN BLOOD REVEALS

BASED ON A TRUE CRIME

MORE THAN BLOOD REVEALS

DIANE THEILER • BECKY KELLEY • JEAN KINSEY

Acclaim Press™
MORLEY, MISSOURI

Acclaim Press
— Your Next Great Book —

P.O. Box 238
Morley, MO 63767
(573) 472-9800
www.acclaimpress.com

Book Design: Samantha Poindexter
Cover Design: Rodney Atchley

ISBN: 978-1-948901-45-1 | 1-948901-45-5
Library of Congress Control Number: 2019949301

First Printing 2020
Printed in the United States of America
10 9 8 7 6 5 4 3 2 1

This publication was produced using available information.
The publisher regrets it cannot assume responsibility for errors or omissions.

Contents

Acknowledgments

We would like to acknowledge all the people who helped us by selflessly contributing their time, materials, and knowledge in our endeavor to create this book. You have our sincerest thanks. We hope we remembered everyone.

We owe much gratitude to the Logan County Library, The News Democrat, and the ladies at the Logan County Archives for going above and beyond their duty to help us locate over fifty-year-old data. We also wish to give credit to Michael Morrow of the African American Heritage Center for furnishing us copies of the FBI files pertaining to this case.

Jesse Riley, Judge Fuqua, and Attorney Lyne graciously shared memories and legal knowledge of the actual case. A special thanks to A.B. Wilhite and Don Neagle for inviting us to the radio program, "Feedback." We also offer our appreciation to everyone who called in to the program.

We wish to acknowledge and thank the following individuals for their assistance in gathering information for our book: Buddy Price, Pete Lehman, Marvine (Pogue) Hunt, Ms. Forgy, daughter of Lewis Forgy, James Penrod, Mr. Forgy's son-in-law, for giving us vital information about the case and allowing us to use their name. Also, a big thank you to Jeanette Shemwel for providing us with Logan County phone contacts.

Dedication

We dedicate this book to Kim Clack without whose persistence it would have never been written. Thank you for pushing us until we saw the importance of the book as much as you did.

Prologue

In a certain area of Logan County, members of the community go out of their way to avoid the dark and twisted road that leads to Martin Cemetery. The stories are a bit vague, but for those who experience the otherworldly happenings, traveling near Peach Orchard Road makes their hearts race.

Stories abound of a floating apparition of a lady searching into the night; for what, no one knows. Many have heard a woman's scream, a man's raised voice, and whispers. But when they went to investigate, nothing was found. A raven is said to follow visitors around the small graveyard. Others claim to have heard tires speeding on gravel, where neither gravel nor tires exist.

Some paranormal experts suggest when people leave the earth suddenly, their souls are left to wander the spot, unknowingly dead, trying to get back home. Residents of Logan County think they know who the man and woman are. They are the souls of Edgar Carroll Harper and Ella Mariah Harper Givens.

Edgar Harper and his daughter, Ella, were kidnapped in December of 1965. Their bodies were found the following March hidden close to the rarely used Martin Cemetery.

Only the killer or killers are certain of what happened that night. Though some were arrested and put on trial, one even pled guilty to robbery, many believe the entire truth never came out.

More than Blood Reveals was written to take a deeper look at the Harper/Givens murder case, go through the evidence, or lack thereof, read through the case files and conduct interviews with some of the major players. The authors hope to pull all the pieces together to determine what may have happened that cold day in December. At the end of the book, the three authors all separately write what they believe happened.

Though the book is based on factual events and evidence, the book itself is a work of fiction. The three Clack sisters do not exist except in the writers' imaginations. They inserted their own ideas as to why things happened or what might have been said through the persona of these three fictional characters. They have no idea why Edgar and his daughter were killed, and can only speculate on several scenarios. The FBI and the police worked the case for many years and they, too, never found the definitive answers to the questions surrounding the deaths of Edgar Harper and Mrs. Ella Givens.

It makes one wonder—what did happen that day in 1965....

BASED ON A TRUE CRIME

MORE THAN BLOOD REVEALS

Chapter 1

December 12, 1965

Ida Clack lay awake, eyes closed, trying to catch a few more minutes of precious sleep. "Take care of Eustice," a voice whispered.

She bolted upright and looked around her empty bedroom. Was that Ella's voice? Ida grabbed her robe and ran down the stairs where her sister Jane sat at the red Formica table drinking coffee. She pulled back the living room curtains and ran nervous fingers down the windowpane. A shiver inched down her spine, gently shaking the pink chenille robe. "I feel something strange in the air this morning—one of those feelings."

"You say that all the time." Jane waved her hand dismissively. "What's going to happen in a town of less than six hundred people?

The rain pounded so against the windows—kept me awake. I've never seen such a hard December rain. I'm telling you now, something is going on right here in Lewisburg, Kentucky."

"Oh, you're probably still tense from that nerve-shattering ball game last night. Looks like we may be going to the state tourney after all."

"That's not it." Ida shook her head. "So much violence on the news. The Vietnam War and all those riots and protests."

Jane sat her coffee on the shiny table. "The world has had violence since Cain killed Abel. There's no such thing as a perfect time in history." Jane pointed a finger toward Ida. "And another thing..."

"Girls." They both jumped as their older sister approached. "Are you two at it already? And on a Sunday morning? You should be ashamed of yourselves."

"Well, we were talking about Adam and Eve." Jane winked at Ida.

"Ida had one of her feelings."

A knock interrupted them.

"I'll get it." Jane hurried to the door.

"Good morning, Miss Clack."

"Why, Eustice Givens. I haven't seen you in a coon's age. How are you?"

"Fine, just fine."

Ida looked him over from where she stood at the window. His tight-lipped smile and taut shoulders stated everything wasn't fine.

What on earth would bring him to their door on a Sunday morning?

"Give my sisters a minute to get decent and come in for a cup of coffee."

"Thanks, but I can't. Just came to get Ella and Edgar so we can head off to Bowling Green. We have a big day planned."

"Ella and Edgar? They aren't here." She turned her head and glanced around as if to make sure.

"They have to be," Eustice said. "I've checked with all the other neighbors."

"Maybe they went for a drive. Looks like the sun is going to come out after all the rain has kept everyone cooped up."

"The car's still in the garage." Eustice looked around behind Jane, as if she might be teasing him for some reason. His eyes came back to hers, and he started to shake. "Where's my Ella?"

"Jane," Minnie said softly from behind her. "Run over and get Lewis Forgy. He can help Eustice look around the house."

"Good idea," Jane said and rushed out the door.

Minnie pulled her robe a bit tighter. "Eustice, have you called the hospital?"

"No, but Ella would have called me if anything would have..."

"Ida," Minnie whispered, "call the hospital, just to make sure." She turned back to the distraught man. "Don't worry Eustice, we'll get things figured out."

He didn't seem to hear her, turning to look up and down Henry Street. He started in one direction then rushed in the opposite back toward the Harper house. "I need to find Ella."

"I'll get dressed and be right there," Minnie shouted at his back. She shed her robe and left the kitchen.

Ida picked up the phone and dialed the hospital. "Lucy, I'm trying to find out if an ambulance came in some time during the night with a man named Edgar Harper. You're not sure? Would you connect me to the emergency room so I can check, please? Thank you." Ida covered the receiver. "Hurry Minnie," she called out. "We'll be going to church before long."

Her voice floated down the stairwell. "I'm hurrying."

"Hello? Yes, Chris, is that you?" Ida picked at a loose thread on her robe. "Chris, it's Ida Clack, the nurse from the fifth floor. Could you tell me if a Mr. Edgar Harper or Mrs. Ella Givens came to the emergency room last night? Yes, I'll wait." She drummed her fingernails on the gold-flecked countertop. "No? Okay, thank you." Ida hung up the phone and lifted the curtain to stare at the Harper house. Jane was right. Bad things didn't usually happen in the tiny town of Lewisburg, Kentucky. She didn't share every time she had one of those feelings, but her feelings were almost never wrong.

Minnie, dressed and ready to go, hurried down the stairs. "What are you doing?"

Ida turned from the window. "Just seeing if I can make out anything from here. They didn't go to the hospital."

The door slammed. Jane leaned against it trying to catch her breath. "I sent Mr. Forgy over."

"Good, I'll go see what I can find out. You two stay here." Minnie ordered.

"I'm going." Jane insisted. "I want to know what's happening too, plus, my boyfriend's a police officer. I might be able to find some clues to solve the case."

"Sometimes I think you started dating a deputy just so you could find out how police investigations go—and to get the inside scoop on anything happening in all of Logan County."

"That's not so. I love Frank," Jane said.

"Just stay here and finish getting ready for church."

She grabbed a jacket and headed out the door.

"Do you believe her?" Jane huffed. "Who does she think she is? I am not going to miss the first real mystery in these parts. Minnie will just have to deal with it." She ran out the door and headed across the street.

Ida looked down at her nightgown. She wasn't going anywhere until she got dressed. She'd let her sisters do the investigating.

***

Jane accepted the harsh look when she appeared at the Harpers. "You're trying to get a story for one of your columns." Jane hissed.

"That's not even entered my thoughts," Minnie shot back. "Eustice doesn't need curiosity seekers at the moment. Go home."

"Don't play the bossy older sister with me. I've as much right to be here as you."

Minnie didn't say a word. Instead she gave a firm knock on the door. Eustice jerked it open expectantly with Mr. Forgy right behind. Eustice's face fell.

"Have you found anything?" Minnie asked.

"No, nothing. The beds don't look like they've been slept in. Breakfast wasn't started." Eustice's voice cracked, but he continued. "I called the hospital to make sure they didn't take Edgar by ambulance; he's got that heart condition, you know."

"Yes, yes. I remember."

"They weren't there."

Jane's mind sped through the clues Eustice listed. She looked around but didn't see any tire tracks or footprints. The rain must have washed them away. "Did you find any muddy footprints in the house?"

Eustice shook his head. "Why?"

"Just thinking. I wonder..."

Minnie turned with a stern warning in her eyes. "Pay no attention to Jane's overactive imagination."

"I was thinking it might be time to call the police," Eustice stated.

"Yes," Minnie agreed. "It will take a little while for Sheriff McMillen to get here from Russellville."

"I'll do that right now," Eustice started to close the door, then pulled it open. "Do you want to come in and wait?"

Jane bounced up the stoop. "Yes, thank y..."

Minnie grabbed her arm. "No, no, we'll be leaving in a few moments," said Minnie. "We'll check on you again after church."

"Okay, thanks."

Wet leaves stuck to their shoes as they made their way back to the house. "I think God would understand if we missed church. We should stay and help our neighbors."

"Jane, we would only be in the way. And besides, we wouldn't want to mess up any evidence before the police arrive."

"Why did it have to rain last night?" Jane grumbled.

"What are you talking about?"

"The rain. It washed away any footprints and tire tracks that might have been left in the yard."

"Why did you ask about muddy footprints in the house?"

"Well, if something happened after it started raining and someone came in the house, there would have been muddy footprints inside," Jane explained.

"Now I understand why you want to work for the police. You're really good at this. Maybe they'll hire you after you retire from teaching." Minnie stepped into the mud room and sat on the blue bench to slip off her rain boots. The blue cashmere coat hanging on the rack caught her eye and Minnie ran fingers through its fur collar. It was the last Christmas gift from Curtis. If only he were still alive, he'd know what to do. Minnie refocused to the tasks at hand.

"If you two are going to church, you better put your butts in gear," Minnie hollered. "We need to leave in five minutes."

Ida shuffled into the room behind Jane. "Sorry, I keep getting distracted." Ida slipped on her beige wool coat and rubbed her mother's pearl pin for comfort. "This whole thing with Mr. Harper and Ella has me out of sorts this morning." Ida murmured as she slid behind the steering wheel. "Who would kidnap an elderly man and his daughter? What would they have to gain?"

"Well," Jane said as she leaned across the top of the cloth front seat. "I've been thinking. Mr. Harper does have quite a bit of money."

Ida turned on her blinker. "How do you know that?"

"He's got that nice house. The farm with the oil wells. They made him president of the bank. They often do that if the person is wealthy or has a lot of stock in the company. I guess investors think rich people know how to manage money since they have a lot of it. Maybe he's refused someone a loan or foreclosed on someone's home. That would make them really angry."

Ida took in a sharp breath. "That would mean it's someone around here. The bank doesn't loan outside of Logan County."

"Oh, Jane, don't start rumors," Minnie admonished. "We just need to wait and see what the police think."

"Yes," Ida agreed. "Don't get people all worked up. There could be a simple explanation."

"Have you ever known Ella not to be somewhere she said she'd be?"

"No, but…"

"There's no buts. Her green Ford's in the garage. Mr. Harper's not in the hospital, and neither he nor Ella can be found. They've been kidnapped. I'd bet my life on it." Jane slapped the seat triumphantly.

"Jane, let's not go there just yet," Minnie interjected. "I'm going to ask the minister to make an announcement in church this morning. Maybe someone knows where they are."

"Good idea, Minnie," Ida exclaimed. "Someone in town is bound to have seen or heard something."

"Humph," Jane huffed. "I think you're barking up the wrong tree. We need action, not all this handwringing."

The three sisters pulled into the gravel parking lot of the Lewisburg Methodist Church. Ida stopped to talk to friends, but Jane followed Minnie to the entrance where the pastor greeted people at the door. Minnie touched his arm.

"Could I have a word with you, please? It's important."

He turned to the small line of parishioners left on the steps of the church. "Good morning everyone. Please have a seat and we'll be starting in a moment."

"I don't know if you've heard," Minnie whispered. "But Edgar Harper and his daughter Ella can't be found this morning."

"Can't be found?"

"Yes," Jane answered eagerly, pushing in front of Minnie. "Ella's husband, Eustice, came to get his wife this morning and neither of them were in the house. He visited all the neighbors and we called the hospital; no one has seen them. Their car is still in the garage, too. I think they've been kidnapped."

Minnie grabbed Jane's shoulder and pulled her back a few steps. "Forgive my sister, Reverend. She's known for jumping the gun on things." Minnie shot Jane a glare and continued. "We're sure there's a simple explanation, but would you ask if anyone saw them last night or this morning?"

"Of course, of course. Shall we get started?" He made his way into the sanctuary. Minnie pulled at Jane's leopard wrap before she followed. "Jane, you have to stop spreading gossip about kidnappings. We don't know what's happened so let's stick to the facts, okay?"

"I'm not a child Minnie; I'm thirty-six years old. You don't need to shush me."

Ida stepped between them. "Enough, you two."

Jane glowered at Minnie's back as she wandered into the chapel and took her place in the choir.

The minister stood at the podium. "Good morning."

"Good morning," the congregation answered.

"I have a special request. Can any of you tell me if you've seen either Mr. Edgar Harper or his daughter Mrs. Eustice Givens last night or this morning?" Murmurs spread through the pews.

"Please, if anyone has seen them, could you stand up?"

William Insco stood. "I was walking along Front Street yesterday somewhere around 4:30, waiting on my wife to get finished at the beauty parlor. I heard Mr. Harper say, 'How ya doin?' and turned to see him going around the corner by the bank. Looked like he was headed toward the post office."

"Thank you, Mr. Insco. Anyone else?"

"I saw Mrs. Givens putting gas in her car yesterday morning," someone said.

"I saw her working in the yard early in the day. Nothing after that," said another.

Brother Mike waited but no one else spoke up. "Friends," he intoned, "Mr. Harper and Mrs. Givens seem to be missing. I want to dedicate this service to their safety. Please pray with me now. "Our Father, who art in Heaven..."

They finished the prayer and the choir began their opening hymn. "When the roll is called up yonder, when the roll is called up yonder, when the roll is called up yonder, I'll be there."

The grim connotation of that song settled over the somber congregation.

Chapter 2

The coffee percolated as Ida sat at the table rubbing her trembling hands. They hadn't stopped shaking since the announcement at church. No one knew anything about Mr. Harper and Ella. Maybe Jane was right. Maybe they had been kidnapped, but who would do such a thing? She walked over and lifted the curtain to gaze at the Harper house. State police detective Sergeant G.C. McMillen sat in his police car.

"See anything?" Minnie's steps were muffled by pink, fluffy house shoes.

"Just the police car. I can't believe this is happening."

"Me either. Ella and I got pretty close after she moved in with her dad. She and I were two of the few ladies on the street during the day. She knows a lot of people and visits them often. Keeps me informed about people for my column. Now and then we slipped in an episode of "Days of Our Lives."

"Soap operas?" Ida turned to Minnie, stunned. "I suppose everyone has some secrets." She looked away. "I'm going to buy some new locks for our doors. We're a prime target, you know? Three women living alone."

Jane entered the kitchen, her face eager as a pup on a rabbit trail. "Oh, poo!" She reached for her mug in the dish drain and poured another cup of coffee. "No one wants three old women. Well, two old women and one younger one." She smoothed her blond coif.

"You aren't that young," Minnie pointed out.

Jane ignored the barb. "We've never locked our doors because we don't have anything valuable. You're letting your imagination run away from you, Ida. Besides, the hardware store won't be open until tomorrow."

"Now Jane," Minnie started. "If Ida wants to put on new locks, she has the right. I have to admit I'd feel a bit safer myself. I'm not even sure where the keys are for our doors. It's scary to think a thing like this could happen so close to us. Maybe over in those trashy apartments in Bowling Green, but not here."

"Oh, you big chickens," Jane announced. "This is exciting."

"Jane," Ida looked at her sister in shock.

"I don't mean Edgar and Ella missing, I'm sure they're fine. I mean a real mystery to solve. It's better than figuring out those predictable Saturday night crime shows. It's almost as intriguing as The Fugitive and it's occurring right under our noses. Wouldn't it be great if I could solve it myself? Snoop out those kidnappers and pounce on them before they know what's happening?"

Ida turned to her younger sister. "Jane, you aren't going to pounce on anyone as skinny as you are. Even if you did somehow prove yourself, no police department has ever hired a woman detective."

Jane flung an offended look in Ida's direction as she plopped down at the table. "Oh, what do you know? Women are being hired in lots of areas traditionally held by men. Have you seen all the women lawyers now? I bet there'll be one on the Supreme Court before long. If I solved this case, some police department around here would hire me. I just know it."

Minnie slid into the chair opposite Jane and took her hand. "I know you've been waiting for a chance like this for a long time, Sis, but you're missing an important point here. These are our friends and neighbors. Your excitement is their pain. Our friends' families are hurting."

"I'm sorry. Of course, you're right. What can I do to help?"

"Well," Minnie looked around the kitchen. "We need to start baking. The Harper family will be arriving. They'll probably get a search going. We could take some food over to the house."

"Yes, that would be good. You and Ida start while I go change out of my church clothes."

"You're not fooling me Jane Elizabeth Clack," Ida shook her finger in Jane's direction. "You'll hide out in your room while Minnie and I get everything going. Hurry up and change and help us cook."

Minnie pulled out her apron. "They aren't going to let us anywhere near the house unless we have a reason to be there. We can all look for anything out of the ordinary once we're inside."

Jane grumbled under her breath, but drained her cup and disappeared from the kitchen.

The sisters locked eyes. Ida shook her head and sighed. "Let's get to work."

Jane returned in a pair of slim brown pants and a pink sweater. "Okay, so when we do go over, will you two keep everyone busy so I can look for evidence?"

Ida jumped as a glass bowl of flour crashed to the floor, scattering shards and dust the length of the kitchen. "Minnie, are you okay? Did it hit you?" She grabbed the broom and dustpan.

"I just remembered," Minnie slapped her hand to her forehead. "A man came to the door last night at Marvine Pogue's while we were playing Rook. He made me so nervous."

"Why would someone coming to the house bother you so?" Jane asked.

"He kept pulling his collar up."

"It is December," Jane answered, "and we had the rain moving in. "It wasn't just that." Minnie stooped down to hold the dustpan for Ida. "He seemed to stay away from the porch light and he barely mumbled, asking if there were any police around. Why would someone want to know that?"

"Minnie," Ida soothed, "if he needed a policeman, I suppose he'd need to ask somebody, wouldn't he?"

"Ida," Jane snapped. "Use your head for something besides a hat rack. If he'd wanted a cop, he'd have asked to borrow a phone to call one and..."

"I guess there could be any number of reasons he'd ask for a policeman," Minnie interrupted. "There were all those strangers in town last night for the ball game, and there was a visitation at the funeral home for A.B. Wilhite's grandfather. Maybe the man was broken down on the side of the road or something."

"I-I don't know," Ida stuttered. "What if this guy was casing the joint?"

"Casing the joint?" said Minnie. "I knew I heard the TV when I was in bed. You were up watching Perry Mason."

"Well, what of it?" Ida replied. "It's legal to watch television."

"Anyway," Minnie continued, "I didn't like the way he was eyeing all the children playing in the living room. Wouldn't have surprised me one little bit if he'd tried to make off with one of 'em. The way he dressed was just plain eerie, with the dark hat pulled down to his brows and collar up past his chin. Real scary."

Ida's voice trembled. "Remember? The last lawman in Lewisburg lived in that same house. McPherson, I think. He moved out just a few months ago. Someone's asking about the police and now the Harpers are missing. It all has to be connected?"

"Pssht," Jane scoffed. "I'm sure it was nothing. Maybe he knew the police officer and was just looking for him. Now, back to the Harper house. Okay, so when we go over, will you guys keep the others busy so I can look for clues? You know, talk about the game, the weather, whatever so I can search?"

Ida turned away from Jane and rolled her eyes. "I'll never understand your enthusiasm over this, and now you want to sneak around the Harper house?"

Minnie turned from the stove where she was browning meat for stew. "It will be embarrassing if you get caught. We all want to know what's going on, but we must be very cautious here, Jane. We can't alienate our friends."

Ida rolled out the dough for a piecrust. "Jane, start some biscuits for the stew."

"Don't boss me around," Jane declared as she took out ingredients.

Ida took a deep breath and counted to five. Mama really had pampered Jane a bit too much, her being the youngest and all. "Okay, fine. Just hurry up. The family will be arriving soon, and you need to keep your mind on cooking for the moment. I promise if you do, I will cover for you while you look around."

"I will, too," Minnie added.

"Deal." Jane smiled and started mixing the dough.

***

Later, Jane proudly held her biscuits aloft as she knocked on the Harper's door. Minnie followed, hugging a pot of stew to her hip while balancing a plate of cookies. Ida straggled behind with her cherry pie. Goldie Watson, the town's nurse, let them in.

"Oh, thank goodness," Goldie sighed. "The family will be here soon and there's nothing in the refrigerator."

"What?" Minnie exclaimed. "Ella always goes to the grocery on Saturdays."

"She did." Goldie picked up a slip of paper. "I found the receipt. It says she spent $14.50. The other $5.50 is in her grocery cup. But there's no food."

"How odd." Jane took the pot from Minnie and sat it on the burner to keep it warm, then rushed back to help with the rest of the goodies. She sat Ida's cherry pie on the counter and sidled up to Goldie. "So, what do you think happened to the food?" Jane leaned against the counter and stared at the town nurse.

"I don't have a clue. Maybe they took it with them. It just doesn't make sense."

Jane went to the refrigerator and peeked in. Sure enough, except for a jar of bread and butter pickles, a butter dish, and a bowl of mayonnaise, it was empty. She looked around. Checked a few cabinets and surveyed the kitchen. When she heard the men talking in the other room, she headed in their direction.

"Jane, they want us to stay in the kitchen." Goldie called after her.

Jane acted like she didn't hear and continued walking, thankful that Ida and Minnie peppered Goldie with questions, so she could get away. She was in such a rush she all but tackled Mr. Forgy.

"Hello, Miss Jane."

"Mr. Forgy, how-how are you?"

"Fine, fine."

"Isn't this just the darndest thing?" Jane asked. "You'd think with both of us being so close, we would have seen or heard something."

"Well, I did see a few things but didn't think anything about it," Lewis Forgy said.

"What did you see?" Jane mentally kicked herself for not bringing a notebook and pen.

"Noticed a couple cars come down the road and turn around."

"Oh. Is that it?"

"No," Forgy continued. "They stopped at the Harpers. I thought they were possibly just having late company."

"Did you recognize either of the cars?"

"Well, I couldn't see too well, you know my eye problem and such. One was a big one, the other small."

Jane nodded.

"You know something else. I called the state police post early this morning. Talked to that Paul Hankins, but he wouldn't come out."

"You asked him to come out? But why?"

"As long as I've known the Harpers, they've left the bathroom light burning night and day. When I got up about six this morning, it was off. Hankins said he wasn't going to wake up two people to find out their light bulb had burned out."

"Really?"

"Yep, I guess we know now that it really was time to worry. Don't know if it would have made any difference at that point. Would you excuse me, please? I need to use the facilities."

"Of course." Jane's mind went through possibilities. Maybe Ella turned the light off to signal for help. Maybe a visitor flipped the light off after using it. She slipped down the hall and stood outside the bedroom door listening to the men inside.

"There's a lockbox here under Edgar's bed that hasn't been touched," Jane recognized the voice of State Police Detective G.C. McMillen.

"Edgar's medicine is still here on his bedside table," Eustice added, "his hot water bottle is in its usual spot, and the spittoon wasn't covered; he always did that right before he went to bed. I found something else I want to show you."

Jane nearly fell into Eustice Givens' arms as he opened the bedroom door. "Would you fellas like some coffee?"

"None for me," said Eustice.

"Please stay in the kitchen, Miss Clack," Detective McMillen advised. "We don't want anyone's fingerprints getting mixed up with others that might be in the house."

"Oh, I'm sorry. I didn't think of that," Jane smiled sweetly. Mr. Forgy joined the other men as they went into Ella's bedroom and shut the door. Jane crept over, stooped down and put her ear against the keyhole.

"These suitcases were always kept in the late Mrs. Harper's bedroom closet," Eustice's voice rose and cracked. "I don't know what's happened—I can't figure this out. Her purse is right here. She never goes anywhere without her purse. Where's my Ella?"

"Now Eustice," McMillen's voice was strong and steady. "You just go in there and have a seat by the phone in case someone calls. I'll look around the house. Go with him, Mr. Forgy."

Jane skittered away as their steps came toward her. Breathless, she entered the kitchen.

"There you are, Jane," Goldie said. "Your sisters and I were just discussing if we should go up to the gas station to get some bread and boloney. It'll be the only place open on Sunday. I have some leftover roast from last night's dinner and I cut up a young fryer for fried chicken I can bring, too. What do you think?"

"I'm not sure. Do you suppose we should wait and see what Detective McMillen wants to do before we fix any more food?" asked Ida. "What if they don't have an organized search until tomorrow?"

"Well that makes sense," Goldie said. "I'll go see what the plan is."

"Oh, I'll go," said Jane. "You know I'm all thumbs in the kitchen." Jane breezed out the doorway. "G.C., where are you?"

He stepped out of Ella's bedroom. "Right here, Miss Clack."

"Do you think we'll need more food? You know, for the search party. Are you planning on organizing one today?

"Yes, a small one." The detective ran a hand over his thick, dark hair. "First, I'm going to call in some help to set up roadblocks and do a house to house search. They'll pursue anything that doesn't seem right. I'll make a few calls on the police radio and get things moving. If you'll excuse me, I need to step outside."

Jane nodded and watched G.C.'s shadow disappear down the porch stairs, then slid into Ella's room. Two suitcases lay open. The blue one on the bed held a hodgepodge of clothes that were Ella's, but nothing she regularly wore. The tan one held her sewing supplies and lay on the floor in such a way that when the door was opened it knocked into the metal strip on the side of the case. A few gaily wrapped packages sat on the pillow. Could Ella have been planning to hide Christmas presents?

"Jane, what are you doing in here?" Eustice stood in the doorway.

"I—I just can't believe she's not here. I had to look for myself. You know what I mean?"

He came to her side and gave an awkward hug. "Yes, sure. Last night around seven I talked to her about going to see our son today and now, I have no idea where she is."

"Have you found anything at all?"

"No. Money's still in her purse. Cigarettes, cigarette lighter, and the keys to her car. Detective McMillen is just as confused as I am. Doesn't make any sense."

"Was the door locked when you got here this morning?"

"The front door was, so I went around back. It was unlocked, but I couldn't find anyone." Eustice stepped over to the suitcase on the bed and closed it. He took a handkerchief out of his pocket and rubbed it over the suitcase absentmindedly. "What could they have that would make someone take them?"

"Now we don't know someone has taken them." Jane rubbed his shoulders as he bowed his head and began to cry. "Oh don't. There could be a very simple explanation to all of this. Detective McMillen is getting a search party together. Let's sit right down here and say a prayer. I'm sure we'll know more before the sun goes down tonight."

Eustice turned his tear-streamed face to Jane. "Do you really think so?"

"I really think so."

A knock on the front door startled them and Jane went to answer. Eustice wiped his eyes and followed.

"Miss Clack."

"Hello Pete, what are you doing here?"

"Just came over to see if I could help.

"I'm sure they could use you. Detective McMillen will be getting a search party together soon. Do you know Eustice Givens?"

"I don't believe we've met."

"Eustice Givens," Jane ushered the young man into the living room. "Meet the best basketball player east of the Mississippi, Pete Lehman."

"Aww, Miss Clack, I'm not that great; Randall Kaufman's good, too."

Eustice held out his hand. "Pleased to make your acquaintance, Pete."

G.C. McMillen rushed into the room. "Dewitt Ryan."

"He isn't here, G.C." Jane said.

"No, no, has anyone checked on him and Miss Hazel to see if they're okay? If this has something to do with the bank, Vice President Dewitt Ryan could have been targeted too."

"I'll go," Jane volunteered.

"I don't want you going over there by yourself."

"I could go with her," Pete suggested. "We can walk over right now."

"Good idea," G.C. said.

As they walked to the Ryan home, Pete asked, "What do you think is going on?"

"I don't know. I really thought this was going to be simple. You know, they took a walk, or went for a drive with someone. But they would be back by now if that were the case. I don't know what to think anymore."

They stood on the front stoop of Dewitt Ryan's home, and Pete knocked. He looked through the diamond shaped window at the top of the door. "I see him coming."

The door opened a sliver and Dewitt spoke to them through the locked storm door. "Hi Pete, Miss Clack. Can I do something for you?"

"We came to check on you," Jane answered. "Have you heard about Mr. Harper and Ella? Do you know anything?"

"Yes, I heard about them. We're fine here, just fine. I'd rather not come out, if you don't mind, a bit of a cold."

"Yes, of course," Jane said. "I'm sure G.C. will be by to talk to you later."

Dewitt closed the door, and Pete glanced in through the window. "Man, he's hiding a .45 pistol behind his back."

"Wow," Jane exclaimed. "Everyone is on edge. Wish we could find a key to unlock this mystery and let Lewisburg get back to normal."

"Miss Clack, I was at the bank washing windows for old man, err, I mean Mr. Ryan, yesterday and two guys wanted to know if we had any law in town. Did I do wrong by telling them we didn't? Did someone kidnap the Harpers 'cause I told them there's no police here?"

"No, no," Jane hugged Pete. "I'm not sure if that incident had anything to do with it, but you need to tell Detective McMillen about those men. Do you think you can give a description?"

"I'll sure try."

"Great, let's get back and see if they know anything more." Jane attempted to cheer up the young man, but in the back of her mind floated an image of Dewitt Ryan holding a gun behind his back.

Chapter 3

Wednesday December 15: 3rd Day Missing

Ida May Clack struggled as she pushed the cart across the nearly empty parking lot. "Wish I could pay someone to do our grocery shopping," she grumbled. The sleet/snow mix didn't help to lighten the mood. She'd have to talk to Bruce about fixing his lot if he expected her to keep buying from his little store. Breathing in short gasps, she finally reached the entrance. The newspaper headline shouted from the vending machine, "$1,000 REWARD OFFERED FOR CLUES IN HARPER-GIVENS DISAPPEARANCE."

Inside, a display piled high with delicious vegetables greeted customers. Her mouth watered at the scent of cinnamon and nutmeg from store-made pumpkin pies. Cheery Christmas songs echoed off the sleek white walls and bounced back toward her.

She rubbed her hands together rapidly, then bent down to rub her knee. Although only forty, she seemed to be developing a bit of arthritis. Cold weather did not help.

Ida pulled tangerines from the table, squeezing and sniffing before putting them in a paper sack. "The first tangerines of the season; Jane will be happy." She grabbed her favorite red potatoes and yams. The specialty foods in the grocery this time of year always made Ida smile. She held up a bunch of fresh herbs. "What will I make with you," she wondered aloud.

"Good Afternoon, Ida. How are you today?" Bruce's smiling face beamed at her.

She blew a lone strand of hair and wished she'd thought to run a comb through it before getting out of the car. "I was better before I crossed your parking lot. When are you going to get those holes fixed?"

"It'll have to wait until spring. You can't fix blacktop in the cold. The potholes will just come right back."

"Oh, I didn't know that."

"Don't you worry, I'll carry your groceries to your car myself."

Ida's cheeks pinked. "I didn't mean to fuss so. I'm..."

"Oh, you were only being honest, and it's appreciated. I want to keep my customers satisfied so they keep coming back." He elbowed her lightly and winked.

"I don't want to cause any trouble, Bruce."

"No problem at all. Let me know when you finish shopping. It's the least I can do since you come all this way to buy your groceries. You live in Lewisburg, right?"

Ida blushed again, and then eyed Bruce with a cautious look. "Yes, but how did you know that?"

Bruce smiled and raised his hands in the air. "Don't worry. I'm not following you or anything. I noticed the address on your check last week when Mabel brought it to me for approval." He rubbed the graying bristles on his chin and caught her eye. "Can I ask why you do your shopping so far from home? Not that I mind. I love seeing your smiling face every Wednesday afternoon. But it is a pretty good distance."

Ida cringed. Bruce even knew which day of the week she came in. "I'm a nurse at the hospital here in Russellville."

"Ah, now that makes sense. But Lewisburg is still in the other direction."

His stare made her uncomfortable. He was right. There were other stores she could stop at on the way home, but she drove an extra fifteen minutes out of the way to visit Bruce's store. The heat in her cheeks increased. What would he say if she told him it was the risqué romance books he sold? Would he think she was a floozy? She swallowed hard and then realized he was still waiting for an answer. "Yes, it is. But I like your store. You've got the freshest produce around. I'd rather eat vegetables than meat."

"Thanks. I do my best. Hey, since you're in Lewisburg, have you heard anything about the Harpers? Any rumors of old man Harper stealing from the bank or something they could be involved in?"

"I'm sure I don't know what you mean. The Harpers are a fine upstanding family." There was an awkward pause as they stared at each other, unsure where the conversation should go next.

"Well, I'll let you get back to your shopping. Holler when you finish." Bruce bounded off a few feet before looking over his shoulder and winking at her again.

Ida sprinted in the other direction. What would he think if he knew she read those novels or how closely she'd been following the Harper case? She glanced at her watch. "Oh my." Ida rushed through the store and then headed for the book section. She pretended to look through a ladies' magazine as her eyes ran over the titles of romances available. A chuckle escaped her throat when she saw a new book called Frisky with Frank. Ida returned the magazine to the shelf and looked around. Seeing no one, she picked up the paperback and put it in her pocket.

The cashier totaled up her groceries, took Ida's check, and went to find Bruce Chandler to help her load the bags in her car. As soon as she disappeared Ida put thirty-nine cents beside the register for the book in her pocket. She would never steal, but she didn't want everyone to know her secret. They might question her morals.

Bruce hurried from the office and took the cart from Ida. She ignored the way her skin felt whenever their hands accidentally touched; somewhat pleasant, but an underlying feeling she couldn't quite place.

"Miss Clack, uh, I'd like to ask you something."

"Yes, Bruce?"

"Well, I was wondering if you'd like to go to a picture show with me sometime."

"That's so nice of you to ask, Bruce. I might. Sometime after the holidays. I'm pretty busy until then."

"I'll ask again later. You can count on it," he said as he closed her trunk and rushed around the side of the car to open her door.

Ida hurried in and sped home, trying to get there before the tea got cold. *I hope I don't pass a policeman.* As she came through the door, arms laden with groceries and placed them on the kitchen counter, she called to Minnie. "I'll be there in a minute." Ida hung her coat in the mud room and gave her mother's pearl pin a rub. It fell off onto the floor. She picked it up and played with the latch. I'm going to have to get that replaced soon.

Her sister placed their mother's treasured teapot on the hot plate, took a seat in her tufted chair beside the tea cart, and laid a napkin across her lap.

"There you are. I thought you were going to be late," Minnie picked up the plate of lemon cookies, offered one to Ida, and took one herself.

"The grocery was so busy today, thought I was never going to get through the line. Is Jane home yet?"

"No, she and Frank should be here any minute." They breezed through the door as the last syllable died on Minnie's lips.

"Girls, I have so much to tell you," Jane gushed.

"Some gossip from one of your students?" Ida frowned.

"No, no. About the investigation into Edgar and Ella's disappearance."

"Jane," Frank warned, "I don't think we should discuss this with others. I told you that in confidence."

"Oh tish-tosh. They won't tell."

"Perhaps Frank is right," Ida stated.

Jane ignored them. "Someone made a ransom demand for the Harpers."

"Really?" Ida scooted to the front of her seat.

"What? A ransom demand?" Minnie questioned. "Maybe you should tell us the story, Frank."

Frank glanced at Minnie's and Ida's expectant faces. "Alright."

He settled himself at the table and rubbed his bald head nervously. "But you have to promise not to tell anyone. Minnie, you can't breathe a word of this in your column."

Minnie raised her right hand and put her left one in the air as if on a Bible. "I promise."

"Me too, me too," Ida repeated.

Jane reached over and patted his knee. "It sure is handy having a police officer for a boyfriend. Have I told you lately that I love you?" Frank blushed a bit.

"Forget that nonsense." Minnie wiped her hands on her apron. "What's happened?"

"Okay, so you know that Mr. Harper's children promised a thousand-dollar reward yesterday, right?"

"Yes, uh-huh," they nodded.

"Heard it on the radio again while I was driving home from the grocery," Ida added.

"Well, right after that, someone called the radio station and demanded money. Sixty thousand dollars."

"What?" Minnie said. "Where did they expect someone to come up with that? The bank doesn't actually keep that much money just lying around."

"Well," Jane pointed out. "You know Edgar Harper is president of the bank."

"Honorary president of the bank," Ida said. "Dewitt Ryan actually runs it."

"I know, I know," Jane snapped. "But he is worth a lot. Maybe someone thought he carried a bunch of cash on him."

"Will you two shush?" Minnie demanded.

"I'm sorry, I'm sorry," they muttered.

"Please continue, Frank."

He smoothed the front of his starched tan uniform shirt. "The FBI said they couldn't come in on the case unless there was evidence it was a kidnapping, so of course we contacted them right away. Almost as soon as we got off the phone with them, the person called the radio station again with more information about what to do with the ransom. Sheriff McMillen sent me over there just in case he called back so I could hear his voice."

"Very good idea," Ida said.

"Shh," Minnie hissed

"Well he did call back, several times. Each time he had another instruction. The kind of bag to put the money in, where to leave it, etc."

"Where are you supposed to leave it?" Jane questioned. "You forgot to tell me that."

"I'm sorry, I can't tell."

"Really Frank," Ida said. "You can't tell us all of this and leave us hanging."

"Well, Ida Clack," Jane teased. "I do believe you're interested in this investigation."

"Hush ladies," Minnie said. "Really Frank. We won't say anything to anyone. Have you ever known one of us to break a promise?"

Frank looked at the floor, then back at their faces. "Alright, but if it gets out, I'll know where it came from. We're supposed to meet them at the bus station."

"When is it going to happen?" Minnie pressed.

"Tomorrow evening."

"Are you all going to be there waiting?" Ida said. "He might catch on something's wrong."

"We're going to be there along with the FBI. We'll be dressed up as workers and travelers. Hopefully, the guy won't suspect anything."

"That makes sense." Ida agreed.

Jane jumped up. "Are there any women FBI agents going?"

"I'm not sure," Frank replied. "We haven't met any of them yet."

"I could go," Jane declared. "I'll go over and have a cup of coffee with Edith at the ticket counter. They'll be none the wiser."

"Now Jane," Minnie chided.

"No, I really want to be there."

"It's too dangerous for you to be there, "Ida warned.

"They're right, honey," said Frank. "I'll be right outside. I'd have to stop you if you tried to go in. Besides, I'm not even sure it's real. The gal at the radio station said the voice sounded an awful lot like one of their regular callers. She said he has an unusual sense of humor."

"Who would do that?" Ida held her hands out in exasperation. "If they were caught it could make them the number one suspect."

"Oh, we've been getting calls from all over," Frank said, annoyed. "Even letters already. Some people claimed to be the one who kidnapped them. Others are psychics 'the bodies are in this lake' or 'they're buried in those woods.' We even had one who told us they were buried alive waiting for money to be paid and another said they took a bus to Mexico, but they didn't know what town. When something like this happens, everyone comes out of the woodwork looking for their fifteen minutes of fame or trying to claim the reward. They think they might get their picture in the paper or hear their name on the radio. It's sad really. Sad for the families to have to listen to all that."

"You're so right," Ida chimed in. "I wish others would respect people's privacy at a time like this."

"Everyone just wants to know what's happening," Frank explained. "It helps them to feel safe if there's a rational explanation why someone would vanish or come to some harm; something that could never touch them in their homes."

"That makes a lot of sense, but it doesn't make me feel any better about the situation."

"Everyone's on edge," Frank said. "We're hoping we can get this wrapped up before Christmas gets here. It's looking like that might be a pipe dream." Frank stood. "Have to get back to the station now. Want to walk me to my car, Jane?"

"Sure."

They departed, leaving Ida and Minnie alone. "It doesn't make sense," said Minnie. "What could the Harpers have that was so valuable? According to Frank, the bank doors weren't tampered with and it doesn't look like anyone tried to get in the vault. They couldn't of course since the vault automatically locks and unlocks itself. What else could someone want?"

"I don't know," Ida worried. "But I hope the police find out before something else happens."

***

The 5:00 bus arrived, bringing the odor of diesel, exhaust fumes, and brake fluid as it parked in the horizontal space in front of the Russellville Greyhound Bus Station. Jane ran her hand over Ida's dull clothes, put on a pair of large tortoise shell sunglasses, wrapped a scarf around the brown wig on her head, and blended into the group of travelers disembarking from the bus. Frank would never recognize her now.

Entering the building, she headed for the row of snack machines, put in a nickel, opened the door of the red metal cooler, and slid the glass coke bottle along the track until she held it in her hand. She placed the cap in the bottle opener and popped the metal top off. Jane spied a chair in the corner, the perfect place to sit and watch.

A man in rumpled clothes pulled a bucket along behind him. Every few feet he tucked a mop into the water and spread a puddle of wetness across the floor. Jane's stomach fluttered as excitement mounted. He had to be an agent. She glanced around. A brown satchel sat on the counter of the ticket booth. Where was Edith? She wondered over to the counter, eyes on the bag, and checked to see if she was in the back. The grey-haired man in the office looked up. Another agent? She lowered her glasses and winked.

The man grinned as his gaze ran down her body. Maybe he wasn't an agent. She glanced away. Frank had to be around here somewhere. She peered out the window and almost choked on a sip of soda. A baldheaded man sat at a table of an eatery across the street. She pulled her regular glasses from her purse and took another look. That was definitely Frank. What in the world was he wearing? Was that a suit? Frank? She'd not seen him in a suit before, not even when they went to the church social. She squinted. Is that a briefcase sitting on the table in front of him?

Jane stifled a giggle. Poor Frank.

The mechanic outside looked her way. She grinned and turned from the window, coming face to face with a hippie. A fellow traveler from the group she'd come in with. He sure looked suspicious. Long straggly hair and dirty beard. Not a typical Logan County resident. It had to be the guy picking up the money.

She glanced at the restaurant window. Where was Frank? She couldn't see him anymore. Wouldn't it be something if she captured this crook by herself? Jane went into attack mode, but before she got into her karate stance, the hippie took hold of her arm, revealing the FBI badge nestled in his palm. Something stirred in Jane. Were the agents going to ask her to help? Maybe Frank had told them she would assist. He was such a sweet guy.

"Ma'am, I'm Agent Thompson," Hippie said in a low voice. "Please don't make any sudden moves, just come with me. Smile and pretend I'm here to pick you up."

"Sure, no problem." Obligingly, she plastered on a big smile. Jane's mind whirled. Here she was involved in a real live investigation. She couldn't wait to see what they wanted her to do.

Once outside, they walked to a black sedan hidden behind the building. "Get in the car, please." He opened the door and they both climbed in. Jane turned around expecting to see another agent in the back seat, with a job for her to do. The hippie took her purse, and handcuffs clicked around her wrists. Jane's eyes opened wide and her heart raced. "What are you doing?" She began to wonder about this guy. Was he even a real agent? Was that a fake badge? What was she going to do now? Where was Frank?

The Hippie started going through her purse. "All clear; no weapons." Another man in obvious undercover clothes—suit too neat to be a traveler, came out of the shadows and slid into the back seat.

Jane jerked at the cuffs. "You know, I can't help you with these things on."

"Oh, you will help, alright. Keep your head lowered." He pulled out her wallet and looked at her driver's license. "Who is your contact, Jane Clack?"

"Contact? I don't have a contact. Hey, how do I know you're real FBI agents?"

The man in the suit pulled out an expensive leather wallet and flipped it open. The gold caught the reflection of the streetlight. These were FBI for sure. They popped questions faster than Jane could keep up. Did they think she was working with the real kidnapper? What was she going to do now? She couldn't tell them the truth. Frank would lose his job. Come on brain. Give me something.

Jane lifted her eyes toward the hippie and chirped. "I come in here often to visit the ticket agent Edith, once or twice a week at least. I just stepped in here to get me a cold drink. Then I saw all these strangers working. I know almost everyone who works here but didn't know any of these people." She gestured back toward the bus station. "Well, I knew something was wrong, so I sat down to watch what was happening. What is going on?"

"I don't believe you," a male voice barked. The man in maintenance uniform appeared from out of nowhere. "Give us names."

A tapping sound interrupted the FBI agent's tirade. Jane recognized a local policeman dressed as a bum. He handed the agent a note. ASK HER NAME.

"We already know her name," the agent said. "It's Jane Clack."

Another note passed. Then silence. The FBI agent got out of the back seat and Frank pushed himself in.

"Jane, what are you doing here?" He said gruffly.

Jane struggled to find a way to let him know she hadn't sold him out. "Frank, I don't know what's happening. One minute I stepped into the bus station to get a soda and the next minute, these men surrounded me." She sniffed and wiped her eyes. "Why didn't you tell me something was happening here today? I wouldn't have come near. Honest."

Frank breathed an audible sigh. "Well, I couldn't tell you, sweetheart. That would have been in open defiance of my orders." He patted her shoulder. "Agent Thompson, I take full responsibility for this. My girlfriend tries to help the police force every time she sees something out of the ordinary."

"And things were definitely out of the ordinary today." Jane stared at him with an innocent facade.

"Have someone take her home."

"I can get home myself."

"And stay there," Agent Thompson barked. "If I see you around here again today, I won't be this pleasant."

Chapter 4

December 18, 1965

The ringing woke Jane from a sound sleep. She grabbed the pink princess phone from her nightstand and shoved hair from her face.

"Hello? Frank? Why are you calling so early? What? Yes, of course I want to go. A few minutes?" Jane jumped up and observed herself in the mirror, while taking the sleeping scarf off her hair. Minnie and Ida appeared at the door. "I'll be ready. See you soon."

"What is it? What's happened?" Minnie demanded.

"They found something." Jane pulled a pair of slacks from a hangar and slid them up over her hips.

"What?" Ida asked.

"I don't know. Frank got permission from Detective McMillen to take me with him, said it wasn't a secret and lots of people would probably show up to watch."

"Darn it, Jane," Minnie snapped. "Watch what? You aren't making any sense."

"Searchers found some articles of clothing late yesterday close to Wolf Lick Creek Bridge. Police and FBI are doing a big search of the area. Jane threw her gown in the hamper and grabbed a shirt from her drawer. "Frank said you guys can come, but he'll be here to pick me up in a minute. Get ready and meet us by the bridge."

"I'm not sure I want to go." Ida exclaimed.

"Suit yourselves, but I'm going." Headlights illuminated the window. "That's Frank. See you later." Jane grabbed her handbag and rushed down the stairs.

***

"Right here!" Jane gushed. "This is where they found Edgar Harper's hat. They found three stockings they haven't confirmed to be Ella's yet, but who else could they belong to? We're standing on the very spot where they found the hat yesterday. Right here at Wolfe Lick Creek!"

"Well, actually it was right over there," Frank laughed as he pointed to a little orange marker. They walked off to investigate further.

Ida lowered her head and pinched the bridge of her nose.

Minnie looked concerned. "Ida dear, are you getting a headache?"

"No, no, the sun's just a bit bright." She turned around and saw two men approaching them. "Who is that guy with Frank and Jane?"

Frank approached. "I'd like you to meet Charlie Shingledecker. He's the guy who found the hat."

Charlie extended his hand as Frank introduced them. He went on to explain he was a member of the Mike Riders, a motorcycle group that works with the Muhlenberg County Rescue Squad and helps with searches in and around the area. "Right now we're helping search for evidence in the Harper disappearance. Guess we lucked out yesterday."

"You sure did." Jane leaned over to look down the hill at Wolf Lick Creek. "How in the world did you get over that bank? That's what, six to eight feet down?"

"I don't mind getting dirty if I can help someone and neither does James Allen. He's the guy who found the stockings a little bit further that way. He pointed to another orange marker down the street. We took everything to the authorities."

"Charlie," Jane asked eagerly. "Can you tell us anything about the stockings?"

Charlie scratched his head. "There were three of them; odd number. They wouldn't tell me what they thought about that, but I'm wondering why in the world there would be three."

"They probably used them as face masks, or maybe tied Ella and Edgar up with them." Jane guessed.

"That's possible," he agreed.

Detective McMillan motioned for Charlie. "Gotta go, ladies. It was nice meeting you." He waved and walked away.

Minnie glanced up as two Army helicopters thundered overhead. "Boy, they sure are loud. Why are they flying so close to the ground?"

"They are looking for bodies and other clues," Jane shouted over the noise. She turned to Frank. "Thanks for bringing me." She threw her arms around him. "I'm so glad I was off today."

Frank leaned over and kissed the top of her head. "It's my pleasure. I knew you'd enjoy it."

Jane looked up as the vast propellers of the helicopters from Fort Campbell whirled by. Excitement radiated from her eyes. "I love it. I guess the police are up there." She pointed.

"Yes, and maybe the FBI. After no one came to recover the money at the bus depot, we still aren't sure if it's a kidnapping. They think it may have been someone from the mental institution over in Hopkinsville that called the radio station." Frank shaded his eyes and looked across the sky, pointing to the second aircraft now far off. "They're searching a five-mile radius of Lewisburg."

"Oh, I hope they find some clues," Jane said hopping from one foot to the other.

"Clues maybe, but I hope they don't find any more than that while I'm here," Ida said.

"Oh, Ida. Don't be like that."

Ida stared at her sister. Jane didn't quite get Ida's fear, but she would never understand Jane's love of crime scenes, either. Jane loved the thrill of the mystery as much as Ida hated it.

"Don't look at me like that. I know you guys think I'm disrespecting Ella and Edgar, but that's not it at all," Jane told them. "I just can't stop the excitement I feel when it comes to attempting to solve crimes."

"I don't think anyone thinks anything of the sort." Frank hugged Jane to his side and turned back to the scene where rescue squads and firemen covered the ground along the creek.

"So, how do they know it's Edgar's hat?" Minnie stood beside Frank, notebook in hand in case she could use something for a newspaper story. "I mean lots of hats look alike. Don't you think it could just be a coincidence?"

"His children told the police his hat would have a brown stain on it and be crushed in the back where he wore it while watching TV in the evenings. When the FBI showed it to them, they all agreed it was his. They even searched the house to make sure it wasn't there."

"What about the stockings? Were they Ella's?"

"Minnie," Jane snapped. "You're interfering with my investigation. So, Frank, what about the stockings? Were they Ella's?"

Frank laughed. "No one knows for certain. They don't match each other, and they don't seem to match any Ella had at the house."

"So why would they be out there so close to the hat? Could they be there by chance, or were they planted there to lead searchers in the wrong direction?"

"Or what about Ella?" Ida asked. "She could have been leaving clues."

"We think they're definitely connected. They aren't worn enough to have been thrown away by someone, they're practically new. Maybe used for facemasks or to tie them up like Jane said earlier. But without more information, we're just not sure."

"Oh, that gives me goose bumps." Pinpricks stabbed at Ida's body as a breeze swept across the road. "How awful. I can't imagine being bound and afraid. Taken away from my home by God knows who to some unknown place. And there's no telling what they did to them after that. I hope the divers find them."

"No divers. It's too cold," Frank explained. "They're dragging." He pointed toward the water. "When you drag, you use a wheel-like contraption with grappling hooks attached, to scoot along the bottom. Sometimes they just use grappling hooks attached to ropes. It all depends on the depth of the water."

"So, you're just trying to hook into..." Ida stopped.

Frank nodded.

She put her hands over her ears. "That's terrible, terrible, please stop discussing it."

"It won't be nice for the family to see what they pull up, but..." Frank stopped at the look on Ida's face.

She stepped away from them as the wind whipped up. Maybe it would drown out their conversation. She caught Eustice's eye where he stood on the bridge. Poor man, he'd be devastated. Her stomach churned just thinking about it. She hoped he wasn't around when they found the bodies.

"Ida, are you okay?" Minnie came to stand beside her. "You've gone pale."

"I'm not feeling well. Just thinking about our neighbors and that..." Ida pointed to the contraption in the lake. "This standing around, waiting for some sort of spectacle is not my ideal way of spending a Saturday afternoon. Well, any afternoon really."

Minnie patted her arm. "Let's get you out of here. We delivered some coffee. Nothing we can do here now." Minnie turned to Frank. "Will you make sure Jane gets home? Ida isn't feeling well."

"Sure will." Frank nodded as he and Jane headed closer to the activity.

"And don't worry," Jane called. "I'll tell you everything you miss."

Ida and Minnie had just pulled away when quiet filled the frosty air.

"Look." Someone broke the silence as the grappling hooks brought up a large bag filled with something.

Jane grabbed Frank's sleeve. "What is it, honey? Do you think it's them?"

"Don't know yet. Could be. It's large enough to hold them. Stay back." Frank walked toward the men.

Jane crept as near the scene as she dared. Enough so she could see anyway. Four men in hip waders splashed to the west bank guiding the heavy canvas bag to the shore. Were they really going to open it right here? G.C. took out his pocketknife and cut a slash in the sack. Thank goodness Ida left, the anticipation was almost too much for Jane. She looked around to see Eustice right behind her, pushing through the crowd with a wild look in his eyes.

As the bag ripped open, the smell of decay hit Jane's nostrils and caused a lurch in her stomach.

The contents rolled out of the sack onto the creek bank. Garbage. Somebody must have dumped a month's worth of garbage in the creek. Jane burst into tears, and so did Eustice.

***

Ida groaned as she heard a loud muffler roar down the street. "I hate all this traffic. I bet everyone in the county has either visited the Harper house or driven up and down Henry Street at least a dozen times. I don't even feel comfortable hanging Christmas decorations outside." She plopped down in the overstuffed chair by the window and laid her head back on the flowered cushions. "I wonder what time Jane got home last night."

"Around eleven," Jane said entering from the kitchen with a mug of coffee. "Frank and I had a late dinner and then talked forever. I kind of like having a boyfriend where hours slip by when you're talking, and you don't even notice." Jane tucked one leg under her as she snuggled into a corner of the couch.

Ida smiled as Jane touched her perfectly teased and sprayed hair-do and then noted her own state of undress, still in her pink robe, positive her hair was a mess. She and Minnie enjoyed their mornings off, taking them slow, and not getting dressed until they had to. Jane on the other hand, never came downstairs unless fully clothed and made-up.

"I talked to so many people yesterday and found out so much. I can't wait to tell you all about it." Jane shifted, pulling her other leg up on the couch.

"I can't wait to hear about your adventure but remember..." Minnie wagged her finger at Jane. "You can't believe everything you hear."

Jane nodded. "I try, but so much happened after the reward was offered."

"Such as?" Minnie leaned forward to catch all of Jane's words.

"This lady, a Mrs. Parker from over in Belton, called to report that on the night of the disappearance, a car parked in front of the Pentecostal church that's being built across from her house. She said it was about 9:30 and it's only thirty minutes away, so it's possible."

"What's possible?"

"That Edgar and Ella could have been in the car." Jane continued. "The car sat there for quite a while—she didn't know what kind it was. She went back to watch a TV program and when she came back about ten minutes later, it was moving around to the back of the church."

Ida shifted in the chair. "Why would that be suspicious? It was Saturday night. Could have been some teenagers looking for a place to neck."

"Maybe," Jane agreed. "But there's an old strip mine behind the church that's flooded now. The police poked around the construction area and didn't find anything. They're going to drag there tomorrow."

"How awful," Minnie exclaimed." I hate to think of them being thrown in a dirty hole somewhere."

Ida rubbed some rosewater lotion into her hands. "Why would someone take them? If money was the primary reason, why would they leave some behind? They had to see the leftover grocery money in the cup when they took the food."

"You're right," Minnie stood and paced. "What about Ella's purse too? And the fact that nothing in the house was disturbed? If they were looking for money and couldn't get into the bank, why wouldn't they try to find some in the house?"

"A bigger question is who Ella or Edgar would let in the house," Ida stated.

Minnie and Jane's heads whipped around to their quiet sister. "What do you mean?" Jane demanded.

"Sometimes I went over to take Mr. Harper's blood pressure if he was feeling a little poorly between his visits with Dr. McEndre. Whenever I knocked, Ella always looked out the curtains before letting me in. I never knew the door to be unlocked, whatever time of day I went over."

"That is strange," Minnie mused. "A few weeks ago, close to dark, I noticed an old rusty truck in their driveway. That tenant of his, Mr. Belcher, I think his name is, knocked and Ella came to the door, but she wouldn't let him in. He held up an envelope and waved it around. Said something about the rent, but she wouldn't open the door. He left without going inside."

"I can't tell you who told me this," Jane whispered, "but Edgar and Ella have been very nervous about something for quite a while."

"Nervous?" her sisters repeated.

"Yes, Mr. Harper reported it to someone."

"Oh, Jane," Ida scoffed. "That was Doctor McEndre. After Edgar's wife Zula died, he had some of the usual grief reactions, plus his heart condition probably made him more aware that death could come at any time. He was 81, after all. Another thing is a lot of older folks get sundowners, you know, where they get agitated and irritable, even fearful, as it gets later in the day. That could explain why they wouldn't open the door after dark."

"That doesn't explain the phone call."

"What phone call?" Minnie cried. "You've never mentioned any phone calls before. Spill it."

"Well, right after Thanksgiving, someone called the house and asked to speak to Edgar. The man said he was from the IRS and wanted to know if he was the president of the Lewisburg Banking Company. He kept Mr. Harper on the phone for quite a while and asked a lot of questions. His son fussed at him for telling so much of his financial information over the phone, but Edgar thought the voice sounded familiar and it was just a friend playing a trick. No one ever called back or came forward to say it was them. The police think this might be connected."

Minnie sat in her favorite chair and plopped her pink house-shoed feet onto the ottoman. "Too bad that call can't be traced."

Jane lowered her feet to the ground and her face glowed with excitement. "I forgot to tell you. I was snooping around at the bridge during the search and overheard two men talking about a special phone they installed in the Harper house right after their disappearance. Sounds like they were expecting a ransom call."

Minnie's eyes rounded. "Do you think they ever got one? I know about the fake call that came to WRUS radio, but I mean a real ransom call?"

Ida looked from Minnie to Jane. "I doubt it. Surely if they did, they wouldn't have dragged the lake. And if they got a call wouldn't they have talked to the victims? They always do on TV."

"Not necessarily." Jane sat her coffee on the side table. "It depends on the demands. But it still doesn't make sense. The FBI would be fully involved if they believed it was a kidnapping. They would have interviewed all the neighbors within sight of the Harper house, and we haven't heard a thing."

A firm knock at the door startled them.

Chapter 5

Jane hurried to open the door.

"Miss Clack?"

"Yes?"

"I'm Special Agent Duncan, this is Special Agent Thorpe." They flashed badges as Duncan continued to talk. "We're here to interview you and your sisters about the disappearance of Mr. Edgar Harper and Mrs. Ella Harper Givens. Do you have some time now?"

Jane, stunned, nodded and pointed the way to the living room, unable to get any words past her throat.

"Mrs. Pryor, we'd like to speak with you first."

Minnie's hands shook as the agent pulled her aside. She'd never been questioned by the police, much less the FBI, and the thought of being accused of something she didn't do frightened her. What would they ask? Would they think she'd hide something from them?

They went to the next room. Jane and Ida scooted to the edge of the couch and stared. Minnie had lived in this house long enough to know they would hear every word. She tried to keep it simple and used great care not to say anything that wasn't absolutely true. Maybe Jane would notice and do the same.

The agent pulled a pen from his shirt pocket and a tablet from his briefcase. He clicked the pen and looked at Minnie. "Mrs. Pryor, how long have you known Edgar and Ella?"

"Oh my, I've known them for many years. Ella visited her parents whenever she came to town."

"How long has she lived across the street?"

Minnie furrowed her brow and thought about his question. "I guess about two years. She doesn't actually live there; she takes care of her father. After his wife's death and his recent heart attack his health started to decline."

He jotted some notes and continued. "Did you know her well? What kind of person was she?"

Minnie, surprised at the gentleness of his questions, relaxed. "Yes, I knew her well. We spent several afternoons a week together watching soap operas and discussing recipes. She helped me with stories I write for some newspapers. Ella is kind and very talented. Everyone likes her. I don't think she has an enemy in the world."

"Do you know why anyone would want to hurt her or her father?"

"No, sorry, I don't have any idea. Can't figure it out. They're good people."

Once Agent Thorpe completed his notes and had her sign them, Minnie returned to the living room where her sisters sat. Jane started to rise.

"Ida, why don't you go next?" Minnie urged. "I'd like to talk to Jane a minute.

Ida stood uneasily and Minnie's heart went out to her. "Go on, Ida. It's okay. You'll do fine."

Minnie looked at Jane. Her legs bounced up and down as her hands rubbed together in rhythm. Minnie knew she was in trouble. Jane couldn't wait for her turn.

"Please don't start a bunch of rumors, Jane. Just stick to the truth. We owe our neighbors that much."

Jane grumbled. "I'm not going to say anything bad about our neighbors. But I am going to ask about some theories I have."

"Jane, I beg you not to."

"Are you kidding? This is the FBI. This is my chance to show I have what it takes to be an agent myself, and maybe get some answers, too." Jane folded her arms across her chest and gave Minnie a warning look. "You can't stop me from answering their questions and you can't control what I say."

Minnie sighed and held her tongue. She could hear Ida finishing up with the agents.

"No, I don't know anything derogatory about them. No problems with the neighbors that I know of, or anyone else for that matter."

"Okay, thank you. Will you send in your sister?"

Jane jumped up before Ida reached the living room. "Don't worry. I'll behave." She gave Minnie a smile and rushed to talk to the agents.

Minnie shook her head. That girl. She would discuss every theory with the FBI as to why someone might kidnap Edgar and Ella, even though she had no proof whatsoever.

"Come on, Ida." Minnie said when she heard Jane talking about a fight between Ella and her sister. "I can't stand any more of this. Let's make some lunch."

When Jane finally emerged, Agents Thorpe and Duncan declined anything to eat or drink and went on their way. Minnie wanted to lay into Jane for spreading gossip, but stayed silent.

"I wonder who else in Lewisburg has been interviewed," Jane mused.

"It's none of our business," announced Minnie.

"Of course it's our business. I'm sure we can solve this with enough clues. I'm going to walk around town and be a little nosy."

"Jane," Ida scolded. "You're going to alienate our neighbors. If you go asking questions like they're suspects, they won't talk to us about anything."

"I'll be discreet. Talk about the FBI coming to interview us and see what nibbles I get. I'll be back in a while."

Jane decided to go to the people she'd seen Ella with. Her first stop was McReynolds General Store.

Mrs. McGehee stood pulling bolts of cloth off a shelf and unrolling them on the cutting table. "Hi Jane, we're getting ready for inventory. Have to count how many yards of muslins we have in stock. What can I get for you?"

"I'm not sure. Let me think. The FBI just left our house, interviewed all three of us. I'm still a little flustered." Jane patted her chest as if her heart beat too fast.

"They visited you, too? They came by here just yesterday. Didn't have much to tell them. Ella came in on the 10th to finish up some Christmas shopping. She did mention at times how lonely it was being away from her husband and all the work she had to do for her father, plus her own housekeeping. It's enough to run anyone ragged."

"Yes, I agree."

"It's hard dealing with aging parents, keeping a marriage going, and enjoying grandchildren. Not hardly enough hours in the day."

Jane nodded. "They do slip by quickly, don't they?"

Mrs. McGehee pulled out another bolt of cloth. "I don't know how she found the time to make all of her clothes. Did you ever notice how well her embroidery was done on her coats? She did that all herself."

"You don't say? Mrs. McGehee, I need to run over to the drugstore before they close. Would you excuse me?"

"Yes, of course. Didn't remember what you came for?"

"What? Oh, no, no. I'm sure Minnie or Ida will get it later. Thanks."

"Oh, I forgot something. The FBI talked to Lucille too, after the hosiery were found. They wanted to know if we sold them."

"What did she say?"

"Told them we didn't sell that brand. I can't recall Ella ever buying hose from us."

"Thank you, thank you. Gotta run."

Mr. Gower from Gower's Pharmacy had little to offer, insisting neither Ella nor Edgar ever shared their personal life with him.

"Anything else you can remember about the night of December 11th? Notice any strangers in the store or on the street?"

Mr. Gower counted pills on the counter before putting them in a pill bottle.

"Nope."

Jane started to leave when she noticed the Greyhound Bus depot sign behind his head. "You sell tickets for the bus. Did anyone buy a ticket that night or the next day?"

"Nope, the police already thought about that. I only sold one that whole week to Mrs. Bennett to go visit her grandchildren over in Hopkinsville."

Jane left and ran into manager Dewitt Ryan locking up. "Hello, Mr. Ryan. What are you doing at the bank on a Sunday?"

"Oh, just doing a little extra work, Miss Clack."

"Mr. Ryan, has the FBI interviewed you?"

"Don't think I'm supposed to say."

"It's okay. They interviewed us, too. Will you tell me what they asked? What you talked about?"

"Well, guess it won't hurt. It's not likely there's any way a secret would be kept in this town."

Jane's mind seized on the word, secret. She listened impatiently as he went through a litany of information that had been parroted by so many others. 'Mr. Harper was a good, honest man. He kept to himself. He knew of no reason why anyone would want to harm him or Ella.' Jane tapped her toe impatiently. When he finished, Jane thanked him and shook his hand. "Thank you, Mr. Ryan. I really must be going." She stepped off the curb.

"Oh, there was that one thing."

Jane turned back. "What thing?"

"On December 13, after they'd disappeared, I received an anonymous call. Never have figured out who it was or what he wanted exactly."

"What did he say?"

"Told me to notify Mr. Harper's son Edward, or another of his sons, and Eustice Givens. Told me to tell them to meet him at the old Hebron Church right away. Insisted there be no publicity. Said all of them would know him."

"Oh my." Darn it, Frank! Why haven't I heard about this? Was Dewitt going to tell her something that would crack the case? She could taste victory, but why was he so all fired slow in telling the story?

"Did they go?"

"Yes, Edward, Eustice, some more of the family went; I did, too. Got there as quick as we could."

"What did he say when you got there?"

"That's just it. No one was there but us."

Jane's hopes deflated. "That's too bad." Wonder if he was hiding and when he saw half the city of Lewisburg there he didn't come out. "I have to go now. Thanks for taking the time to talk to me."

Jane headed toward home with little more to tell her sisters. A police car sat in front of Mrs. Crafton's place. Jane slid between the Crafton's home and their wash house, listening for the slightest tidbit of information about the case. What was going on? Did Mrs. Crafton know something they didn't?

"Just a few shirts. Inis has been feeling poorly and got a little behind on the laundry."

Shoot. Jane snuck back toward the street but her shadowy form outside the window alerted Mrs. Crafton of her presence.

"Oh, who is that? What are you doing?"

"I'll take care of this," a deep male voice answered.

Jane tried to hide behind a forsythia bush, peeking between branches to make sure he didn't see her. A hand grabbed the back of her collar.

"I got her, Mrs. Crafton."

Mrs. Crafton came outside to see Jane's shirt grasped firmly in the hands of the large, beefy policeman. He must have been over six feet and close to three hundred pounds.

"You can put her down, Buffalo. Jane, what were you doing?"

Jane's mind whirred. "Uh-uh, I was trying to cut around to the back of the house so my sisters didn't see me. They'd put me to work on some Christmas chore."

Mrs. Crafton hid her smile behind her fist. "I'm sure you remember Marshal Lawrence 'Buffalo' Ellis?"

Jane smoothed down her blouse then extended her right hand. "Yes, of course. Glad to see you again, Marshal. Do you have any inside information on the Harper case you'd be willing to share?"

The marshal laughed. "As I tell dozens of people daily, I know nothing new. Gotta run. Nice seeing you."

"The pleasure's mine," Jane answered.

"Hey Jane. Haven't seen you in a while. Where you been keeping yourself?"

"Oh, the usual, work, church, volunteering, dates with Frank."

"Isn't it awful, the Harpers, I mean?"

"Yes, no one seems to have any ideas of what happened. When was the last time you saw Ella? I know she brings her dad's laundry here."

"About a week before she disappeared. She had to rush off that day but sometimes she'd sit and talk for a couple hours while I worked. Over the months she's been at her father's, I got the feeling she was lonely."

"Really? What did you talk about?"

"How she missed her husband, seemed to be crazy about him. He came up from Quality about every other night to stay at the Harper house. She went home frequently too. It's no wonder she had to go over to Dr. Dodson in Russellville for nerve shots. All that taking care of others, she barely had time to take care of herself."

"She certainly was busy. Did the FBI talk to you?"

"Sure did. Couldn't tell them much except that thing about McPherson, but I'm sure it was nothing."

Jane tried to hide her surprise. "McPherson?"

"The police officer, Barney McPherson."

Jane tapped a finger against her cheek, then put her hand behind her back and crossed her fingers. "Oh, I remember now. He moved in and out of town so quickly, I almost forgot about him."

"Well, I'm not saying he followed her, but when she was here visiting, he drove up and down the street real slow, more than what seemed normal. It happened so often, I teased Ella about him being sweet on her. She told me he even drove up to their house at night and turned around. She didn't like that, never gave him any encouragement."

"I knew she wouldn't," Jane nodded. "Either way you look at it, it's weird. He could have had some romantic thoughts about Ella, or he could have overheard something and maybe he was watching her in order to protect her."

"Never thought about it like that," Mrs. Crafton picked a speck of dust off her apron.

Jane glanced around as if someone might be listening. "Did you hear that about three weeks before they disappeared, that renter of his, Mr. Belcher, came after dark to pay them? They wouldn't open the door."

"Really? There's just so many oddities to think about I don't know how the police can decide who to investigate first."

"We're all on edge." Jane glanced at her watch. "I have to go now. I'll drop by again soon for another chat. Something more pleasant, I hope."

All this time, everyone had focused on Edgar Harper and his money as the reason for the disappearance. What if it was Ella? It does seem odd though that the strange guy that stopped at Marvine Pogue's asked if the policeman was at home. That's where Barney McPherson used to live before he moved to Russellville. If I tell Minnie and Ida, they won't want to pry. I'll just mosey on over there before they can stop me. Jane rushed home and pulled her keys from her purse. She eased open the door of the Buick and turned the key. Her sisters came to the door and she waved at them as she sped off.

Jane crept around to the back of Barney McPherson's house. She couldn't believe it was so easy to find out where he lived. Just a few questions at the grocery and the clerk gave directions to the house. She loved small towns.

If he were holding Edgar and Ella, he'd have to put them somewhere out of sight where they couldn't be heard. Around the back of the house, she found a root cellar with a heavy lock. Jane laid her head on the wooden door, trying to hear anything.

A small sound rose from the dark depths. Through cracks in the door she could see a faint light and smell the earth floor. The sound came again. Could it be a muffled scream? Did McPherson have them tied up with gags in their mouths? Jane looked around for anything to get the lock off the door. A shovel lay against the privacy fence. She took it and shoved it at the hinge of the door. A piece splintered as it bounced off. The sound became louder. She hit the hinge again.

"Stop right there."

Jane turned around to see G.C. McMillen.

"Oh, G.C. I'm so glad you're here. I think Ella and Edgar might be in this cellar and..."

"Do you know whose house this is?"

"Yes. Barney McPherson's."

"What are you trying to do?"

"Someone told me they thought he might be infatuated with Ella, and I got to thinking what if it wasn't Edgar they were after but Ella."

"Barney McPherson?"

The sound came again. "There, there, you see? Doesn't that sound like someone with their mouth gagged?"

G.C. stopped to listen. "I'm sure there's a reasonable explanation."

"That's right, there is." Barney McPherson stepped around the house.

"Could I see what's in your cellar, Barney?"

"Yes, of course." He reached under a flowerpot near the back door and pulled out a key. He unlocked the door and threw it back. Jane started down first, but G.C. grabbed her arm.

"Wait here, please." G.C. went down first and Barney followed close behind.

What if he hits him in the head? What if he shoots him? What if he shoots me?

"Miss Clack, you can come down now."

"Are you sure G.C.?"

"Yes, there's no danger."

Jane carefully picked her way down the stairs and saw the two men staring down into a box. Inside, everything seemed to wriggle at once. G.C. turned on his flashlight to reveal a mama cat and her kittens.

"Aw, how sweet. But why lock them down here?"

"Neighborhood children were coming to see them and leaving the door open. I was afraid a dog or something else might get in and hurt them, so I started locking it when I wasn't home. Anything else? Do you want to take a tour of my house?"

"Well..."

"Jane," G.C. said sharply, "We meet here for card games on Friday nights. Don't you think a house full of police might have noticed something? You're barking up the wrong tree. Please go home and let us handle the investigation."

Jane turned and slunk back to the car. Another dead end. Dead end? She hoped not.

Chapter 6

December 25, 1965

Come and see, come and see." Jane bounced on Ida's bed. "Santa Claus came."

Ida rubbed the sleep from her eyes. "For goodness sakes, Jane. Santa hasn't come to see us in about thirty years."

"He really did this time. Come on." Jane pulled Ida up and dragged her down the stairs to the back hall. "Here," she threw Ida's long camel-colored coat over her shoulders.

"Wait, why do I need this?"

"We're going outside. Hurry and put your boots on. It snowed overnight. It's a white Christmas." Jane jerked the door open and pulled Ida down the concrete steps and around to the front of the house. A bright yellow Volkswagen Beetle gleamed in the early morning sun. A gold bow glistened from the top of the car. A large tag hung down the side with "Jane" written in pretty script.

"What in the world?" asked Ida.

"Santa came and gave me a car," Jane danced around in a circle, grabbed some snow and threw her arms in the air. "Have you ever seen anything more beautiful in your life?"

Ida walked to the back. "What's this?"

"That's those new crazy daisy stickers. You know, flower power and all that jive."

"Crazy daisy? Flower power? All that jive? Are you speaking another language, Jane?"

"No, it's just things kids say today. There's no harm in adding new words to my vocabulary. Anyway, what do you think? Do you like my new car?"

"Where did it come from?"

"Well, Frank wanted to get me something really special for Christmas, so..."

"Jane," Ida chided, "you didn't let him buy you a car."

"No, of course not. I let him make the down payment and after 48 payments of $32, it will be all mine."

Ida's mouth dropped open. "Thirty-two dollars a month? How can you afford that and the insurance and upkeep? Why, they're saying gas might even hit forty cents a gallon next year. I think you should take it back."

"Don't worry about it. I've been saving, and teachers get a raise after the first." She laid her cheek on the hood and stretched her arms out. "Isn't it wonderful?"

"Yes, Jane. It's wonderful. Can we go in now? I'm freezing my keester off."

"Sure, let's go in. You start the coffee. I'm going to wake up Minnie."

"You're pretty brave. You know how grouchy she can be in the mornings, especially when she's woken up. She might throw you off the bed."

"Aw, it's Christmas. I bet she thanks me. After all, guests will be arriving soon." Once Jane repeated the ritual of the car, Minnie checked the turkey she'd put in the oven in the wee hours of the morning and settled down for the only break of the day.

"Open these," Jane said as she handed Minnie and Ida bright red packages with silver ribbons curling over the sides. "I can't wait for you to see them."

Minnie and Ida quickly unwrapped the paper to find identical white boxes and lifted off the lids. Beads spilled out onto the floor.

"Heavens to Betsy," Minnie blurted out. "What is this?"

"It's beads," Jane said. "Aren't they cool?

"But Jane," Ida said. "We're supposed to make our presents to each other. You're breaking our tradition."

"I did make them."

"How?" Minnie asked.

"I used Frank's fishing line and picked the beads up at the five and dime. I threaded each one myself."

"Wow," Ida admired her royal blue strings. "That must have taken you a long time."

"It took me a whole month. Frank let me hide them at his place. Don't you just love them?"

Minnie stood and held the strings of purple and red beads over her head. They reached down and puddled on the floor. "Yes dear. I love them, but can I ask you one teeny-tiny question?"

"Well of course, Sis. Ask me anything."

"What am I supposed to do with them?"

"Yes," Ida echoed. "Where do they go?"

"Where do they go?" Jane asked. "Why they can go anywhere. In a doorway, over a picture, around a lamp, hanging in a window; any place you think needs a little jazzing up."

"Ah," Minnie said. "Now I see. Thank you. I'm sure I'll find the perfect spot for them."

"Thank you." Ida repeated. "I can tell you worked hard on them." She slid the beads under the tree and pulled out the rest of the gifts to exchange.

Once the gifts were done the doorbell rang for the first of many times that day. Before they could shake a stick every corner of the house held a few people deep in conversation, telling jokes, or reminiscing about Christmases past.

All the people and noise caused Jane to feel a little claustrophobic and she stepped outside. No one would miss her. Minnie's party was a success, there were plenty of people to socialize with and the sisters couldn't be happier. They had put a lot of effort into this celebration. Well, Minnie and Ida had.

Jane pulled a pack of cigarettes from her pocket and put one in her mouth. The new menthol flavor advertisement promised the Pall Mall brand was "clean and natural." The models in Cosmopolitan looked so serene and beautiful with a thin cigarette perched daintily between two fingers. After lighting it, she took a few puffs. The heat burned her throat and she began to cough.

"What the heck?" The magazine had made it seem so glamourous—even a tad rebellious. "You've come a long way baby." She'd read an article about supposed health benefits, but it hadn't said anything about how nasty they tasted, or how bad they smelled.

Jane ground the half-finished cigarette under the heel of her white go-go boot. So much for that idea.

After the fiasco at Barney McPherson's house, Frank hadn't spoken to her for several days. 'If you embarrass me one more time in front of my colleagues, it's over.' It was the first time Frank had ever threatened to break up with her. Jane knew he was still hiding something from her, but she was going to have to be more careful with her investigation. She folded a piece of gum into her mouth before stepping back inside.

Minnie wiped her forehead with her hand. "Whew, there you are Jane. Take the blackberry jam cake to the sideboard and see if anyone needs refills of eggnog or cider."

Since Minnie's family couldn't be home for Christmas, Jane and Ida had encouraged their older sister to invite friends for the day and Minnie had embraced the idea. God bless her big old heart, everyone she thought might be alone this holiday received an invitation, and most of them accepted.

An old man sat at the kitchen table, his bald head, shiny as glass, reflected the overhead light. A tuft of hair sprouted from above each ear, and he talked nonstop about his granddaughter in Dunmor. Who was this man anyway? She didn't remember him. Beth, from McReynolds Store, sat beside him. Jane gave them a smile as she passed.

She set the cake down and wandered into the living room to find Frank entertaining guests. She had to smile when she saw him standing at the punch bowl, dipping eggnog to the folks hanging out by the side board. A grin stretched across his face as he "Ho, ho, hoed" and wished those standing there a "Merry Christmas."

He motioned for her, and she glided over as if she had a book on her head and didn't want it to fall. The past few weeks had been grueling for Frank and he needed this day off duty to relax and have a good time.

Pulling her to his side they stepped away from the group and he leaned to whisper in her ear. "Don't go over to the other side of the room. Tom and Mr. Forgy are discussing tobacco crops and trucking. We both know you couldn't care less if dark tobacco sold for 29.7 cents a pound on the floor last week, or that Woodrow Thompson and Chester Ezell's names were mentioned on the radio for having the highest bidding price in Bowling Green? I, on the other hand, wouldn't mind that a bit, so I'll head that way in a minute if you'll mind the eggnog.

Her eyes sparkled with laughter. "You just saved me from certain death. Thanks."

"Don't mention it."

They returned to the eggnog table together, where Frank jumped right back in the conversation. Jane's gaze however wandered the room, taking in everything.

Getting the eight-foot pine home on top of the Buick was no problem. The man from the Christmas tree lot had hauled it up there and tied it down. Convincing her sisters to help her get it in the house was a different story.

"Why do we need such a monstrosity, Jane?" Ida barked. "I broke a nail and have tar stuck to my hand. Do you know how hard it is to get that off?"

"The smell will fill the house and remind us constantly of the season," Jane countered.

"We don't even have enough ornaments and tinsel for it," Minnie surveyed the huge tree with a critical eye.

"Picked those up already. We just need to get it on the porch and Frank will bring it in."

Later, their negativity was put to rest when they plugged in the Christmas bulbs and turned out all the lights.

"Beautiful," Ida sighed.

"Told you so," Jane sassed.

The pine added to the gaiety of the sights around her. Its colorful bulbs hidden between the branches filled the room with a festive feel. Greenery dotted every available flat space. Some nestled around candles, while others rested behind decorations on the mantle and sideboard. Holiday music played lightly in the background and the murmur of conversation filled the room. Somehow, they had pulled it together and made it work. Minnie would be so proud.

A young woman came up to Jane, hand extended. She stared for a second before shaking herself out of her musings.

"I don't believe we've met, I'm Catherine Snyder."

"Pleased to meet you."

"Same here."

"Are you here to visit family? Do you live far?"

"I live over in Dunmor. Barry Jackson is my cousin." She waved in his direction. "His mom was a second mother to me when we were young. I spent every summer at his house. Of course that was before they moved here when I was in college or I'm sure we would have met before."

"Did you have a pleasant drive over?" Jane put into practice all the polite social conversation her mother had drilled into her daughters from the time they were born.

"Oh, I didn't drive. I planned on being here almost three weeks and you never know the weather here. I won't drive in snow, so I took the bus here."

"When was that?"

"The evening of December 11th, I'll be here until January 2nd."

December 11? Jane felt lightheaded. Why had she never thought of who might have taken a bus or taxi into town instead of out of town? "So, did anyone ride into town with you? Anyone get off here in Lewisburg?"

"No, I was all by myself. Gave me time to finish Neil Simon's latest book, "The Odd Couple." Not a big fan, myself. Two guys living in an apartment in New York. Just couldn't associate with anything."

"No one got off the bus while you were on it?"

"There was this one guy who got off in Dunmor."

"What did he look like?"

"Dark clothes, a hat. Didn't notice much because I had my nose in the book the whole time."

Dark Clothes, hat? Dunmor wasn't too far away. Could it have been the same guy that visited Marvine Pogue's that night? Did he double back to throw suspicion off of him? Jane was so deep in thought she almost missed the next part of Catherine's sentence.

"It's not important to the disappearance though, or so the police said when they interviewed me."

"Interviewed you?" Jane's eyes widened before she could tamp down her shock. "Interesting. Would you excuse me please?" She launched herself to where Frank stood, grabbed his arm and pulled him out the door before he could react."

"What honey? Do you want a little dessert before dinner?" He reached for her waist, but she sidestepped him.

"You didn't tell me there were interviews with people on the bus, probably taxi services too. How could you?"

"Now Jane, there has to be some things kept under wraps. Besides, that was the FBI interviews, not our department. From what I could tell by reading them…"

"Reading them? You were allowed to read the FBI interviews? Where are they? When can I see them?"

"Darlin', we're not allowed to take them out of G.C.'s office. They're strictly in his control and no one can get to them except him."

"You have to give me a chance to read them, you have to."

"No, Jane. Absolutely not."

"But..."

"No buts. This is the FBI we're talking about. That information is classified. You already almost cost me my job. I will not go to jail for you."

Jane looked down, her voice wavering. "I'm sorry, Frank. You know I'd never do anything to hurt you." She ran a finger under her eye as if to catch a tear.

Frank took a deep breath. "Look, you know I love you, but I'm not taking that chance."

Jane's voice cracked. She started to speak, then stopped. He was right. She certainly didn't want him to end up in jail because of her.

"Frank, I'm sorry."

"It's not going to work."

"Okay."

"What? No crying? No fighting?"

"No. You're right. I don't want to hurt you. I want to help. Besides, it's Christmas. Let's talk about it later."

"That's a great idea." Surprise registered in his voice. "I promise I'll find some other way to get you involved, but we have to wait until more is happening so they don't focus on you and your connection to me." He put his hand under her chin and lifted. "Okay?"

"Okay." She threw her arms around him. "Thanks."

The door swung open revealing Minnie with garland wrapped around her neck. Someone must have sneaked in their own flask of Christmas cheer.

"Come on you lovebirds. We're sitting down to dinner."

People were squished around card tables covered with white tablecloths in every inch of space in the dining room. Every folding chair they'd borrowed from the church was occupied and everyone awaited the carving of the turkey and ham so they could form a buffet line. The incredible smells from the traditional Christmas dishes sitting around the room had people wiping their mouths before ever taking a bite.

"Frank," Minnie held up a carving knife and fork. "Would you do the honors before some of these people start chewing on each other," she laughed.

"My pleasure."

Everyone filled their plates and gathered at their tables. They joined hands for the blessing and dove into the food, barely stopping to pick up a fork. Jane sat in the corner beside Frank with her ear cocked to pick up different snippets of conversation. No one seemed to be talking about the Harper case. She looked across at the bald man she'd noticed talking to Beth McReynolds earlier.

"Have we met?" Jane asked?

"I think so, but it's been a long time. I used to help your brother-in-law Curtis at harvest time. My name is Lawrence Tabb, they call me Spud because of all the blue ribbons my potatoes have won at the Kentucky State Fair."

"Wow," Jane feigned interest. "Are you originally from here?"

"Yes. My wife's gone now, and my children and grandchildren are scattered to the wind, except one daughter I have over in Allensville, but I'd rather not talk about that."

"Oh, I understand."

"I heard two of my grandsons were in town recently to visit her, but they didn't come see me."

Minnie shot Jane a warning look and shook her head just slightly. Jane frowned back at her and shrugged her shoulders, confused.

"That's too bad," Jane soothed.

"No, it certainly is not."

"Would I know them? What's their names?"

"I won't even say their first names but their last name is Brown. I doubt a fine upstanding woman like you would know them. Their dad taught all of them boys nothing but how to cheat and steal from people. Several of them have been in the penitentiary, and if you ask me that's where they all belong." He was on a roll and couldn't slow down. "You know, it wouldn't surprise me if they were involved in this whole Harper thing. They came into town a few days before and left right after. Wouldn't surprise me at all. I even told the FBI agent that when he questioned me. He seemed kinda shocked".

FBI? Jane's eyes flew to Frank as he covered his laugh to stop food from flying out of his mouth. "Now, that's something you don't hear every day."

"I don't behold to lowlife. Not even my own kin. Bible says if a man wants to eat, he must work, not steal." Spud said between bites. And another thing..."

"I'll tell you," Ida interrupted. "This thing's got me in a bundle of nerves. The FBI has been questioning everybody in our neighborhood. Did polygraphs, too. They didn't learn anything more than they already had, I think. Guess they believed us, because they didn't put us through any lie detectors."

"They didn't have reason to suspect us." Minnie changed the subject. "Let's talk about something more cheerful. Like desserts. We got several to choose from."

"Choose?" Frank bellowed. "I want them all."

The dining room once again, filled with cheer. Jane made sure to save room for her ambrosia Jell-O dessert. That Italian cream cake of Ida's had her name on it, too.

After the successful Christmas feast, most of the ladies stayed to help with the dishes, while the men loitered around the fireplace, drinking apple cider, eating roasted chestnuts, and swapping tales about hunting rabbits and running coon dogs.

Minnie gave everyone a small tin of gingerbread cookies as they left. She blushed as they all oohed and ahhed over them.

"I'll be right back," Jane told Ida. "I'm going to walk Frank to his car."

They held hands and walked the short distance to Frank's cruiser. "Only a quick kiss tonight, darlin'. I have to get on patrol."

"But what about those Brown brothers? They came to town right before they disappeared and left right after. Did the police ever check them out?"

"How did you know about them?"

"In a town this small, could there be really be any secrets?"

"Since you didn't find out about them until now, Jane, I guess there can." Frank chuckled.

"Spill it, Frank. What about Mr. Tabb's grandsons, the Browns? Are they suspects?"

"Now don't go spreading this around town, but yes, they were. We were looking for them because they passed some bad checks around. Then we learned one of the brothers drove a big car like the one Mr. Forgy saw leaving the Harper driveway. They'd come in just before the disappearance of the Harpers and left soon after, which really made us suspicious."

"Frank..."

"Their mother and a sister live here but the other brother and sister who lived here left for Connecticut.

"It's them, it has to be them. You guys solved the case. When are they going to be arrested?"

"Hold on, there's more. The other brother left here and returned to his home in Florida. That's why we had such a hard time tracking him down. They both seemed to be on the run, but when we caught up to them, they were cleared. They don't have any connection to the Harpers or Givens, and you know Ella was not going to open that door to strangers and the door jamb wasn't broken. It wasn't them."

"Oh Frank." She reached up and hugged him tight. "How disappointing."

"You're going to have to let me go sweetie or I'm going to be late for work." He gave her a deep kiss. "Now get in the house before I call in and take you for a midnight ride."

Jane giggled and high-tailed it back to her sisters. She closed and locked the door.

"That didn't take long." Ida said.

"Oh Ida, I thought you'd be in bed."

"Had to have one more piece of chocolate pie. Was afraid you'd get up in the morning and eat the rest of it." Ida placed her plate in the sink and ran a little water on it to wash it.

"Still doing dishes?" Minnie questioned as she came in wearing her pajamas.

"Only this last one."

Minnie gathered her two sisters into a big hug. "Thank God for the true meaning of Christmas. We have surely been blessed today."

"Let's get to bed," yawned Ida. "I, for one, am going to sleep in tomorrow." The other sisters nodded in agreement.

"Merry Christmas, sisters," Jane said. "I'll be up in a few."

She waited until they disappeared before grabbing her notebook. Writing quickly, she noted everything she'd found out about the case that day. She understood Frank couldn't help her, and she respected that he stood up to her and hadn't backed down. But that didn't mean she couldn't try to find out a few things on her own.

Chapter 7

December 31, 1965

The bells rang as Minnie struggled up the old church steps. She regretted waving away her sisters' help so they could run ahead and begin the preparations for the celebration after services. Her legs hurt from the chilling cold weather, but she refused to miss the New Year's Eve service or the fun and games afterwards.

"Good evening, Minnie. Your knee giving you trouble?" Marvine Pogue took her arm.

"Thank You." Minnie walked with her into the white clapboard building. Wooden pews stretched to the altar of the old country church. Minnie groaned. "I don't know if I can make it all the way up to the choir this evening."

Marvine patted her arm. "Let's sit here in the back row. Molly may be strict about the choir being in their seats on time and ready to hit those high notes, but she'll understand if you need a night off."

Minnie followed her into the pew and sank onto the blue cushioned seat. The choir was already seated, song books on their laps open to the first hymn. Her friend Tom, who sat beside her on stage every Sunday, and any time there was a special service, searched the audience. A look of relief crossed his face when he spotted her and he gave a little wave. Well, she hadn't missed a church meeting since the day her husband died, and only then because her sisters insisted, she shouldn't go, just to stare at his empty seat.

Tom smiled at her, scratched his white beard, smoothed his gray speckled hair, and straightened his tie. The oak paneled door from the vestibule swung open and everyone scrambled to their seats as the Pastor came to the podium.

"Let us pray."

Minnie stayed seated as everyone around her rose. Tom's rich voice an octave above the others, stayed in time with the music, but he craned his neck often, watching to see if she stood. What a nice man, so sweet of him to be concerned.

The pastor's deep voice reverberated around the room. "As the New Year starts, today is a good day to make a decision concerning our Savior. No one knows when they will be called home. What their fate will be."

Minnie's attention wandered back to her throbbing knee. Using the tips of her fingers, she massaged it, hoping to relieve the pain before going to the fellowship hall afterwards.

Once the service finished, Marvine helped Minnie to her feet. "Are you going to be able to stay for fellowship?"

"I wouldn't miss it. Just glad I don't have to walk down steps. You go on, I need to find Ida and Jane. They're here somewhere preparing for the party."

Marvine looked up the aisle. "Here they come now. I'll see you in a bit." She waved at them then turned away and wandered off.

"Minnie, are you okay?" Ida said as soon as she got close.

"What happened?" Jane asked.

"I'm fine, you two. My knee just hurts. It's my arthritis."

"I can take you home," Ida offered. "I don't mind at all."

"A-hem."

Minnie turned around. "Tom, it's good to see you. You know my sisters, Ida and Jane."

"Of course, I do. Hi, ladies." He turned back to Minnie. "I was very concerned when you didn't show up in your seat. Is everything okay? You look pale."

"Oh, I'm fine. My knee is bothering me. I didn't think I could climb the steps to the choir loft."

"I can understand that. Will you be staying for the New Year's party then?" A hopeful look filled his face.

"Sure am, wouldn't miss it."

"Good, I hope your knee won't keep you from moving around the room, I know how social you are. I can go with you and hold onto your arm. See you in a bit."

"No wonder you insist on coming to church every Sunday." Jane's gaze followed Tom as he left the sanctuary. "I think there's more to you and Tom than you've let on.

"He is a good-looking gentleman." Ida nodded.

"Now, Jane, you know I come to service for the Lord. Tom has nothing to do with it." Minnie snapped, and nudged Jane aside. As she headed for the fellowship hall, Minnie was sure her red cheeks gave her away.

Jane and Ida hurried to catch up. "Oh, Minnie. Don't get mad," Ida called. "We were just teasing."

"I know you were." Minnie marched on, ignoring her pain. "Just not in a good mood tonight, sorry." They entered the room at the back of the church.

"Maybe we can stay a bit and then leave," Ida soothed. "There's no need for you to suffer all night." Ida met Minnie's stare. "Unless of course you want to be with Tom." Jane laughed out loud as Ida stifled a giggle.

Children played musical chairs on one side of the room and pin the tail on the donkey on the other. Minnie smiled as a few tails wandered off course and almost got the bystanders. Adults talked in groups while some cheered on their children. If only she could walk around and engage in conversation. Minnie found the closest table and sat down as her sisters joined the crowd to mingle.

"Here you go, Minnie." Tom put a cup of punch on the table and joined her. "How's the pain?"

"Oh, I'll be fine, thank you."

"Yeah," Tom nodded. "When you get to our age, everything seems to fall apart."

"Don't I know it?"

Tom seemed content to sit with her and they chatted about the weather, church events, and even the Christmas party.

"Minnie, I've been meaning to ask you something for a while now."

"Yes?"

"I, well, I want. Would you—would you like to go out for coffee and pie after church next Sunday?"

A blush warmed her neck and she glanced away to gather her composure. Of course, she wanted to go with him. Couldn't he tell? She lifted her face to him. "I'd love to."

Ida seated herself at the table. "You're all flushed Minnie. Is your knee hurting that bad?"

Frank and Jane approached, Jane's blonde hair bounced on her shoulder as she walked up, her face full of excitement.

"Minnie do you want us to give you a ride home?"

"Are you leaving so soon?" Minnie asked.

"Frank just got a call. It's official business, and he has to go. I'm going with him." Jane bent down and whispered, "they found Edgar's wallet." She squeezed Minnie's arm and did a little dance, then bent to Minnie's ear again. "I can't believe it. It's exactly what we needed. Another clue."

"Now Jane, they want me there right away." Frank said. "You should take your sister home."

She stopped and looked at Frank. "What? I want to go with you."

"But honey, it's dark and I don't have an extra flashlight."

"I keep one in my glove compartment. Never know when it will come in handy."

Frank tried to shake his head no, but his resolve weakened. "But Sweetie," Jane's voice oozed honey, "you always say how detail oriented I am, how I can catch on to something even seasoned detectives miss."

"Yes, but…"

"Please, please, please. I'll just listen, I promise."

"Well..."

She grabbed his hands and swung them around. "Thank you."

"But one word and you'll have to stay in the car."

"Yes, dear."

"Minnie," Tom said, "I know you're ready to go. Let me take you home."

"Oh Tom, that would be great, if you truly don't mind." Ida replied. "I just volunteered to do the countdown at midnight."

Tom rose, "I don't mind at all." He took Minnie's elbow and helped her to stand.

"Well if ...if you're sure." Minnie stammered. She saw Ida and Jane grin at each other and wink. Why, they'd done that on purpose. Those sisters of hers were matchmaking. It was a good thing it was Tom, or she would have put them in their place. As it stood, she wanted to finish their conversation. Just a few minutes ago he'd asked her out on an official date.

In a low tone, Minnie asked Jane, "Did they say where they found the wallet? Was it anywhere near the place they found the hat?"

"No, it was actually in the opposite direction, over on Sportsman Road, near Russellville. You know, right on the edge of Lewisburg. That's what—about fifteen miles away from Wolfe Creek Bridge?"

Frank tugged on Jane's sleeve. "We have to go."

Ida hugged them. "Happy New Year's, you two. Be careful."

"Oh, don't worry about me," Frank said. "And I'll take care of Jane." He hugged her against him. "Nothing to worry about."

The excited look on Jane's face told Ida and Minnie there could be plenty to worry about.

"Just be careful," Ida repeated as they left.

"You wait here inside the door, and I'll pull the car around," Tom told Minnie.

As soon as Tom disappeared, Minnie turned to Ida. "So, you're going to do the countdown, huh? I could've sworn the pastor did that."

Ida blushed. "Uh...well..."

Minnie shook her finger. "No more lies." She pulled Ida into a big hug. "Thank you." Minnie winked and stepped out the door, leaving a shocked Ida staring after her.

Frank's car passed with Jane in the driver's seat, leaning forward as if she could make the automobile move faster. Poor Frank.

***

Jane pulled her yellow bug into the police station in hopes that Frank would be available for lunch.

Eustice pulled up beside her and got out.

"Hi, Eustice." Jane greeted. "How are things going?"

He kicked at a rock and eyed the small building that housed the Sheriff's Department. "Same old stuff. They spend too much time on things that aren't important. God knows I've visited this tiny station too much in the last twenty-two days. And yet, here I am again."

"What are you here for this time?"

Sheriff Sweat said they have another clue. He'd better be telling the truth. I'm really tired of being interrogated and blamed for the disappearance of my wife."

"Aw, Eustice. They don't really think that do they? You're kidding right? "

"I'm not kidding. They've spent so much time on me the real kidnappers have probably gotten away. They even gave me a second polygraph test."

"I'm so sorry."

His boots pounded the ground as he and Jane made their way into the station to find out what they'd discovered this time. Of course, Jane already knew what this was about, but the sheriff would kill her if she told Eustice before he did.

"This had better be good. I'm in no mood to mess around, and I definitely don't want to hear about a psychic who claims to know where their bodies are. Heck fire, they're not dead. Why are people trying to say they are?"

Jane didn't know what to say so she just nodded.

Eustice jerked open the door and stepped inside. Sheriff Sweat came out of his office and held out his hand. Eustice hesitated for a second before accepting it in his firm grasp.

"Hello, Gene. You got news for me?"

Jane slid onto a bench by the door. If all went well, she'd get to witness Eustice's reaction firsthand.

"Let's go into my office."

Sheriff Gene Sweat sat behind the desk and invited Eustice Givens to take the seat opposite him. Eustice shook his head, "I prefer to stand."

The sheriff left the door open, so Jane only had to slide down the bench a little to see what was happening. Gene opened his desk drawer and withdrew an envelope. He pitched it the short distance between them and Eustice caught it in his hands.

"Do you recognize that?"

Eustice flipped the yellow envelope up and a wallet slid into his palm. He opened it and read the license in the little window pocket. His eyes widened. "Are you serious? This is really Edgar's Wallet?"

"You tell me."

Eustice looked at the wallet again. "Where? How? Did you find anything of Ella's?" He stumbled, caught himself and leaned against the desk.

Jane, afraid to move, stayed in the background praying they wouldn't notice her and shut the door.

The sheriff held up his hand. "Sit down, Eustice, and we'll see what we can figure out. Eustice sat heavily in a chair.

"The wallet was found on a deserted stretch of highway just above Russellville. US 431 to be exact. Sportsman Road. Jerry Wilham, a Russellville construction worker, told me one of his workers found it. Jerry was bulldozing and helping Mr. Bill MacGoodwin with his seeding. Anyway, it was found by the side of a road, next to a drain."

Eustice stood. His gaze never leaving the wallet. "All his cards, papers, and driver's license are still in here. Does anyone know if there was any money?"

"Did he usually carry a lot? Maybe for show?"

"Oh no. Mr. Harper wasn't like that. I bet he never carried over $50. They didn't get much if that's what they were after. But that just doesn't sound right. Why wouldn't they go through the house looking for money? I mean, they didn't take Ella's money out of her purse, or even investigate the lockbox under Edgar's bed."

Jane sat still as stone on the bench not believing her luck. Here she was hearing first-hand the latest info on the wallet. Now Frank wouldn't have to worry about telling her.

"That's what I was thinking. Why all the trouble for so little money?" Sheriff Sweat continued. "Why didn't they just rob them at home and not take the risk of a witness seeing them?"

"I guess we're right back where we started," Eustice sighed, "except we have a new place to search."

"Now Eustice. You know we've searched everywhere. They could've thrown that out a hundred miles from their destination. We still don't know what direction to look. We just need you to wait by the phone until we know something more."

"So, you're telling me you called me all the way down here to tell me you found a new clue, but you're not going to do anything with it?" Eustice kicked the little wire trashcan across the room. Wadded paper tumbled out. "This is my wife we're talking about. What if it were your wife, Gene? Would you sit idly by and just wait?"

Gene's face reddened, but he didn't move. "Now Eustice."

"Don't you 'Now, Eustice" me. Are you going to help me or not? I need to find my wife."

Gene rubbed his chin. "Okay. Okay. Yes, I'll get another search going. Give me time to get some people together. I guess that's the best place to start. Maybe you can grab anyone you know and meet me out at Bill MacGoodwin's farm.

"I'll help," Jane piped up.

Both men turned in surprise.

"I know my sisters will help, too. Come on, there's lots of people we can ask. Let's get started." Jane left the station and ran to her car before the sheriff could reprimand her for eavesdropping on their conversation.

Late that afternoon, around two hundred volunteers including Jane and Ida, swarmed the woods around Bill's farm. Minnie sat in the car and watched the searchers. Joining hands, they struggled through the cockleburs and brush searching for anything of significance to show Eustice and the sheriff. When nightfall came without any new clues, Sheriff Gene Sweat called off the search.

Jane felt helpless as she watched Eustice walk to his truck. He would go home alone to an empty house once again. She had hoped... prayed...that this time would be different.

Chapter 8

February 1, 1966

Jane organized her thoughts before approaching Minnie with her newest idea. Feeling antsy since Frank wouldn't let her help with the investigation, Jane had thought of a different way to stay involved. Why couldn't they do a little private investigating of their own under the guise of writers? FBI agents were interviewing people all over the county. There were only a few hotels, so their car would be easy to find. Minnie could use some of what they found for her columns. It might take a little persuasion, but she was sure she would convince her sister. She had to be careful not to anger Frank further. Valentine's Day was coming, and she expected a trip into Nashville for a romantic dinner. Maybe even some champagne.

After hearing Jane's plan, Minnie hesitated. Following the FBI around could lead to big trouble. The idea of getting statewide recognition for her column won her over and she finally agreed. That night when Frank made his usual phone call, Jane picked his brain to learn as much as she could without exposing their scheme. The next day they arose early and found the dark Sedan with the official license plate in a motel parking lot next to the Tasty Freeze in Russleville; it was the same Sedan Jane had been handcuffed in. This time getting caught wasn't an option. Frank might never speak to her again.

Excitement oozed from the women as they set out on their secret rendezvous. Minnie carried a briefcase and wore a business suit. Jane, clad in dress slacks and heels, maneuvered with some difficulty as she tried to keep up with the FBI car,without arousing suspicion. Gravel crunched as they traveled out Russellville's graveled Rural Route Four. The big car pulled into the drive of a two-story frame house.

"Hmm, wonder what this is about?" Jane commented.

They drove on past and pulled over onto the shoulder of a side road where some tall weeds hid the car. Jane got out and ran to part the plants so she could see.

"Jane, get back in the car," Minnie hissed. "You aren't going to see anything from here and we'll see the car leave." Their gaze never left the house until the FBI sedan backed out of the drive and headed toward Russellville. Jane cranked the Buick. "Here goes." A faded mailbox stood beside the road as they turned into the drive. Darn, no name, Minnie would just have to play it by ear. Jane knocked on the door of the white frame house and stepped in front of Minnie when the middle-aged woman answered the knock.

"Hello, I'm Janice Cook. This is Minerva Payne, you might recognize the name from reading one of her columns in the newspapers."

"No, I don't. Can I help you? Do you need directions or something?"

Jane answered, "I hope you can help us. You see, we were supposed to meet the gentleman from the FBI here, Special Agent Allen. We hoped you might have some information that would interest Minerva's readers. Just any little tidbit, and she'd be glad to use your name in her article. I'm her private secretary and will write your statement exactly as you say it." She held up her steno pad.

"Sorry, Miss Cook. I'm a private person and I do not give you permission to use my name in any newspaper."

A little, white-haired lady toddled in from the other room, waving a hand in the air. "I'm the one who called them. It was me. If there's a reward, I get it. My name is—"

"Mother. Stop. Do not give these people your name."

Jane stepped closer, not allowing Minnie to get in a word. "You don't have to tell us your name. We'll keep it out of the paper. And if your information leads to finding Mrs. Givens and Mr. Harper, we'll guarantee you will receive the one-thousand-dollar reward. Won't we Minerva?" Minnie nodded to Jane.

"Yes. Yes, of course, we will. I'll personally deliver it. I'll even let you read the article before it goes to print. You can change anything you don't like."

The lady who opened the door stepped between them. "This is my mom, and I don't want her hounded. Please excuse us." The younger woman placed her hand on the doorknob, slowly pushing it closed."

"I understand," Minnie turned away. "Please forgive us. We wouldn't want to cause any problems."

Jane didn't want to leave, but acquiesced to Minnie's snug grip on her arm as she pulled her toward the car. Jane's eyes widened and mouth formed a silent objection as she pointed toward the older lady following them. "Wait…"

"Hold on a minute." The elderly woman tossed her head toward the white frame structure where her daughter stood on the porch. "This is my house and I say who comes and goes. I'm telling my story. It might help them find that missing banker and his daughter." She beckoned to Jane and Minnie to follow her inside.

"We want to respect your daughter's wishes. It's not worth causing friction in a family." Minnie smiled at the ladies and opened the door of the Buick.

"Then I will call the radio station and tell them. Somebody in this town will believe this old lady."

"Okay, Mom, you win." The daughter threw up both hands. "You ladies might as well come in. She's not going to rest until she crows it to the world."

Minnie and Jane followed the women into the house and thanked them for the interview. They all seated themselves around the cherry dining room table. "This is a lovely lace tablecloth," Minnie said.

"I crocheted it myself." The older lady replied. "Now about that morning, the morning it was discovered they were missing, there was a wreck right out here on our road. I saw the wrecker pulling off the car and there were several cars following it. All the cars followed the wrecker except for this big black Chevrolet, had an orange or yellow license plate. It crossed the railroad tracks and turned in, I tell you, right there in that abandoned farmhouse's old drive. I saw the people in it clear as day. Two men and a woman. She was sitting in the middle and slumped over. A man, he was sitting on the passenger side, had a handkerchief across his mouth. There's a big pond on the property and I'd bet my life that's where they put the two of them. I'm trying to get the police to drain it. It's just a hazard anyway with nobody living there."

"Is that the end of the story?" Minnie asked.

"Yes, I told the FBI everything. I hope they do something about it right away. I'm going to get that reward. No need to keep my name out of the paper. Everybody will know it soon enough. It's Louise Moore."

The woman's daughter stood. "I think it's time to go ladies. You have your story." She escorted Minnie and Jane to the door while her mother wandered into the living room and switched on the TV. The daughter opened the door and stepped out on the porch behind them. "Just so you know I was here when the wrecker went by, too. My mother is a little feeble minded and she likes the police shows. She confuses real life and TV sometimes. There was a car that turned into the farm, but it wasn't black, it was blue. There were four people in it, but there was no lady slumped over and no handkerchief. The car was too far away to see more than the number of people in it." She nodded and closed the door. Jane heard the lock click firmly in place.

When the two imposters returned home, Ida read Jane's notes. "I'm not sure about this. The daughter doesn't want you to use their names, even though the mother doesn't mind. The story sounds a little vague for a paper to print, but I don't know. I'm sure the FBI noticed she'd forgotten all about the incident until she learned of the reward."

"Thought about that when the woman first mentioned it." Jane said. "The daughter seemed to be scared or hiding something, but I'm not sure either one should be taken seriously. I think it could be made into an interesting story."

"Jane, you know that woman was only trying to protect her. She didn't want her name all over the papers and on the news with those low-life hoodlums running around Lord knows where. They might come looking for her mother. I want to become a professional newspaper woman, but I have to protect my sources, too. If something happened to them, I'd never forgive myself."

Frank pecked on the glass pane and stuck his head in the kitchen door. "Anybody home in here? What's that you're cooking, Minnie?"

Jane quickly slipped the stenographer's pad in a drawer. No need for Frank to see that, but Frank was one up on her. He stared at Minnie's back as she stirred the pot on the stove, then he glanced at Jane. She slid an Emory board across her nails, seemingly intent on a hangnail.

"I have something to share with you ladies, some interesting tidbits about the Harper case. Jane's been complaining that I haven't told her much lately, so thought I'd share something that came down today. If you're interested."

Minnie's back stiffened. Jane's eyes fluttered with excitement. This could be the beginning of a closer relationship if he was ready to share things about the case again.

"What was it honey? What happened?" She put down the Emory board and blew on her nails.

Frank straddled the back of a kitchen chair and pitched his police hat on the sideboard. "I got a call at the police station today from a woman out on Rural Route Four."

Minnie stirred even faster.

"You did?" Jane feigned innocence.

"Yep, had to call Agent Thompson about it. You remember Thompson don't you Jane?"

She remembered. As if she could ever forget someone who put handcuffs on her and shoved her in a car. Jane dropped her hot face and nodded.

Frank continued. "It seems like two ladies in a Buick paid some FBI witnesses a visit today."

"Jane opened and closed her mouth a couple of times before words could form on her lips. "Do they know who?"

"We have our suspicions. They used the names Janice Cook and Minerva Payne. Do those names sound familiar?"

Jane bristled. "I don't know anybody by that name do you Minnie? Why do you think we would know them?"

Minnie continued to stir her soup.

Frank wrinkled his brow." Minerva Payne and Janice Cook. I would have thought you two could have been more inventive than that. I am surprised. Thought Minnie was the one person in the world that would always tell the truth I can't believe you both fed those people a mouth-full of lies."

"Now you listen here, Frank Carter. Minnie did not lie; I introduced us I told them our names. I told them we were working for a newspaper. All Minnie did was follow my lead, and she never said one word that was not true. You're not allowed to speak to my sister that way."

Minnie stepped up behind Jane and placed her hands on her shoulders. "Thanks for defending me Jane, but I did follow your lead, and I did go along with everything you said. So, yes, I did lie even if I didn't speak the words. Not very proud of it either."

Frank laughed. "Actually, I thought it was funny, but I doubt Thompson saw it in that light. I convinced him that these witnesses didn't add anything to the case and because of the older lady's dementia, we couldn't even use her testimony. Kept him from trying to find who you two were. You know you girls could get in trouble. I think it might be called interfering in an FBI investigation. You didn't hurt anybody, this time, and you didn't do any damage to the case. But in a different situation you could have, and I believe they would prosecute you. So, give me your word you will never do something like that again."

"You got mine, Frank. I should have known better."

"Me, too." Jane added. "Frank does this mean you're not mad at me? I do seem to get in trouble a bit for my natural curiosity."

"Just a bit, you do seem to be a meddlesome Maddie. I'm not mad—this time. Just concerned." He hugged her close, kissed her forehead.

"I do have a suggestion. One I thought about during the drive out here. You've always wanted to be in law enforcement. School will be out in a few months for the summer. Why don't you go to Western University and sign up for a course or two in criminology? With enough credits, you could apply for a private investigator's license before school starts. I don't know what subjects you need or how many credits because I've never done anything like that, but it's definitely something to check out because investigating is in your blood. A smart gal I know, who happens to be dating me, always says we need to follow our hearts. Think about what would make you happy, sweetheart."

Ida and Minnie clapped their hands. "Bravo, bravo."

Jane stood stunned. "Oh Frank, honey, you've made me so happy. And my sisters, too. I just don't know what to say except that, yes, I am going to do just that."

Minnie bit her bottom lip for a moment before she spoke. "Frank, I have one thing to add. I promised not to be underhanded again, but I, too, have an idea. You're aware I write freelance articles now and then for various newspapers. I think I'll work up a few stories about the Harper case from a neighbor's point of view. Ask people what they feel may have happened to Edgar and Ella, then try to sell the stories to other papers throughout the region. Who knows, my own column and byline could become syndicated. I would be open and honest to everyone. No more Minerva Payne. Just plain me – Minnie Pryor. Even the FBI should have no problems with that.

"Minnie, that's an excellent idea. I will feed you any information I legally can."

"I'll help you." Ida offered.

"So will I," Jane chimed in.

Thus began Minnie's new focus in life.

***

March 25, 1966

Minnie aimlessly stirred the hot cocoa as a tear channeled down her cheek, eroding a curvy trench through her pancake makeup. It had been over three months since their neighbors disappeared and this was the day of the week she and Ella usually watched a soap opera together.

"Why are you up so early?"

Minnie jumped. "Ida, you gave me a fright. Thought you'd be asleep for a few more hours since you worked so late."

The phone interrupted them and Minnie grabbed it.

"Hello? Hello? Frank? Could you speak up? Where are you?"

"I'm calling from a pay phone. Randall Adler found a half pair of broken glasses on Sunday. The optometrist just confirmed they were the same type that Ella wore. I tried calling Jane at school, but she wasn't there. Do you know where she is?"

"Yes. She had to take the class on a field trip to Mammoth Cave. What's happening?"

"There's a large search party headed for the old Martin Cemetery on Peach Orchard Road."

"Did they find anything else?"

"Yes, some of Edgar's papers and one of his fountain pens. Also…"

"Also, what?"

"I'm sorry to have to tell you this, but two bullets were found under gravel that was laid back in January. This may be it. Gotta go."

"Ida and I will get some things ready and head that way. Frank? Frank? He hung up on me. Ida, get a pot of coffee started."

"What's going on?"

"Randall Adler found some broken glasses the other day and Ella's optometrist confirmed they were the brand she wore."

"Where?"

"In Martin Cemetery, Peach Orchard Road. They're getting a search party together."

"Martin Cemetery?" Ida shivered. "What an awful place. People even mentioned a crow out there that follows visitors around. I read somewhere once that a single crow is supposed to be a bad omen."

"Oh, Ida. There's thousands of crows. Every one can't be a bad omen."

Let's get some things ready and head out to the cemetery."

Ida put on some coffee and retrieved the big thermos from beneath the sink.

Minnie didn't move. Now that it seemed things were coming to a tragic end, Minnie dreaded the story that might be coming soon in her bi-weekly column in the Daily News. She'd felt a tinge of guilt over the excitement and extra interest her column had garnered from using words like "anonymous sources" and "FBI." More and more, people called into the newspaper office for her since she'd switched the focus from the usual social column to the mystery of the missing father and daughter. But at what cost? She'd promised readers to follow the whole thing through to the end, and that's just what she intended to do.

Reporting on her neighbors' visitors and positive news such as college scholarships and military inductions gave her joy. But she'd also enjoyed the research involved with the mystery.

Mr. Harper's wallet found on New Year's Eve hadn't revealed any more clues, but this new one was more ominous. Ella's broken glasses signaled she had been there sometime after she disappeared. Pages of notes from Edgar's little pocket notepad wouldn't have been discovered in the area if they hadn't been there not long ago. Their neighbors from across the street had most likely come to a bad end. How could this happen in a town so close-knit that you couldn't swing a cat without hitting someone you knew? Could it really be someone in Lewisburg who did this, as many rumors suggested? This was a community of trust where neighbors went out of their way to help each other. At least, it used to be.

"Are you almost ready?"

"Oh, Ida. I was a thousand miles away."

"You know Jane's going to be upset with us if the bodies are found while we're there and she isn't."

"Now Ida, the bodies could be found whether we're there or not. Jane had to go on the field trip with her class. We didn't find out about it until it was too late to tell her. Let's finish up and head out."

"Should we really go out there?"

"Yes, Ida. There's been a lot of suspicion and pointed fingers. If the bodies are found today, neighbors will need to come together and start the healing process. We can help with that."

Minnie poured the hot cocoa in a large thermos, placing it in the picnic basket with coffee and muffins. "Bundle up. It's a bit brisk out this morning. Spitting a little snow. You know how March weather is here in Kentucky. Like Mama always said, if you don't like the weather right now, just wait a few minutes."

Ida wrapped her pink knitted scarf around her neck, rubbed her mom's pearl pin and picked up the basket hesitantly. "Are you sure we should go out there where those people are searching? What if they–what if they find them?"

"Well, I'm praying they will. It's time for some closure for poor Eustice, the Harpers' and Givens' families too; closure for the whole town. Can't imagine anything more grating on one's mind than not knowing what happened to loved ones."

Ida's fingers traced the weave of the basket. "You're right, but I'm having a hard time. I don't want to actually watch people uncover the remains of our neighbors. Ella was not a stranger or even just someone we knew, she was our friend." Ida squeezed her eyes together.

Minnie wrapped Ida in a one-armed hug. "It's terrible for all of us to think about, but what would the alternative scenario be? Never discovering them and their family never finding out what happened? Would you want that for them?"

"No, of course not I just..."

"Come on, Ida. The searchers will need food and drink. Besides, if we don't have a good reason for entering the search area, we'll never get any new information to try and help solve the case."

They loaded up Minnie's old Buick, taking Hwy 431 to Peach Orchard Road. Sleet hit the windshield and dribbled down the sides of the car. As they crossed the bridge, the car fishtailed. Ida's hands gripped the steering wheel until her knuckles whitened. "Hope the roads don't get any worse."

"Me, too," Minnie said. "The grass has already greened up for spring and trees are blooming. Too much snow and ice and we won't have pears this year. Also, it could mean a snow day for schools tomorrow. Jane would be wanting to drive all over in that weather and search for clues."

"How many people do you think will be here?"

Minnie frowned. "The news has gotten all over town, but who knows how far the word has gotten. Big newspapers from every major city within 100 miles are trying to get a scoop. The police requested that only people they trained for searches come to the cemetery. Guess they're afraid of how strangers might take advantage of the situation. Plus, they don't want people swarming all over if the bodies are found, might destroy evidence."

"I can understand that." Ida shivered.

"Are you cold?" Minnie asked. "I can turn up the heat."

"No, just got the sensation Mama always called someone walking on my grave. I don't like the thought of going out there by a cemetery to search for dead bodies."

"It's sure enough spooky. Dead, twisted trees about to fall over." They slowed as the blacktop gave way to gravel. Mists from the early morning sleet and rain rose off the fields. "Oh look," Minnie exclaimed. "Cars everywhere. Look at that little red convertible. Doesn't even have the top up. Hope he didn't drive far like that."

Ida pointed to the press pass hanging from the rear-view mirror. "Minnie, it says *The Courier-Journal*. There are newspaper people here all the way from Louisville. They must think they're going to find something important."

People stood out along the road, throughout the gravestones, and dotted the nearby hills. "Folks seem to be everywhere." Ida parked and wrapped a scarf around her head. "I wish I could just sit in the car." Ida pulled herself from the vehicle. "But I guess that wouldn't work."

"No, Ida, nobody is going to stop their search and come to you. They'd lose more time than the day is long."

"I'm sorry, I just don't want to see the decomposed bodies of Ella and Edgar after three months."

Minnie gestured all around them. "These people are cold. If you keep yourself busy—don't think about that, you'll feel better. There's Frank. Let's go talk to him."

The frosty grass dented under their feet as they trudged up to Frank, deep in conversation with Tony Hutcherson, a local farmer.

"I promise, Frank. You know me. I don't talk out of my hat. This isn't something someone told me; saw it for myself. Sometime around 9:30 the night they disappeared, a car was parked here with the lights on pointed toward the gravestones. I could only see their silhouettes, but they were yelling. I couldn't hear what they said, but it seemed serious."

Frank jotted in a notebook. "Thank you. Somebody will be coming to talk to you about that soon."

"Okay, thanks. And could ya, could ya," Tony's eyes darted from side to side, "could ya keep my name out of the papers? Don't want anyone coming after me or my family."

"Of course, I understand."

"Hi Frank," Minnie said.

"Minnie, Ida." He tipped his hat. "Did you see all these people? Reporters, gawkers, members of the Russellville Rescue Squad, even some from Nashville. One reporter came all the way from Louisville. Said he was assigned, let me see if I can get his exact words 'to view the intense search now taking place.' The latch on his pretty red convertible over there is broken and he didn't even bother to get it fixed; drove a hundred and fifty miles in this cold drizzle so he could get a byline."

"The darn fool will catch his death of cold," Minnie exclaimed. She glanced in the other direction. "Poor Eustice. He's been at every search so far."

"Yes, and at the police station almost every day. I don't think he's slept more than a few hours at a time in all these months."

"So, is there any way we can get through here?"

"Sorry, only authorized people are allowed past this point."

"We're not going to search. Only hand out coffee, cocoa, some muffins we made."

"Yes," Ida agreed. She flipped back the kitchen towel and showed the muffins. "Hopefully we'll be long gone if they're found."

"Well, alright. But make it quick."

Minnie observed one searcher turning over every mound of dirt, large or small. He poked in each pile of brush, turned over every particle of wood, leaving nothing unexamined within the radius of his arms. He'd then step a few feet in another direction and begin again.

"I'm going to work my way to that man." Minnie pointed her chin toward the area. "You head in the other direction."

They separated and started working. Minnie's basket was nearly empty by the time she reached the man, but she handed him a muffin and a half cup of coffee. "Hello, I'm Minnie Pryor. It's a nice thing you're doing, coming to help with the search."

"Thank you, Miss Pryor. I'm Vane Brown."

"Do you know the Harpers?"

"I'm a neighbor of Eustice Givens, Ella's husband."

"You're so kind to come all the way from Quality."

"I couldn't be anywhere else today. I've known this family for many a year. I just pray the Lord will soon lead us to the solution. Poor Eustice can't take much more." Vane Brown's head swung slowly from side to side like a pendulum.

"My thoughts exactly." Minnie followed him down the creek bed. "Do you smell something, Mr. Brown?" Minnie sniffed the air. "Something strange?"

"Oh my God, look!" A purplish-blue something protruded from under dried foliage. He fell to his knees, tossed aside brown leaves and brush until a wooden plank fell away to reveal a foot. Using his bare hands, Mr. Brown dug until he uncovered enough to ascertain he'd found Edgar and Ella. "Over here!" he exclaimed. "I found them!"

Minnie turned her back and covered her mouth. She hadn't expected to be this close to the discovery. Hot bile roiled in her stomach and she felt faint. State Trooper McMillen fired a gun, announcing the search was over, the bodies had been found.

The crowd moved toward the gunshot. A few men attempted to hold Eustice back, to no avail. With the strength of a frightened stallion, he wrestled through the crowd to view his wife. He was there as the searchers removed the last of the branches and barn lumber that covered father and daughter. He was there when they discovered them lying head to head face down in a shallow ravine. Eustice was there staring at his wife, covered with bruises, dried blood and clothing ragged and torn. He dropped to his knees, threw back his head and howled. Echoes filled the valley and bounced off the tops of the hillsides.

The reverberations stabbed Minnie's lungs as if she was the one doing the screaming. Maybe she did. Her once vibrant neighbors lay dead behind her. They must have suffered profusely. What type of human monster would commit such a hideous crime? Eustice continued to wail. He was still on his knees when all was quiet once again.

A rumble like thunder seemed to be edging near her. Minnie looked up to see people charging in from every direction.

"Stop!" Frank called, to no avail.

Women with smiles on their faces suddenly turned and lost their collective breakfasts on the cold ground. Men turned away while cameras flashed and reporters peppered first Vane Brown, then Eustice with questions. "How do you feel?" one shouted at Eustice.

How does he feel? Minnie wondered. His wife is just found like this with all of these people as witnesses to his pain and this jerk asks how he feels? Minnie glanced around the roadside and the cemetery. Ida. Where was Ida? Finally, she swept her eyes past the Buick. Ida sat inside, her head bowed, hands covering her ears.

Eustice's voice rang behind Minnie as she walked to the car, begging the reporters not to take pictures of his wife like that.

"I'm so glad you're here," Ida said as Minnie opened the door and slipped into the driver's seat. "Can we go, please? I don't feel like I've accomplished anything here today. I can't sit idly by and watch this sideshow. If I were braver, I'd tell all those people they look like vultures circling prey."

"Hush now. The world needs gentler souls, especially these days. You've been a big help today."

"Do you think so, Minnie?"

"I know so. We better go. Jane will be home soon and wanting us to fill her in on what she missed."

"Wish I could have missed it, too. I'll never forget Eustice's cry. It broke my heart. These hills will ring forever with his grief." Ida covered her ears, filtering out the echoes. "You won't tell Jane will you, Minnie? About me I mean."

"Tell her what?"

"That I couldn't be there when our neighbors were found?"

"There were muscular farmers down there, some of the strongest men I've ever seen, who had to come back up the hill. They couldn't take it. This type of business makes a lot of people go weak in the knees. Anyway, Jane will be so busy picking our brains she won't be interested in anything else."

"Okay, can we go home now?"

Minnie patted her shoulder. "Of course, dear."

Chapter 9

March 26, 1966

The green and yellow fields, alive with new March growth, captured Ida's attention from her perch in the cramped back seat of Jane's little Volkswagen. Minnie didn't want to take unnecessary trips in the big old gas guzzler now that gas hit the thirty-five cents per gallon mark. She and Minnie wanted to stay home, but when Jane wanted something, she just wouldn't rest until she got it.

"Don't know why you wanted to drive back out here, Jane." Minnie held tightly to the grip bar as Jane flew around another curve.

"Me either." Ida agreed. "Gives me the creeps."

"I just want to see the recovery scene," Jane replied. "You two got to see it yesterday. There aren't a lot of clues to who killed the Harpers. Maybe I can get some ideas from the crime scene that might help."

"I don't think we should go there again." Ida wrung her hands together. "I've got a bad feeling."

"Ida," Jane lectured. "The bodies were found and no one else is missing."

"Don't badger her Jane," Minnie scolded.

"Jane, look out!" Ida grabbed the headrest.

Minnie and Ida squealed simultaneously. Jane locked the brakes and the right front tire left the road spitting gravel. A battered green pickup barreled toward them.

Minnie covered her face and peeked through her fingers as the truck squeezed past.

Jane turned. "Oh my gosh." She pointed to a blue Fairlane rounding the corner behind them.

The swerving pickup crossed the line again and sideswiped the car. The Fairlane spun and rolled down a shallow ravine. The truck hurried on its way as if nothing happened.

Jane slammed the car in park. Ida grabbed the first aid kit and climbed out onto the rocky road. Shading her eyes she peered at the wrecked car, glad it had landed right side up. The driver's side looked like a giant accordion. Ida ran toward the scene.

"Let's go help," Minnie said.

Jane tugged at Minnie's arm. "What do you think we're going to find down there?" She pointed to the crumpled blob of metal. "I mean, I can talk about blood and guts all day, but actually seeing it in person. I'm not good at situations like this."

"Come on ya'll. Somebody needs help. Hurry!"

"Ida needs us. That's all I know." Minnie crossed the street and looked down at the car.

Ida bent down and looked into the broken driver's window. She immediately jammed two fingers against the man's neck and felt a weak pulse. "He's alive, but he's bleeding profusely. Minnie, go find a phone. Call an ambulance."

"Jane, look in the trunk. Find a tire tool, a jack, something to pry the door open. Minnie, be sure to tell them we need the fire department, too."

Jane struggled down the slope with the tools, stopping to take a breath as she looked over the scene. "I've always heard you should never move someone hurt in an accident."

"I know, but he's bleeding badly. I need to slow it down. Now get over here and help me." She forced the skinny end of the jack handle into the jammed passenger door and pried. It moved slightly, creating a steel on steel screech. Jane flinched, but continued to help push and pull until the door shifted enough for Ida to wriggle through.

"Thank you, God," Ida whispered. "Now please help us get him out of this car." Her nurse's brain ran at high speed. She checked the pulse again. Hang on! A John Deere hat slid to one side, exposing a laceration above his temple that would need several stitches. His left arm hung at an impossible angle, and blood soaked his jeans where something had sliced his leg. She looped the good arm around her shoulders, then reached around him.

"Ida, I don't think we should move him," Jane yelled.

Ida pointed toward the hood where smoke rolled upward. "We don't have a choice."

Jane's face paled. She grabbed Ida's arm and pulled. "We need to get far away. Now! Come on, Ida!"

"Jane, I don't have time to argue. I am getting this man out of here, and I need your help."

"Please get out of that car."

Ida ignored her. "If you can hear me, sir, I'm here to help." She leaned forward and situated her arms around his chest. Ida strained as hard as she could to heft the man over the gearshift in the floor. She ignored the pain in her arms and shoulders and lifted the top half of the man's body onto her lap.

"Hurry. I think I see a flame."

"I need you to pull him out."

"But..." Jane took a step back.

"I'm trapped until he is out."

"What do I do?"

"The door has to be opened wider."

Jane slipped around the door and climbed up on the running board. She put her hands against the frame and pushed with all her might, but it only moved a crack. Her sweaty palms slipped and she nearly fell face first into the window.

"Wipe your hands on your skirt and try again. The smoke is getting to me." Ida coughed.

This time, Jane put her shoulder into it and pushed like a linebacker. Slowly, the door moved another few inches. "Is that enough?"

"Try and see."

"What do I do?"

"Put your hands under his arms, lock your hands around his chest and lift. Jane got into position and heaved as Ida guided his legs over the gearshift. His shoulders stuck in the doorway. Jane pushed the door with her bottom and pulled until he finally scraped down the car and onto the ground.

Ida scrambled out and they dragged him as far as their energy allowed. Ida slumped on the ground for a few seconds before grabbing the first-aid kit.

Minnie pulled up and yelled, "The ambulance is on the way. Should be here in twenty minutes."

"Twenty minutes," Ida exclaimed. Could he make it that long? She noted his pale face, his low pulse, and decided no, there was too much blood. No time to waste. Ida knelt beside her patient and looked into his weak, bleary eyes. Not sure if he could hear, she touched his cheek and spoke to him. "Can you tell me your name?" His eyes met hers, but he didn't answer. She whispered to God asking for help. "Jane, take off your slip and tear it into strips. Hurry."

"No, it's new."

"Do it." Ida yanked at Jane's half-slip, dropping it to her ankles. Jane stepped out of the garment and bit the cotton material to start a tear.

"Minnie, find some water and wet a rag. Wipe his forehead." She squatted beside the near-lifeless man and patted his cheek. "I need you to fight. What's your name?" Ida went down on her knees atop the rocky ground and tore his shirt off. She continued talking in soft, assuring tones.

"Rennie."

"What?" Ida said. "Oh, your name is Rennie. Well, Rennie, my name is Ida. Breathe as normal as possible and stay awake." Without looking away from the gray eyes focused on her, she said, "someone hand me a couple of strips of cloth and find me a stout stick."

Ida folded a piece of petticoat and pushed it tightly against the wound, blood continued to gush. Time for a tourniquet. "Jane, I need a piece of wood, rock, anything."

"Whatever for?"

"To prop up Rennie's legs. We must keep blood flowing to his vital organs. Minnie, give me a strip of rag. She wound the cloth around Rennie's thigh, then tied a series of knots. "Slip the stick through this square knot, twist it tight to slow the bleeding. No, hold it firmly."

"Like this?"

"Yes, that's good. Jane, wipe his brow. Watch his pallor. If he turns blue, let me know. In the meantime, gals, give me your coats. I don't want him going into shock."

"My coat? My leopard coat?" Jane questioned, yet she unbuttoned her precious fake fur as she spoke.

A tear slid down Minnie's cheek. The blue cashmere coat was the last gift Curtis had given her, but she didn't say a word as she slipped it off.

Ida carefully placed her and Jane's coat on the injured man first, then put Minnie's on top.

Jane admired her sister's kind-hearted benevolence even amidst the trauma. "Rennie's passed out, Sis." Jane swiped his face with a wet cloth.

Ida bent down and listened to his heartbeat fading away. She'd ridden on ambulances while getting her nurse's degree. Long buried facts and information floated into her brain. "I haven't-I haven't done this in a long time." Ida placed Jane's hands on Rennie's chest. "Thrust ten times as soon as I tilt his head and breathe into his mouth." Ida checked to see if there were any visible obstructions, pushed his head back. She pinched his nose and breathed into his mouth two times, then instructed, "push. And one and two and..." The sisters got into rhythm.

An explosion interrupted them and Jane fell back on her bottom. Ida instinctively covered the man with her body to shield him from any falling debris.

Jane stared at the burning car. "That could have been us!"

"Jane, you need to focus here. One and two and..."

Ida glanced at her watch, where is that ambulance? The distant sound of a siren was the sweetest music she'd ever heard.

The emergency workers took over and whisked Rennie off to the hospital. State Trooper, G.C. McMillen also arrived.

"Can anyone tell me what happened?" He looked toward the Volkswagen. "Did you ladies hit him?"

Jane didn't give anyone time to answer and stepped forward to give all the details. Soon the state trooper knew all about the accident and the hit and run driver who appeared drunk. Before she could mention Frank's name for the third time, the trooper rushed to his radio and ordered an alert for the pickup.

One of the fire truck drivers touched Ida on the shoulder. "The other ladies tell me you are responsible for saving the accident victim's life."

"Not me alone. We did it together." Ida motioned toward her sisters.

"It was all her," Jane bragged proudly. "We wouldn't have known what to do."

"I think you're bleeding, Miss." He pointed to Ida's arm. "May I take a look?"

"Oh, this isn't my blood. It's Rennie's."

"I don't think so ma'am. Looks like your arms are cut and blood seems to be coming from your knees."

Ida frowned and looked herself over. "I must have scratched myself a bit freeing him from the car, but it doesn't hurt. I'm sure it's okay."

The fireman furrowed his brow and flashed a toothy smile. "Ma'am, with this much blood, I'd feel better if you were checked out in the ER."

Jane piped up. "Well take care of her."

Minnie herded them into the car, settling Ida into the passenger seat. "Well ladies, I think I know what my next column will be about."

***

March 28, 1966

Sadness hung heavy on Minnie's heart and she lagged behind as they entered Price Funeral Home. Ella Givens murdered. Why? No one knew, not even the police. A closed casket meant no one would see the beating her friend went through. Thank God.

Colorful flowers decorated every surface of the room; a complete contradiction to the solemn mood of the crowd. The whole community respected Edgar and Ella, and it showed.

Minnie murmured a few hellos as they approached the two caskets sitting head to head. Her mind flashed back, visualizing the bodies found the same way and a tear slid down her cheek.

Ida and Jane joined Minnie at the casket. Ida reached out and touched the pink roses on top of Ella's.

"She would have hated these. She didn't like roses, or pink."

"Frank, about the case..."

"Hush, Jane," Minnie shushed. "This isn't the time and place for that. We're here to grieve our friends."

They made their way around the room, greeted neighbors and dabbed their eyes when the tears began to fall. The brutality of the murders had shocked everyone concerned. How would this little community go forward?

Buddy Price, whose father owned the funeral home, spotted Minnie and headed her way.

"Hello, Mrs. Pryor."

"Hello, Buddy, how's the Harper family holding up?"

"Pretty good, considering everything. Eustice is pretty distraught."

"Of course, of course. This is all just confounding. Why would someone kill them? It doesn't look like anyone tried to get in the bank."

"Really? How do you know that?"

"I can't reveal my sources." Minnie stopped and looked around. "You can't tell anyone this now, promise."

"I promise. Believe me, when you work at a funeral home, you have to keep a lot of secrets."

"The vault wasn't even closed that night."

"What? Are you sure, Miss Minnie?"

"Yes. With the big basketball game going on, the booster club wanted to put the money in the vault, rather than have someone take it home until Monday. After they counted it, Dewitt Ryan was supposed to take it to the bank, but decided to wait until Sunday after church."

"Wow. I've been out of sorts since this whole thing started. I'm having that new house built, you know?"

"Yes, I heard."

"I went out three times the first week they were missing to make sure someone didn't bury them there before the basement floor was poured. I even had the police come and check."

"Mr. Price," someone called from across the room."

"Excuse me, back to work."

Ida walked up to Minnie. "Are we going to follow the funeral procession or go right to the church?"

"Best I can remember from a wedding I went to a long time ago, Quality Missionary Baptist Church is pretty small. I think we should go ahead. I'll get Jane and Frank."

They gathered in the Buick for the short drive to the church. "Looks like a lot of other people had the same idea," Frank pointed at the gravel lot already filled to overflowing. They followed the stream of mourners to the church and managed to get half of the last empty pew.

Jane looked around curiously and even stood to get a better look at some people.

"What are you doing?" hissed Minnie. "Sit down."

"I read that the murderer will often come around the family, especially at the funeral. I'm trying to see if there are any strangers."

"Jane," Ida fussed. "They have family spread out all over the Commonwealth, Indiana, and Florida. We can't possibly know all the people here. Conduct yourself properly."

Jane huffed and sat down. Frank patted her hand.

The double doors at the back of the church opened and the caskets were carried in. Edgar Harper's friends Grider Watson, Orville Hill, Bob McReynolds, Joe McReynolds and Irvin Baugh carried him to the stand at the front of the church.

Eustice entered, dressed in gray, hat in hand, head bowed, as he followed Ella's flower draped casket. It was carried by Ralph McReynolds, Shelby McCoy, Gus Gray, Grady Porter, Justice Perry, and Vane Brown. Eustice's shoulders began to shake and his son put his arm around him.

Edgar's sons and daughter walked with their spouses and followed the procession with their children trailing after them. All went to the reserved seats at the front. Anyone who followed the hearses to little church found places to stand in the back.

"Let us bow our heads and pray for the families of our dear departed loved ones," the preacher said.

After burial in the Quality Missionary Baptist Church Cemetery, the Clack sisters and Frank climbed into the car and waited their turn to exit. "Are we going to the Harper house?" asked Frank.

Minnie sniffed and dabbed her eyes with a lacy handkerchief. "Yes, for a bit. We have some food to take over to the family."

"I can only stay for a minute," Ida exclaimed. "I have to get to work a little early."

"You've been awfully anxious to get to work lately," Jane observed. "Do you have your eye on a certain doctor or something?"

Ida blushed from her chin to the roots of her hair. "No-n-no." She stammered. "I just like to be punctual."

"Sure," Jane teased.

"I-I-you know, I want to get the next head nurse position that comes up."

"Uh-huh."

"Oh Jane," Minnie scolded. "Leave her alone. Nothing wrong with going in early and talking to your friends." Minnie looked at Ida and winked then laid her head back on the seat and closed her eyes.

***

Ida fluffed her hair, straightened her uniform then pecked on the door of room 207. Just one more check on Rennie, and she'd head home.

"Come in," a weak voice answered.

"Hello, Rennie, do you mind if I come in? Thought I'd stop by and see for myself how you're faring."

His lips parted to show a row of perfect teeth amidst a few days worth of stubble. "Better than the first time you saw me."

"You remember. I wasn't sure if you were conscious enough after the accident."

He reached out, and Ida stepped closer. "I want to thank you for saving my life."

Heat washed over Ida's face. "I only did what any medical professional would have done. I'm glad we happened to be there."

The door opened again. Rennie introduced his mother, Jennifer and dad, Reynold, Sr. "Mom and Dad, this is my guardian angel, Ida Clack."

Trying not to flush, Ida offered her hand to Rennie's parents. "I'm no angel, just a nurse here at the hospital."

"Well, whatever you are, you're an angel to us. Isn't that right, Reynold?"

"Yes, little lady. We owe you for saving our boy's life."

"It wasn't just me. My sisters helped."

"Well, you give them our gratitude please." Jennifer answered.

"Don't let her tell you she's not an angel. I was pinned in that car and couldn't move. Could barely think clearly when those arms," he pointed to Ida's arms, crisscrossed with scratches. "Those arms wrapped around me and lifted me up out of that car. No mortal as small as she is could do that. I heard her talking to God. She's my guardian angel, I'm telling you."

Ida opened her mouth to refute him, but his mother shook her head no, so she said nothing.

"Mrs. Simmons, would you like to go to the cafeteria and have a cup of coffee with me?"

"Sounds like a good idea, Ida, but please call me Jennifer. Reynold, you stay and chat with Rennie for a few minutes? We'll be back soon."

Ida and Jennifer took the 2nd floor elevator down to the cafeteria. Since it was almost midnight, the only thing available was coffee and a piece of pie in a vending machine. The place was deserted and quiet, perfect to chat.

"Ida, Rennie said some weird things, do you think he hit his head too hard?"

"He may be confused from the trauma. The head injury seems slight, but please voice your concerns to the doctor. He'll check thoroughly."

"Thank you, dear."

"When I stopped by to check on him this afternoon, he still remembered my full name. That's a good sign."

"I agree with my son; you're an angel."

Ida dropped her chin and smiled shyly. "Thank you, but I'm just an ordinary person who happened to be in the right place at the right time."

Jennifer returned the smile. "Why were you and your sisters traveling Peach Orchard Road? It gives me the willies. Now more than ever. Do you live back there?"

"No, we just wanted to revisit the place where we found the Harper-Givens bodies the other day."

"We? Were you in the search crew?"

"Well, Minnie, my older sister, and I were delivering the searchers some baked goods and drinks."

"See, you are an angel of mercy."

Her calm laughter made Ida relax. "No, no, just helping out."

Jennifer took a sip of her coffee.

"We live in Quality. I have no idea why my son was on that curvy, gravel road."

"He did mumble something yesterday about tomato plants."

"I guess that makes sense. He does put in a garden every year."

"You lived in Quality? Do you know the Givens?"

"Somewhat. In a small farm community, you tend to know everyone, but not truly know them. We ran into the Givens several times at church socials and such. It sure was a shame how Ella and her father died. I can't remember anything like this happening in tiny Lewisburg."

Ida listened intently, hoping the woman would give a hint into the personal lives of Ella and Eustice, but she didn't say any more than Ida already knew.

Jennifer continued. "Ella was a kind lady, maybe a little eccentric. She smoked cigarettes but never touched a drop of alcohol. She spoke her mind, but always remained a lady. I can't imagine anyone doing vile things to her."

"And Eustice, do you know him?"

"I know him enough to say hello when we pass on the street, but he mostly keeps to himself. Never does anyone any harm, but never mingles in a crowd either. A hard-working farmer. Honest, I reckon. Never heard anyone speak ill of him. Well, how did we get off on this subject? I thought we broke out of Rennie's room to discuss Rennie."

Ida stood to put her empty cup on the tray for dirty dishes. "That we did. Sorry, I get easily sidetracked onto the Harper-Givens case because they are always on my mind. The funeral was this morning. We live across the street from their home." She pushed two on the elevator button.

"I didn't know that. You should have caught me up instead of me running my mouth. This case bothers me so. Do you know anything new?"

What should she answer? Minnie and Jane would have her head if she told any secrets. She would be very discrete and say only what she'd read in the papers.

"You know the police will only let out so much information. I did hear the house would be rented out soon." Ida rubbed the back of her hand. "I heard a rumor Eustice would pay $1,000 for information for who killed them, but he'd be broke if someone claimed the reward." Ida cringed hoping she hadn't said too much.

The elevator stopped on Rennie's floor. When they quietly opened his door, the two men were having a snoring contest. The women turned and stepped out of the room.

"I'm going to run along home now," Ida said. "Tell Rennie I'll check on him tomorrow after I finish my shift. I work seven until three."

Jennifer hugged Ida. "In that case, I'm sure we'll see each other again soon. Thank you, Ida."

"You don't need to thank me, just doing my job."

"And is it your job to check on a person who isn't a patient of yours twice a day and on your breaks? Even take his mother out and calm her nerves?" She grinned.

"Well, this is different, I was there when…"

"Yes, you were, and that's the job of an angel."

Chapter 10

Ida put the groceries away and kicked off her nursing shoes. She took a long sip from a glass of lemonade, then leaned back in the easy chair.

Her eyes closed a moment. Why did a vision of Rennie's face appear before her? He was just a patient at the hospital, like hundreds of others each year. She'd never saved someone before though. Maybe that's why she felt the need to check on him all the time.

What about Bruce? He helped her put the groceries in the car today, then asked her out again and waited expectantly. She turned the radio up loud and avoided the question.

Bruce appealed to her in a physical way, but with Rennie, his trusting eyes pulled her in. The way his lips curved up just a bit when he smiled made her stomach flip a little. He was down to earth and honest. She yawned, turned her head to the side, and smiled.

Minnie discovered her there an hour later. "Wake up, sleeping beauty. Someone on the phone wants to speak to Nurse Ida Clack."

"Huh? Who? Nurse Ida Clack?" Could it be Rennie? Ida reached for the phone. "Yes, this is Ida Clack. Yes. Oh, I don't know. Well, yes. I suppose so. At the hospital tomorrow? How about four o'clock. Okay, but what about my sisters? They helped, too." Ida pushed Minnie's head away from the receiver. "I'll tell them. Thank you so much. We'll see you tomorrow at four." She hung the phone up and squealed.

Jane walked through the door and tossed her jacket on the chair back. "Ida, did you remember to get the S&H Green Stamps today? I'm saving up for that new color TV."

Ida squealed again and grabbed Jane's upper arms.

"What's all the commotion? Sounds like a pigsty in here."

"Oh, Jane, we are going to be featured in the Local Hero Section of the Russellville News-Democrat."

"Have they heard I've been searching high and low for clues in the Harper case?" Jane asked. "You think they'll want to hear what I think of the investigation so far? Do you sup..."

"Jane," Minnie stopped her. "I don't think this is about you and the Harpers. I think it's about the car accident."

"Yes," Ida nodded. "They want to do an article about us."

"Honey," Minnie said, "I'm so happy for you, but you don't have to include us. We will not steal one moment of your thunder. Will we Jane?"

"Uh, of course not. But you will mention me won't you, Ida. Tell them I..."

Minnie interrupted. "I'm so proud of you. We'll be there for moral support if you need us. Or stay away if you want."

"No, no. I need you. I asked the reporter to wait until 4:00 o'clock so we could all meet together after Jane gets home from work. I'm sure they'll want to ask you questions. I could never have saved Rennie without your help, and I plan to tell the press exactly that." Ida dropped her head shyly. "Plus, I want you to meet him and his parents tomorrow. They are the ones who nominated me for hero of the month."

"You're sweet on that man. Aren't you?" Jane pestered.

"He is nice, but we're just friends." She turned and took her glass into the kitchen. Her sisters didn't need to see the flush creep into her cheeks.

***

Rennie took Ida's arm and leaned on a cane as he escorted her out of the hospital conference room. He winced and she grabbed a nearby wheelchair. "Well I'd say we did pretty good in there."

"Reporters can certainly fire questions quickly," she sighed. "I'm glad you were there to help me." Impulsively, Ida ducked her head and kissed him on the cheek. Mortified, she straightened quickly and pushed the chair faster. Maybe if she drew his attention to something else, he'd forget she did that.

"Well, I suppose our families have become acquainted with each other by now. Wonder how many of our childhood secrets were exposed while we sat in there sweating it out with the reporters."

"Probably more than we'd care to know. Mom tends to talk about me to anyone who will listen."

Ida grinned shyly, glad he didn't mention the kiss. "I'm sure Jane knows everything then. She's a pro at asking questions to get people to spill their guts."

Rennie turned to face Ida and took her hand. "Do you think we can get them discussing our childhood diseases so we can sneak off and get more acquainted?"

"Well here's the celebrities," Mr. Simmons joked as they stepped off the elevator joining the rest of the group. Jane and Minnie popped questions about the interview, but Rennie's mom just looked at them and smiled with a twinkle in her eye. "My Rennie probably needs to lie down," she said. "Let's go to his room for a bit and discuss all this."

"Good idea," Minnie agreed.

"Don't worry," Rennie whispered to Ida. "We'll spend more time together soon."

After Rennie rested awhile, loud conversation and laughter dominated their table as they enjoyed their cafeteria food. Ida's mind continued to wander.

Rennie yawned.

"Dear, I have suddenly gotten a headache," Mrs. Simmons announced. "I'm afraid your dad and I must leave."

"I'm sorry, Mom, but I'm sure our friends will understand if you want to cut the evening short."

"I have to get up early for school tomorrow," Jane added. "Are you ready to go Minnie?"

After they all agreed, Jennifer dropped the other shoe. "We rented an apartment here in town to be close to Rennie while he recovers, but Reynold can't see to drive at night. We'll need the car to come back tomorrow. Can one of you ladies drive us home in your car and someone else drive ours?"

Ida's heart dropped all the way to her knees. Rennie looked at his mom and then at Ida.

Jane piped up. "I'll drive your car to your apartment and Minnie can follow us." She elbowed Minnie.

"Yes, yes, of course. That will work out well. Ida, you stay here to see Rennie back to his room and make sure he's settled for the night. Jane and I will be back to get you in a little while."

"I guess that will be alright," Ida eyed Rennie.

"I need to get back in time for nighttime meds anyway." He pulled Ida's chair back and held her sweater out.

Jane smoothed her hair. "I told you she was sweet on him," she whispered in Minnie's ear.

"You think?"

Mrs. Simmons hugged Ida and kissed her on the cheek. "Even angels need help now and then," she said softly.

Ida escorted Rennie back to room 207.

"What a day," he sighed and scooted onto the bed.

"Are you in pain? Should I get the nurse?"

"No, no. Someone should be around in a minute with my pills. Come sit with me."

Ida took the seat by his bed. She picked up his hand; it felt so natural. Stunned, she quickly turned it over and checked his pulse. His knuckles hit the bedrail and he groaned. "I'm so sorry. It's just, I just, are you okay?"

Rennie held up his arm. "Well you did hurt me. If you kiss it though, it might be all better."

Rennie laughed at the surprised look on her face.

"Oh, you're teasing." The wheels squeaked on the shiny tile floor as the night nurse pushed the medicine cart into the room.

"Here you go, Mr. Simmons. There's a pain pill, an antibiotic to make sure you don't get an infection, and a little something to help you sleep." She stood watch as Rennie dutifully swallowed each one, then rolled the cart out to repeat the procedure with the other rooms on the floor.

"You know," Rennie said, "I'm going to owe you big time when I get out of here."

"No, no." Ida objected. "I was just..."

"Doing my job." Rennie finished for her. "Is that all it is, Ida? You're here this late because you're just doing your job?"

"Well, your parents wanted to take me to dinner."

"Rennie grasped her hand and pulled her to him. Taking her cheek softly, he put a light kiss on her lips. His head dropped to the side. "Are you sure that's all?"

***

"Stop that bellyaching, Jane," Minnie admonished. "We're out to have fun."

"I didn't get that police job because those officials make harder tests for women than men. Even Frank would have failed."

"Hey, wait a minute." Frank gave her a playful punch on the shoulder.

Tom maneuvered the car around a sharp curve. "You three quit the squabbling and tell me where to go. I'm not familiar with the lake area and if you don't help me, we'll all end up in the water. I'm a farmer, not a fisherman."

They all laughed and reminded him they were headed for the diner on Lake Malone for their famous fish.

"Since I heard the station mentioned back there, is it okay if I ask how the Harper case is coming along? Last I heard, the FBI was questioning Eustice Givens and giving him polygraphs. Is that true?"

"Well, partially true." Frank answered. "I guess it's ok if I tell you about poor Eustice. You're right, Tom. For a while, he was the prime suspect."

"So, the lie detector got him off?"

"Not exactly. He never totally passed it."

"I didn't know that." Minnie said.

Jane added, "He never exactly failed it either."

"Now how can that be?" Tom asked. "I thought you either passed or failed."

"Me, too." Minnie looked at Jane, who sat grinning like a Cheshire cat because she knew something first.

"I'm afraid this discussion will have to wait, because Tom needs to make a right at the next turn, we're almost there."

Minnie stared out the window. "The killers traveled this very road, didn't they? And they had to cross Lake Malone, also."

As Tom parked the car, lights from inside Malone Fish Hole unveiled the tears traveling down her face. "Something this tangible makes me think of Edgar and Ella, tied up and crammed in a car." She shivered visibly, and Tom squeezed her hand.

"Let's not talk about this until after dinner," Tom suggested.

"Yeah," Jane commented. "I'm hungry, and Frank, as always, is absolutely starved."

The others, knowing Frank's love for eating, shook their heads and laughed.

The guys led their ladies into the café, and found an empty booth. The fish platters with their tantalizing smells were barely served before a familiar face entered the diner. Lewis Forgy took the booth behind them and Eustice Givens joined him soon afterward. They passed a few pleasantries before Eustice reached over the back of Minnie's seat and patted her shoulder. She couldn't dream what he wanted, but he soon told her.

"Ms. Pryor, er that column of yours, I noticed you haven't mentioned me in it. I wish you would. Tell the people I didn't kidnap my wife."

"I'm sorry, Eustice, I didn't mention you out of respect, but I'd be glad to do it. I'm sure you're innocent, but once I start interviewing others for the article, I am honor bound to tell both sides. Is that okay?"

"Sure. I'm positive you won't find out more than I'm a cantankerous old grouch," he grinned. "Just my nature, I suppose."

"Oh, I'm quite positive I won't uncover anything new." Minnie thought about that polygraph and prayed she'd told him the truth. She didn't want to cause him any more pain.

Deep in thought, Minnie stayed quiet on the way home. Planning the next day's activities tied her mind tighter than a shoestring. She would make a trip to Quality. Jane would insist on going along, of course. Somehow she had obtained a list of FBI interviews, which made her valuable.

The first stop she made the next morning was to visit Burns Gas Station. Mr. Burns said Ella stopped by the morning of the kidnapping. "Seemed her normal self," he said. "Didn't seem like anything was wrong." As the two ladies started to leave, Grady Porter pulled in, ready to talk.

Mr. Porter claimed to be Eustice Givens' oldest and best friend. "I have to admit he's got peculiar ways. Doesn't get along with any of his neighbors—or his father-in-law. Minnie wrote furiously.

Porter took out a red bandana and wiped his face, then went on to say the Givens' didn't have a good relationship at all. "She wasn't a good wife to him."

Jane couldn't hold her tongue a minute longer. "Why do you say that? Ella Givens was..." Minnie, standing behind Jane, kicked her slightly on her ankle. Taking the hint, Jane hushed.

Grady Porter continued. "She spent most every night with her father. Don't know more than what I said. Nothing specific, anyways. But I'll tell you one more thing about Eustice. He got into a heated argument with Bob Russ, a tenant of Mr. Harper's. When Russ started to jerk Eustice from his car, Eustice pulled a knife on him."

Jane and Minnie allowed Porter to rattle on without interruption. "On the night of December 11, 1965 and the next morning I noticed the light on in the house and barn, so I assume Eustice Givens was home all night. The last time I saw Ella Givens though was Friday when she left the farm. Look, I don't know why they are missing, but I'd be willing to bet it has to do with money. Both the Givens and the Harpers worshiped money."

Ella's beautician Mrs. Justice Jenkins gave quite a different story. She'd never heard Ella complain about her husband. Not once. And as for Eustice, yes, he didn't get along with others in the neighborhood because he is a bit peculiar but that doesn't mean he's involved.

"I've heard they were having marital problems and they've even been separated a few times, but who knows if that's true."

"Where did you hear that?"

"Over the phone. From the Baptist Preacher and that storekeeper over in Huntsville. I think his name was Elliot.

When Jane and Minnie settled in Jane's Volkswagen on the way to interview Monroe Davidson of Penrod, Kentucky, Minnie suppressed a laugh, but Jane didn't suppress anything. Through her bubbles of laughter, she burst out." I'm sure glad we got Brother Mike!"

"Yes," Minnie said, "Can you see him telling tales on the phone about a member of our congregation?"

"I can't see that. There sure is a lot of gossip around here. You don't know what's truth and what's hearsay. I'm glad I live in Lewisburg."

"I haven't seen anything to make me think Eustice Givens is involved. The most I've gotten is he is a very peculiar man. We heard that word, peculiar, mentioned enough. He must be hard to get along with. And does every married couple not have a quarrel?"

"Never seen one yet who didn't. Bet you and Curtis even had a few."

Minnie laughed. "A few. But the mention of separations and marital trouble does bother me. Well, I'm ready to bring this questioning to a close. I'm not getting much of anything I need for my column."

"No, I haven't seen much yet either, but I would like to finish our list since we're here, then we need to interview Eustice, you know, and there are several people in Lewisburg we haven't talked with."

Monroe Davidson repeated what he had told the FBI. He made an anonymous telephone call to Eustice Givens and the same to Edgar Harper about contacting an attorney in Indiana for information about Harper's business concerns. He worked for Harper a few years before and in that capacity worked with Attorney Norvell regarding all of Harpers business affairs. At that time Norvell was evasive in answering questions, which caused Davidson to be suspicious of him.

"I wonder," Jane mused. "Do you think the crooked attorney could've been embezzling Mr. Harper's funds and Edgar found out? Wouldn't that motivate someone to murder? I mean I've seen it on TV."

"Sure seemed suspicious to me," Davidson explained. "That's all I know."

Minnie thanked Mr. Davidson, then she and Jane traveled on to visit a Mr. Harrison who said he'd heard rumors over the last few years that the Givens' we're having marriage problems. "I talked with John Givens, a relative of Eustice's. He told me Eustice and Ella had an argument on Friday, the night before she and her father disappeared, but he didn't give any specifics."

"Thanks for the info," Minnie shook Mr. Harrison's hand and they turned to go on to their next stop.

"Wow," Jane said. "That's something we haven't heard before. Think we can locate John Givens?"

"We're sure going to give it a good try."

When the ladies finally found John Givens, he agreed to an interview.

"I've known Eustice since we were kids, he's my cousin. Heard rumors. About two or three years ago Eustice and his wife started having trouble. I have no idea what the problem was, and I swear to you I never told anyone about an argument that day or any other for that matter. The FBI came to me like I was the one spreading rumors about an argument, but it wasn't me. I don't know who it could have been."

"Thank you, John," Minnie turned to Jane. I'm ready to go back to Lewisburg, regroup, and begin there. We'll end with Eustice. She gathered her notes and crawled into Jane's little car. "What do you think about Eustice now?"

"Not sure. He admitted he was a grumpy grouch. I don't see much more than that."

"No one's accused him of being malicious. The FBI didn't arrest him. I don't plan on throwing suspicion his way just because he's a peculiar man with a temper."

"I think I agree, Minnie, but let's snoop around Lewisburg a bit. Ella had friends she spent time with. Let's see what they say. If a good friend lets it out she was suspicious of Eustice, then that's something else entirely."

They drove home each in deep thought, ready to kick off their shoes, brew some tea, and rest. Minnie would get started again tomorrow. Jane couldn't take off another school day.

The next morning, Minnie squinted in the bright sunshine and walked across the street to Lewis Forgy's house. She knocked, then knocked again. Finally, the curtain moved slightly and Mr. Forgy opened the door. He kept the chain on and talked to Minnie through the crack. She noticed how his hands shook as he raised them to smooth his hair.

"Mr. Forgy, I'm doing some interviews for my column. For this one, I'm talking to people about Eustice Givens. Do you remember the last time you saw him at Mr. Harper's before the disappearance? Any arguments you might have heard? Anything that might help solve the case?"

"I'm worried, Minnie. Worried that I might have to testify if they find who did this. Someone who would kill an old man and his daughter would kill anyone, wouldn't they?"

"I guess, maybe."

"That's all I have to say. Don't use my name." Mr. Forgy shut the door.

Minnie finished her notes and walked to the post office. Employee Mrs. Hinton said she saw Ella Givens and her father on the morning of the kidnapping, but saw nothing out of the ordinary. She told Minnie the couple only received regular mail, government checks, banking business, and utility bills.

Minnie spotted Marvine in line at the window and turned toward her, but stopped in her tracks. Eustice Givens was tapping Marvine on the shoulder. When she looked up, he said very calmly, "I hear that you think I am guilty of kidnapping and killing my wife and her father."

"Ah-uh, yes, I did say that. I'm not going to lie to you. I have always felt you had something to do with it."

Eustice turned and walked out of the post office as if no one had accused him of a horrible crime.

Minnie, open-mouthed, didn't know what to say. Marvine shrugged her shoulders, lifted both hands, and said, "I couldn't lie to him. I do think he's guilty."

Minnie said her good-byes and left the post office. She was through with interviews for today. Only Eustice remained.

"As luck would have it, Eustice was across the street at the Harper House doing yard work. Minnie walked to him, notebook in hand. "Hi, Eustice." She didn't mention a word about the post office and hoped he didn't either. "I'll be finished with the interviews for the column as soon as I ask you a few questions. Is this a good time?"

"Go ahead, I don't know anything new to say that's not already in the paper, over the television, the radio, and on the lips of everybody in Lewisburg."

"I understand. All I need is an explanation of the polygraph. I'm sure you want your side of that told."

"All I know is that I heard so many explanations from so many people telling me what they thought happened. Guessing what could have taken place. I had dreams, vivid dreams. You can't imagine all the scenarios running around in my head. I wasn't sure what was real and what people had told me. I was in no shape to comprehend if I had told the police all I knew. That's why the polygraph showed that I wasn't telling everything. But I know nothing about what happened to my wife and her father. Now people look at me and tell me they think I may have committed murder. Mrs. Pryor. I promise you I'm not a killer."

Welcome to the Neighborhood
By Minnie Pryor
Dear Readers, Mr. Eustice Givens requested I do interviews with his neighbors, friends, and foes, inviting each of them to express any reasons or proof that pointed to his innocence or guilt. I obtained many comments containing both good and bad character references, some of which I'll list below. However, I acquired nothing that would lead me to believe him a ruthless murderer. His statement to me was: "You know I'm the one who lost the most. I lost everything. I lost my wife; I lost my life. Now people look at me and tell me they think I may have committed murder. Mrs. Pryor. I'm not a killer."

Harper Home Now Closed, But Not Case

FROM THIS HOUSE in Lewisburg, bank president Edgar C. Harper and his daughter were lured or forced to their deaths a year ago this month. The house is among the assets of estate which suit filed this week seeks to settle. House is now locked up. In picture taken last year, Guy McMillen, left, then Logan County sheriff, was discussing case with a Lewisburg citizen.

Det. G. C. McMillen

...He Was Assigned From Beginning

December 13, 1965

Few Clues Found In Lewisburg Case Disappearance Of Banker And Daughter Baffles Authorities

Lewisburg, Ky. - Authorities reported few clues today in the weekend disappearance of the 81-year-old president of Lewisburg bank and his 49-year-old daughter.

***

But state police said they are assuming foul play and have flashed an all-state alarm for the pair, Edgar Harper, president of the Lewisburg Banking Co. and wealthy oil well owner and his daughter, Mrs. Eustace Givens of near-by Quality.

Logan County Sheriff Guy McMillen termed the disappearance "baffling" but said due to the lack of clues he would say the case is a kidnaping.

State Police Det. Sgt. Guy C. McMillen said progress of the investigation has been discussed with agents of the Federal Bureau of Investigation and FBI agents said they are keeping a close watch on the progress of the probe to determine if federal laws have been violated.

Police said Harper and Mrs. Givens disappeared from the Harper home here Saturday night without a trace.

Relatives (husband) said they thought the disappearance occurred before the pair retired for the night Saturday. The beds were made and there was no indication they had been slept in.

Sheriff's deputies and members of the family kept an all-night vigil Sunday but dawn came with no contact from the missing pair.

"We are still without clues but we are going to search various buildings in the area and farms in Butler and Logan counties," said Sheriff McMillen.

Officers and members of the family discounted any possibility that Harper and Mrs. Givens would have left suddenly on a trip without notifying relatives.

***

"Besides the Harper car was still in the garage and all signs indicate they left suddenly," said the sheriff.

McMillen quoted Eustice Givens, husband of the missing woman, as saying his wife frequently spent the night with her father, who had been a widower for about three years.

The sheriff said the disappearance was discovered before 8 a.m. Sunday when Givens telephoned the spacious Harper home and got no answer.

Givens said he and his wife had talked about taking some fresh meat from their farm and some tobacco stalks to a son in Bowling Green Sunday.

When Givens arrived at the Harper home Sunday he was in a farm truck loaded with tobacco stalks with which to mulch the son's lawn in Bowling Green.

The stalks were never delivered and the son joined other members of the family in keeping a vigil at his parents' home Sunday, waiting in hopes of a telephone call that did not come. Eustace Givens told police that when he arrived at the Harper home he found the back door unlocked and no one at home. Givens said his wife's purse, containing money and the keys to her father's car, was in the house and the car was still in the garage.

Givens was the last person known to have been in contact with the pair. He told police he talked with his wife by telephone Saturday night.

Relatives said Harper usually took a hot water bottle to bed with him and it was in its normal place when not in use.

A Saturday night rain at the scene obliterated all car tracks making it difficult to obtain a lead in that direction.

Alarm for Harper's well-being mounted last night after it was discovered medicine he took daily for a heart condition and high blood pressure was found in his house.

Relatives speculated that Harper would not have left his medicine behind if he planned to leave his home for an extended period.

***

Givens told the sheriff he telephoned the Harper home Saturday about 7 p.m. and told his wife he would pick her up at 8 a.m. yesterday to go to Bowling Green to visit their son.

This was the last known contact with Mrs. Givens and her father, the sheriff said.

Givens said he telephoned the Harper home again early yesterday to tell his wife he was in route but got no answer. After driving to the home and finding his wife and father-in-law gone and Harper's car in the garage, Givens notified the sheriff's office.

"There was no sign of a struggle or disturbance, but two empty suitcases, belonging to Harper, were found moved from their customary storage place. The back to the house was unlocked but a front storm door was still locked." The sheriff said.

Following a search of the house, officers joined officials of the bank where Harper is president in an investigation there but found nothing missing.

$1,000 REWARD **$1,000 REWARD** **$1,000 REWARD**

For Information Leading To Whereabouts Of

Edgar Carrol Harper, 81 **Mrs. Ella Maria Givens, 49**

Missing From
Their Home At
Lewisburg, Ky.

Edgar C. Harper, 81, D. O. B. 10-10-84, 5 ft., 8 inches, 170-180 lbs. Gray thin hair. Blue eyes. Last seen wearing brown pants, brown sweater, flannel shirt. Wears glasses, has no teeth. Has scar on chest from lung surgery.

Mrs. Ella Maria Givens, 49, D. O. B. 12-27-15, daughter of Mr. Harper. May have had dress and white sweater. 5 ft., 5 inches, 125 lbs. Dark brown hair, hazel eyes. Wears glasses, has false lower teeth. Yellow gold band wedding ring. Had wrist watch.

Mr. Harper, president of Lewisburg Banking Co., Logan County, Lewisburg, Ky., and his daughter vanished from his house the night of Dec. 11, 1965. Foul play feared. Mr. Harper's heart and blood pressure medicine, false teeth left behind. His billfold, containing personal papers but empty of money, found near Russellville, Ky. Dec. 31.

Family offering $1,000.00 reward for information on their whereabouts.

Contact Logan County Sheriff's office at Russellville, Ky., or Kentucky State Police or any police officer.

Logan County Sheriff Gene Sweatt

Russellville, Ky.

December 14th

Still no clues in missing couple case.

Police officials in Lewisburg, Kentucky have found no clues in the disappearance of banker Edgar Harper and his daughter Mrs. Ella Harper Givens. It was discovered that the pair were missing on Sunday morning December 12.

Investigating officers, headed by Sheriff Guy McMillen, his son, State Detective G.C. McMillen, chief deputy and sheriff-elect Gene Sweatt and state troopers, had expected that a ransom call, if one was made, might go to the bank after it opened yesterday morning. A kidnapper familiar with the bank would know that the bank vault was sealed during the weekend by a time lock. But, the officers said last night, no ransom demand had been received. There was speculation that such a call would go either to the Harper home or to DeWitt Ryan, the bank's manager and cashier. Bank officials said Harper had no keys to any of the vaults.

If robbery was the motive, why was nothing disturbed in the house and no money taken? A medical assistant at the Lewisburg office of Dr. Roy McEndre, Goldie Watson, reported that Eustice Givens came to her house between 8:30 and 9:00 stating he could not find his father-in-law or wife.

Later that day, she visited the house and found the kitchen to be bare of groceries except for a coconut pie with one slice missing. This was in spite of evidence that Mrs. Givens had went to the grocery the day before. The receipt and change of $4.50 sat in a cup on the kitchen counter. Mrs. Harper's purse, containing $8.00, lay on her bed undisturbed and a lockbox under Mr. Harper's bed went untouched.

Harper's family said the banker received a telephone call during the Thanksgiving weekend from a man who identified himself as an FBI agent and asked whether Harper were president of the bank. Harper concluded that the caller was a friend playing a joke, according to Sweatt. No one has come forward to say they made the call.

The banker had suffered two coronary attacks and took four heart pills and two blood pressure pills daily. The medicine was found at his home and family said that if he planned to leave for any length of time, he would have taken it with him.

Man pointing out where the wallet was found.

Men stand above Wolf Lick Creek Bridge, where Mr. Harper's hat and three individual hose were found."

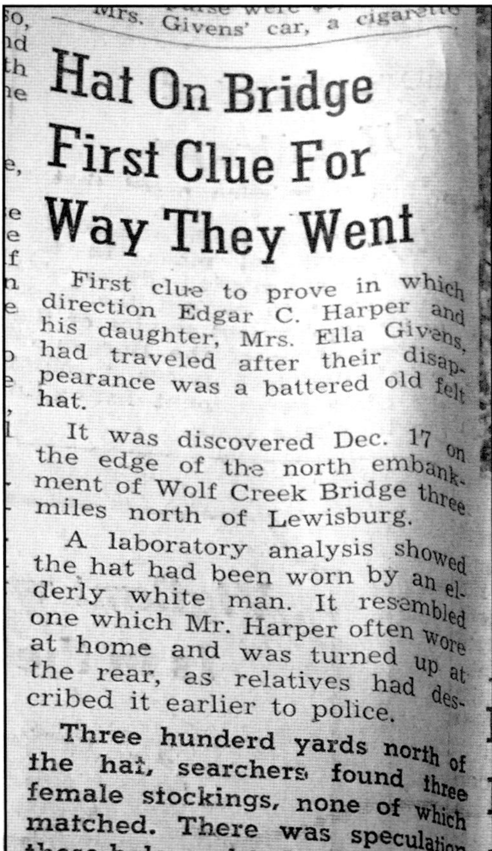

Hat On Bridge First Clue For Way They Went

First clue to prove in which direction Edgar C. Harper and his daughter, Mrs. Ella Givens, had traveled after their disappearance was a battered old felt hat.

It was discovered Dec. 17 on the edge of the north embankment of Wolf Creek Bridge three miles north of Lewisburg.

A laboratory analysis showed the hat had been worn by an elderly white man. It resembled one which Mr. Harper often wore at home and was turned up at the rear, as relatives had described it earlier to police.

Three hunderd yards north of the hat, searchers found three female stockings, none of which matched. There was speculation

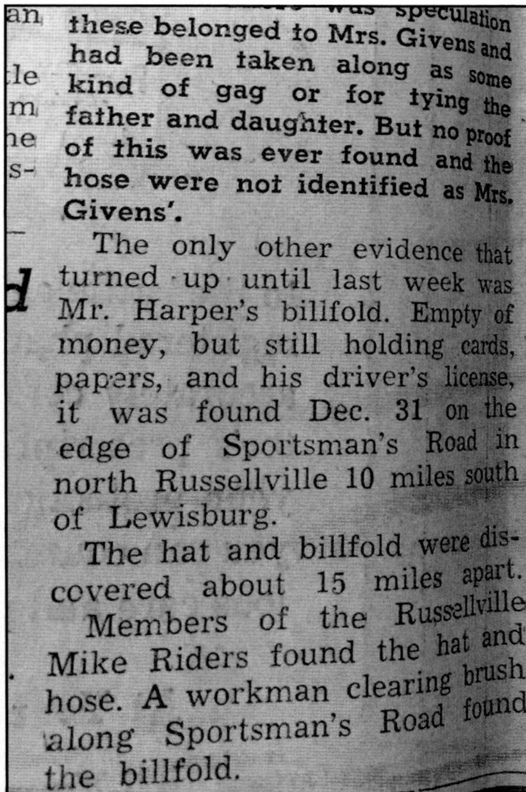

these belonged to Mrs. Givens and had been taken along as some kind of gag or for tying the father and daughter. But no proof of this was ever found and the hose were not identified as Mrs. Givens'.

The only other evidence that turned up until last week was Mr. Harper's billfold. Empty of money, but still holding cards, papers, and his driver's license, it was found Dec. 31 on the edge of Sportsman's Road in north Russellville 10 miles south of Lewisburg.

The hat and billfold were discovered about 15 miles apart.

Members of the Russellville Mike Riders found the hat and hose. A workman clearing brush along Sportsman's Road found the billfold.

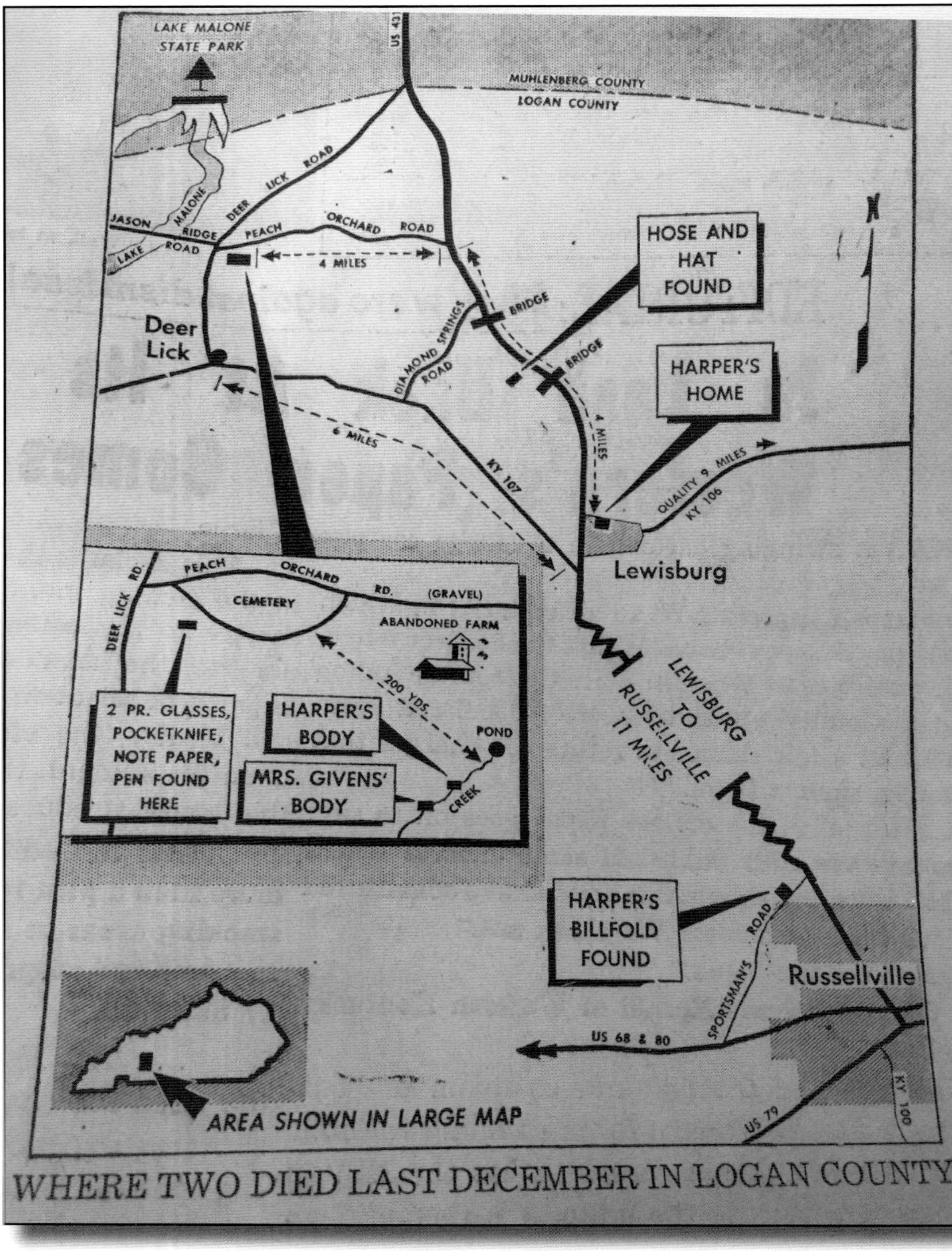

WHERE TWO DIED LAST DECEMBER IN LOGAN COUNTY

Searchers looking for Edgar Harper and Mrs. Ella Harper Givens.

Plank that covered the bodies

Edgar Harper Had A Mystery Caller

Edgar Harper's family has told police that the Lewisburg banker received a telephone call during the weekend last Thanksgiving.

It was from a man who identified himself as an FBI agent.

"Is this the Edgar Harper who is president of the Lewisburg Bank?" the man asked.

When Harper said it was, the man hung up.

The banker thought it was a practical joke, he told friends. But was it?

The identity of the caller has never been learned.

BRUTALITY ADDS TO SORROW FOR VICTIMS OF MURDER

The savage and wanton slaying of a gentle, elderly Logan County banker and his faithful, loving daughter has outraged this community and shocked the nation.

Edgar C. Harper and Ella Maria Givens were not just names in headlines. They were flesh and blood people, our neighbors and fellow citizens.

The normal sorrow that comes to any family when it loses an honored father and good woman who was wife, sister, and mother as well as the child who cared for an elderly, ailing parent, has been compounded by the brutal manner in which their lives were claimed.

These senseless acts of violence do happen—and often in communities where we say they couldn't happen.

Motive, identity of the killers are not known, but we do know that the law officers working on the case have given it a full measure of competence and evidenced great zeal to effect a solution.

Meanwhile, as our sympathies go out to the bereaved family, we ought to resolve as neighbors and good citizens that no other innocent persons be harmed in this tragedy. By that we mean that our desire for justice should not overcome our restraint when it comes to spreading rumors or making remarks that could cast unfair suspicion where it does not belong.

State Police Detective G.C. McMillen and Sheriff Gene Sweatt examine Mrs. Givens' broken glasses.

Who Would Know?

Littered Beer Cans Near Cemetery Indicate Woods A "Party Area"

The secluded Martin Cemetery, near Lake Malone, is about eight miles northwest of Lewisburg on a gravel portion of Peach Orchard Road. It is about five miles west from the road's intersection with U. S. Hwy. 431 and a few hundred yards east of the road's intersection with Deer Lick Road.

Littered beer cans on the abandoned Martin farm give testimony that it is something of a "party area."

The fact that such a spot was selected for the concealment of the bodies of Edgar C. Harper and Mrs. Ella Givens lends strength to a growing belief that the crime was committed by someone who knows that section of Logan County. But police say they have no real proof.

The bodies were found 200 yards below the cemetery. They appeared to have been dragged from the cemetery. At the cemetery's edge, possessions of the victims have been found scattered through the brush. These include Mrs. Given's glasses, a ball-point pen and some sheets of paper containing faded business notes thought to have been made by Mr. Harper, glasses fragments and a pocket knife which could have belonged to the banker, and a pack of gum of a type he favored.

Discovery of so many clues indicate the crime could have been committed by amateurs or someone rendered careless by drunkenness and rage, police say.

But then—nothing yet learned really proves this.

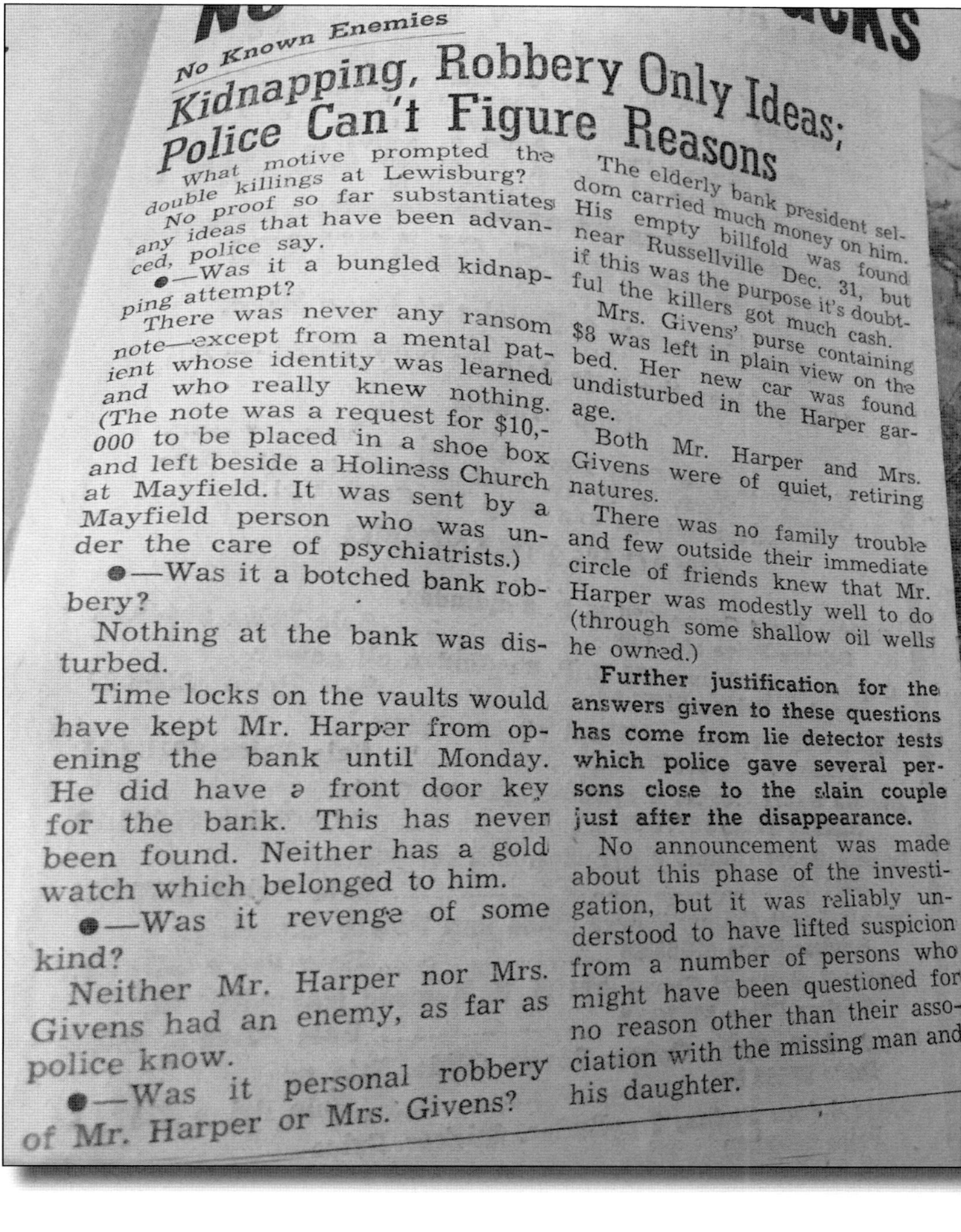

No Known Enemies

Kidnapping, Robbery Only Ideas; Police Can't Figure Reasons

What motive prompted the double killings at Lewisburg?

No proof so far substantiates any ideas that have been advanced, police say.

●—Was it a bungled kidnapping attempt?

There was never any ransom note—except from a mental patient whose identity was learned and who really knew nothing. (The note was a request for $10,000 to be placed in a shoe box and left beside a Holiness Church at Mayfield. It was sent by a Mayfield person who was under the care of psychiatrists.)

●—Was it a botched bank robbery?

Nothing at the bank was disturbed.

Time locks on the vaults would have kept Mr. Harper from opening the bank until Monday. He did have a front door key for the bank. This has never been found. Neither has a gold watch which belonged to him.

●—Was it revenge of some kind?

Neither Mr. Harper nor Mrs. Givens had an enemy, as far as police know.

●—Was it personal robbery of Mr. Harper or Mrs. Givens?

The elderly bank president seldom carried much money on him. His empty billfold was found near Russellville Dec. 31, but if this was the purpose it's doubtful the killers got much cash.

Mrs. Givens' purse containing $8 was left in plain view on the bed. Her new car was found undisturbed in the Harper garage.

Both Mr. Harper and Mrs. Givens were of quiet, retiring natures.

There was no family trouble and few outside their immediate circle of friends knew that Mr. Harper was modestly well to do (through some shallow oil wells he owned.)

Further justification for the answers given to these questions has come from lie detector tests which police gave several persons close to the slain couple just after the disappearance.

No announcement was made about this phase of the investigation, but it was reliably understood to have lifted suspicion from a number of persons who might have been questioned for no reason other than their association with the missing man and his daughter.

A man points to where each of the victims were found lying in a shallow ravine.

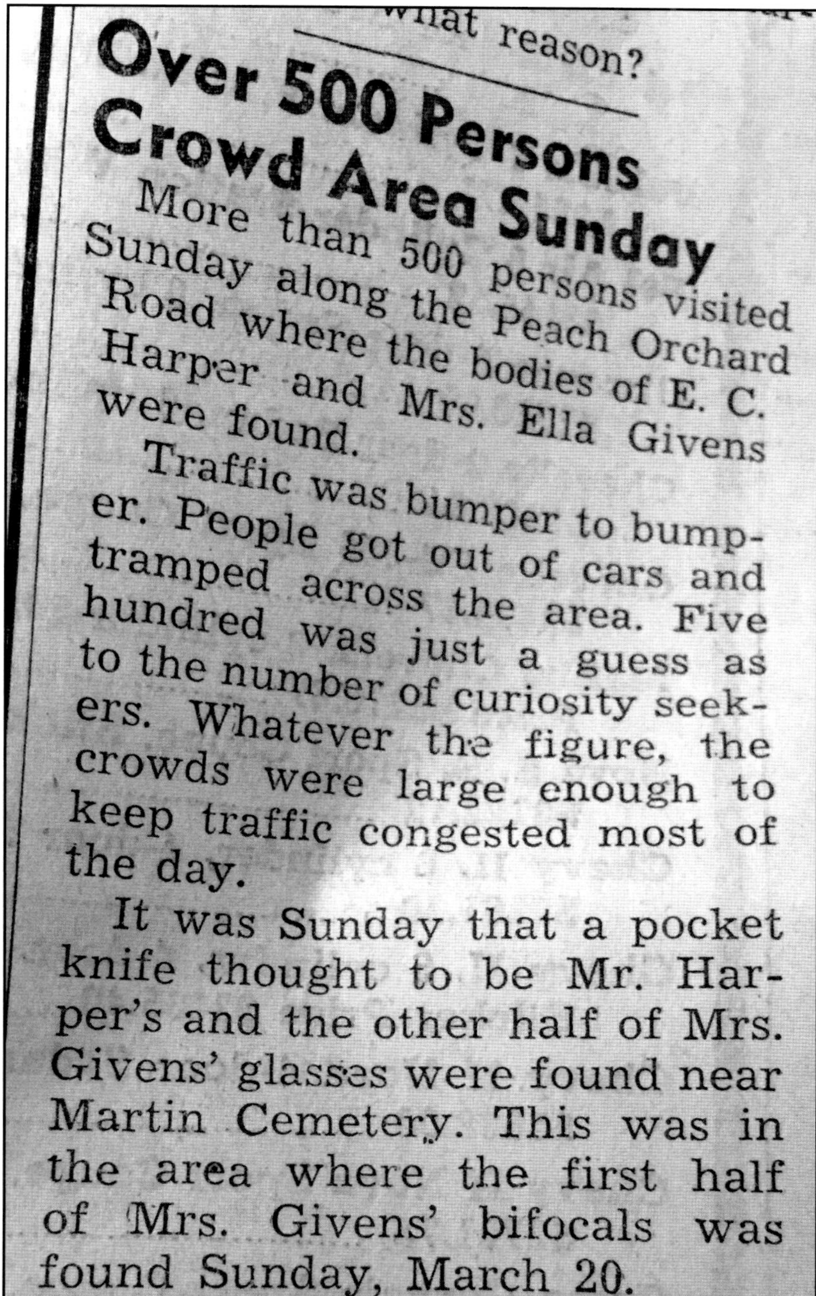

...what reason?

Over 500 Persons Crowd Area Sunday

More than 500 persons visited Sunday along the Peach Orchard Road where the bodies of E. C. Harper and Mrs. Ella Givens were found.

Traffic was bumper to bumper. People got out of cars and tramped across the area. Five hundred was just a guess as to the number of curiosity seekers. Whatever the figure, the crowds were large enough to keep traffic congested most of the day.

It was Sunday that a pocket knife thought to be Mr. Harper's and the other half of Mrs. Givens' glasses were found near Martin Cemetery. This was in the area where the first half of Mrs. Givens' bifocals was found Sunday, March 20.

With so many people in the area, could some crucial evidence have been damaged?"

Above: Final Burial

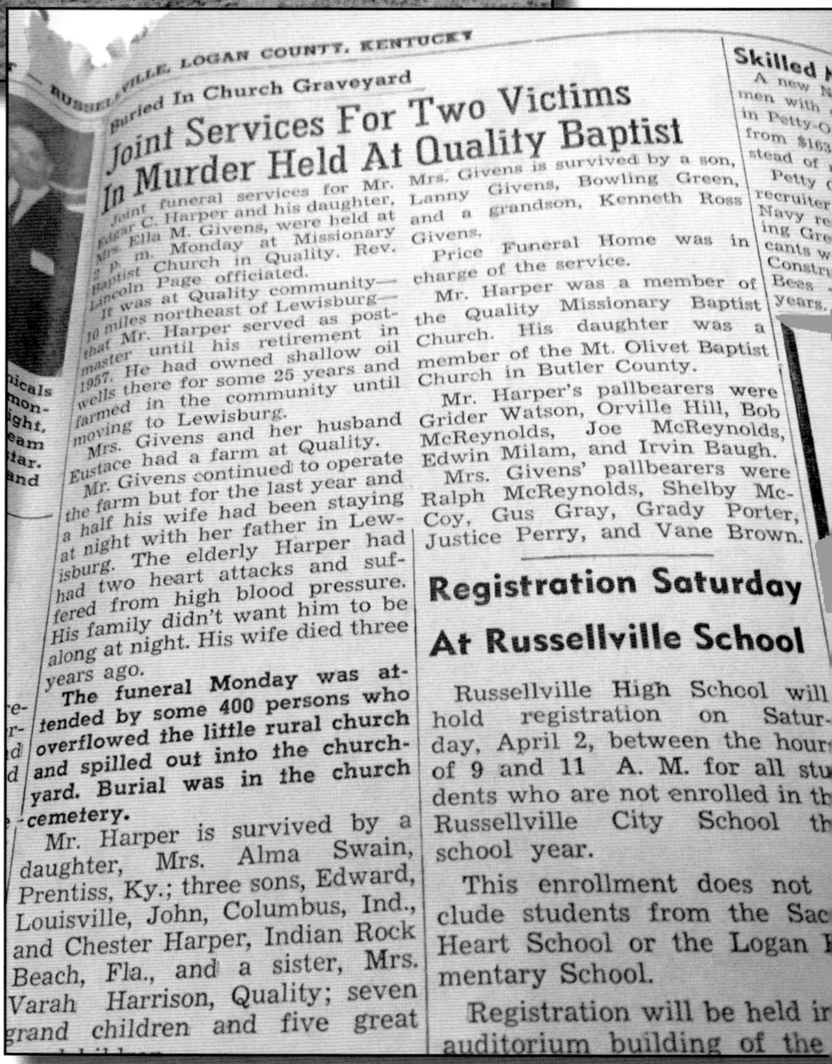

RUSSELLVILLE, LOGAN COUNTY, KENTUCKY

Buried In Church Graveyard

Joint Services For Two Victims In Murder Held At Quality Baptist

Joint funeral services for Mr. Edgar C. Harper and his daughter, Mrs. Ella M. Givens, were held at 2 p. m. Monday at Missionary Baptist Church in Quality. Rev. Lincoln Page officiated.

It was at Quality community—10 miles northeast of Lewisburg—that Mr. Harper served as postmaster until his retirement in 1957. He had owned shallow oil wells there for some 25 years and farmed in the community until moving to Lewisburg.

Mrs. Givens and her husband Eustace had a farm at Quality. Mr. Givens continued to operate the farm but for the last year and a half his wife had been staying at night with her father in Lewisburg. The elderly Harper had had two heart attacks and suffered from high blood pressure. His family didn't want him to be along at night. His wife died three years ago.

The funeral Monday was attended by some 400 persons who overflowed the little rural church and spilled out into the churchyard. Burial was in the church cemetery.

Mr. Harper is survived by a daughter, Mrs. Alma Swain, Prentiss, Ky.; three sons, Edward, Louisville, John, Columbus, Ind., and Chester Harper, Indian Rock Beach, Fla., and a sister, Mrs. Varah Harrison, Quality; seven grand children and five great

Mrs. Givens is survived by a son, Lanny Givens, Bowling Green, and a grandson, Kenneth Ross Givens.

Price Funeral Home was in charge of the service.

Mr. Harper was a member of the Quality Missionary Baptist Church. His daughter was a member of the Mt. Olivet Baptist Church in Butler County.

Mr. Harper's pallbearers were Grider Watson, Orville Hill, Bob McReynolds, Joe McReynolds, Edwin Milam, and Irvin Baugh.

Mrs. Givens' pallbearers were Ralph McReynolds, Shelby McCoy, Gus Gray, Grady Porter, Justice Perry, and Vane Brown.

Registration Saturday At Russellville School

Russellville High School will hold registration on Saturday, April 2, between the hours of 9 and 11 A. M. for all students who are not enrolled in the Russellville City School th school year.

This enrollment does not clude students from the Sac Heart School or the Logan mentary School.

Registration will be held in auditorium building of the

3 Bullets Recovered, Autopsy Shows Banker Shot Once, Daughter Twice

A preliminary report from autopsies conducted on the bodies of Lewisburg banker Edgar C. Harper and his daughter, Mrs. Ella Givens, showed that each had been shot.

Mr. Harper was shot in the neck. Mrs. Givens was shot in the head and chest. The bullets were recovered but were reportedly in badly mutiliated conditions. They were thought to be either .22 caliber or .25 caliber.

At the creekbed where the bodies were found near Peach Orchard Road, Mr. Harper was lying face down and Mrs. Givens was lying on her back.

Officers theorized they may have been shot elsewhere, then dragged down a ravine to the creekbed where they were covered with boards and brush.

The bodies were first taken to Price Funeral Home and then sent to the University of Kentucky Medical Center at Lexington where autopsies were performed by a University pathologist.

A complete report was to be submitted to county and state authorities later this week.

The bullets were sent to the State Police laboratory at Frankfort for analysis.

Autopsy

Why Beatings And Bullets? Police Puzzled

If any one of the bullet wounds suffered by Edgar C. Harper or Mrs. Ella Givens could have been fatal, why were they beaten so ferociously?

This puzzles police attempting to establish a motive to the killings of the Lewisburg banker and his daughter.

A complete autopsy disclosed Mrs. Givens had 15 scalp wounds and a fracture, Mr. Harper had six wounds on the head. She had been shot in the head and chest, he in the neck.

Still missing are Mr. Harper's keys—including one to the front door of the Lewisburg Banking Co., of which he was president. The elderly banker had no access to the money vaults. A watch of Mr. Harper's may or may not be missing. There is some confusion as to whether he owned one, police say.

A new and plausible theory to explain three unmatched hose found scattered along Hwy. 431 north of Lewisburg is that they were used as masks.

The women's stockings were discovered in December not far from Mr. Harper's hat, near Wolf Lick Bridge not far from the intersection of Hwy. 431 and Peach Orchard Road. Mrs. Givens had on socks and canvass sport shoes when the bodies were found.

Where couple's bodies were found.

There May Not Be Another Year For Killers At Lewisburg

THE KILLER or killers of Edgar Harper and his beloved daughter Ella may not win another year of freedom. Conversations with law officers still working on the case convince us that a diligent pursuit of several leads and theories which they have may bring a solution or an arrest before another 12 months elapse.

We share the belief of many Lewisburg residents that Mr. Harper and Mrs. Givens were murdered by someone familiar with the community and the Peach Orchard Road.

The hiding place in the ravine near the cemetery on Peach Orchard Road wouldn't be a concealment area known to outsiders, in our opinion. We find it hard to believe that strangers could so easily remove the father and daughter from the house at Lewisburg without at least the assistance of someone familiar with the house or known to the banker or Mrs. Givens.

MOTIVE? Money is always a good motive. Anyone brutal or stupid and coarse enough to commit this crime could have been of a type of mind to have thought that the banker had access to either the vaults of the bank, which he didn't, or kept large sums of money at home, which his family vigorously denies.

A year before the slayings, an attempt was made to enter the Lewisburg Banking Co., with an acetylene torch. Although the effort was made by a person who displayed welding skill, the attempt to break in failed. Police admit there could be a link between the attempted robbery and the murders. The savagery with which the banker and daughter were killed, the beatings as well as the multiple shootings, indicate a cruelty that must have had a great element of frustration. Did the burglar who visited the bank in 1965 go to the Harper house in the hopes of forcing the banker to help him enter the vaults? Did he take a companion along to help overpower this harmless elderly man and his faithful daughter who stayed with her ailing father at night?

IF THERE were two killers, the chances for identification are more than doubled. While the great majority of citizens in North Logan and Butler County are law abiding, the community has, like every rural area, an element of hoodlums, men with criminal records who might be susceptible to the temptations of attacking an old man and a helpless woman for the gain of money.

These men and their friends elsewhere are known to police. Their neighbors know them, too.

There are many men who have worked on this case and who want desperately to solve it — men like Guy McMillen, the former sheriff, G. C. McMillen, the State Police detective, Sheriff Gene Sweatt, who was chief deputy when the murders occurred, Deputy Clyde Darden, Commonwealth Attorney James C. Lyne, FBI agent John Alden of Bowling Green, the State Troopers and other officers assigned to Logan.

Logan Countians have not forgotten this crime, and their police give no indication that they have forgotten either. Actually, the killers could be known. From what we have learned, there is no cause for citizens to think that key officers aren't staying on the trail of the murderers. And no reason for those who committed this awful deed to think so either, wherever they are, under surveillance even at this time, perhaps.

A year after the murders, no one had been arrested.

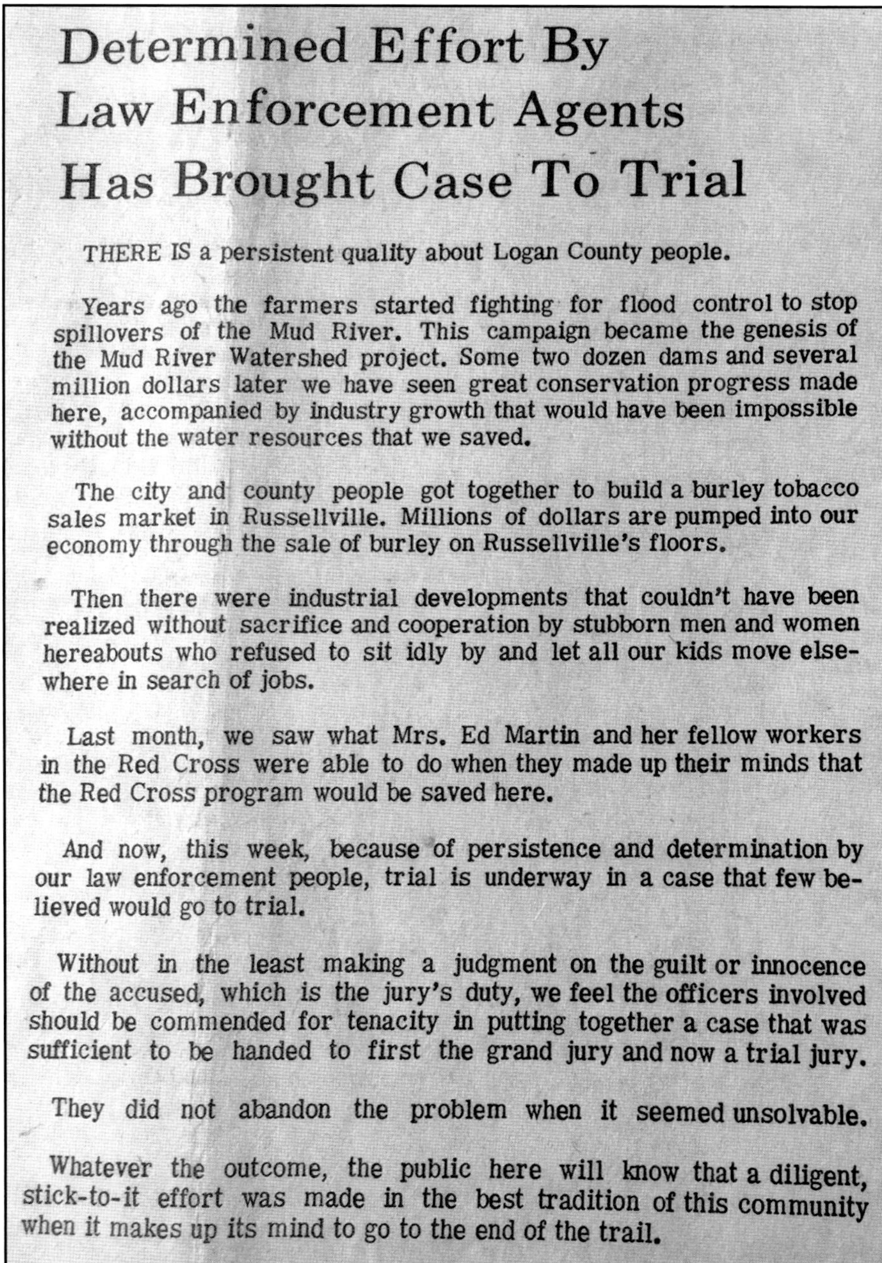

Determined Effort By Law Enforcement Agents Has Brought Case To Trial

THERE IS a persistent quality about Logan County people.

Years ago the farmers started fighting for flood control to stop spillovers of the Mud River. This campaign became the genesis of the Mud River Watershed project. Some two dozen dams and several million dollars later we have seen great conservation progress made here, accompanied by industry growth that would have been impossible without the water resources that we saved.

The city and county people got together to build a burley tobacco sales market in Russellville. Millions of dollars are pumped into our economy through the sale of burley on Russellville's floors.

Then there were industrial developments that couldn't have been realized without sacrifice and cooperation by stubborn men and women hereabouts who refused to sit idly by and let all our kids move elsewhere in search of jobs.

Last month, we saw what Mrs. Ed Martin and her fellow workers in the Red Cross were able to do when they made up their minds that the Red Cross program would be saved here.

And now, this week, because of persistence and determination by our law enforcement people, trial is underway in a case that few believed would go to trial.

Without in the least making a judgment on the guilt or innocence of the accused, which is the jury's duty, we feel the officers involved should be commended for tenacity in putting together a case that was sufficient to be handed to first the grand jury and now a trial jury.

They did not abandon the problem when it seemed unsolvable.

Whatever the outcome, the public here will know that a diligent, stick-to-it effort was made in the best tradition of this community when it makes up its mind to go to the end of the trail.

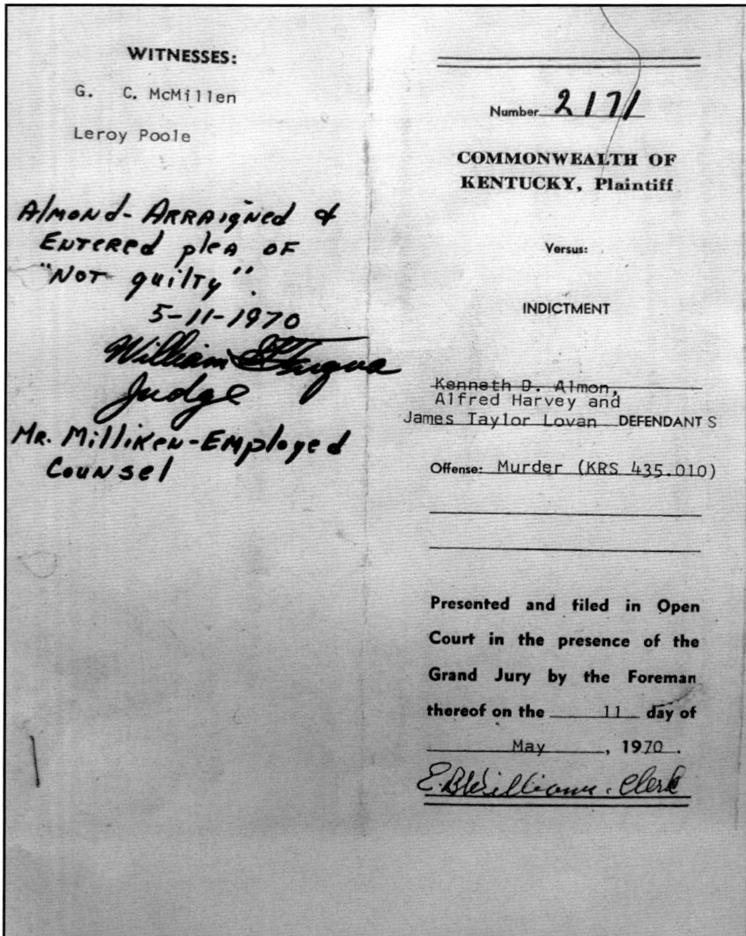

WITNESSES:

G. C. McMillen

Leroy Poole

Almond- Arraigned & Entered plea of "Not guilty". 5-11-1970 William [illegible] Judge

Mr. Milliken-Employed Counsel

Number 2171

COMMONWEALTH OF KENTUCKY, Plaintiff

Versus:

INDICTMENT

~~Kenneth D. Almon,~~
Alfred Harvey and
James Taylor Lovan DEFENDANT S

Offense: Murder (KRS 435.010)

Presented and filed in Open Court in the presence of the Grand Jury by the Foreman thereof on the 11 day of May, 1970.

E. B. Williams, Clerk

After all three men were accused and arrested, the grand jury handed down indictments for all three on charges of murder and kidnapping. The men were Alfred Harvey, Kenneth Almon, and James Lovan.

WHERE WAS Harvey? A phone call from Alfred Finley Harvey, above right, to James T. Lovan may prove to be a crucial defense point for Lovan. The defense claims Harvey called Dec. 11 from Missouri when the State says he was in Kentucky. Harvey is seen with Logan Sheriff Jim Johnson and deputy sheriff Morris Kisselbaugh. -Staff photo by J. J. Johnson.

Alfred Finley Harvey.

Kenneth Delaney Almon with Sheriff Jim Johnson.

James Taylor Lovan

May 1, 1970

Three Charged in Logan 1965 Kidnap-Slayings

Russellville, Ky. – A four-and-a-half-year police investigation climaxed Tuesday night when a schoolteacher and two penitentiary inmates were charged with murder in connection with the 1965 kidnap-slayings of an elderly Lewisburg banker and his daughter.

Kenneth Delaney Almon, a 37-year-old father of four and a science teacher at Webster County High School. Almon has no prior arrests.

James Taylor Lovan, 35, Almon's brother-in-law who has been imprisoned at Eddyville State Penitentiary since Oct. 3, 1967, when he began serving a total of 15 years on three five-year counts of schoolhouse breaking and entering, hog theft and storehouse breaking and entering.

Alfred Finley Harvey, 25, also an inmate at Eddyville, imprisoned since March 9, 1966 when he began serving a life sentence concurrent with a 21-year-sentence for armed assault with intent to rob and for armed robbery.

Almon, a student at Western Kentucky University in 1951 and 1952, was arrested Tuesday at his Providence home by State Police detective G.C. McMillen, Russellville, and Logan County Sheriff Jim Johnson.

Police officers said Commonwealth Atty. James C. Lyne, Russellville, had instructed them to reveal nothing about the investigation except the names of the accused.

McMillen said the details of how the investigation led to the charges being placed against the suspects would not be made public until they were brought out in trial.

He said the case is still under investigation and that other arrests may be made.

Officials were asked if any Logan Countains might be implicated, but offered no comment. Sheriff Jim Johnson who was elected sheriff last year, promised voters he would solve the killings if elected.

Police officials close to the investigation say robbery is still considered the motive in the 1965 slayings. Officials will present evidence Monday to the Logan County Grand Jury. If indictments are returned against the three suspects, a preliminary hearing tentatively scheduled for 2 p.m. Monday will not be held.

LEAVING PARKING lot on way to Courthouse at Hopkinsville, Judge Wm. G. Fuqua, left, carries robe bag and tape recorder. At right, Mrs. Mary Smith, court stenographer.

Christian County Courthouse

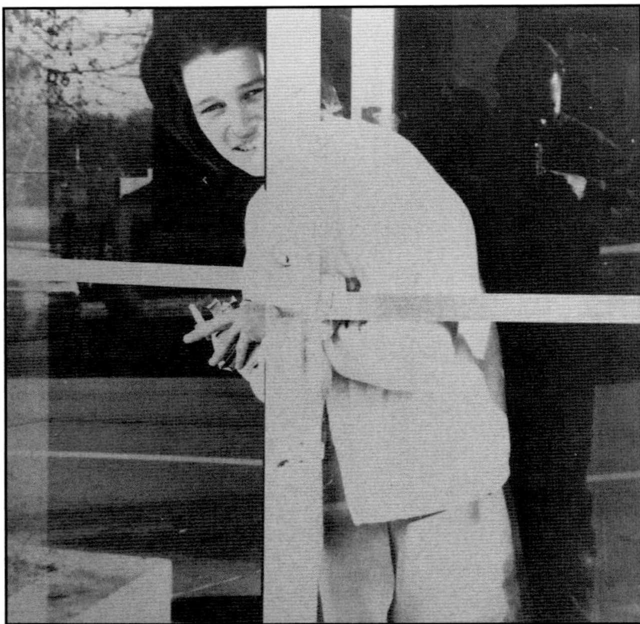

Above: Carolyn Brown Hampton

Dixie Satterfield said the woman came to his office with Donnie Almon, a brother of Kenneth, and Donny Boyd, a friend. He said she didn't seem drunk or drinking to him, that he couldn't smell liquor on her breath and she didn't appear to be under the influence of any drugs.

Shortly after noon, they started taking a six-page statement from her, he said. Mrs. Helen Ogden, a law firm receptionist, was there, and attorney John Milliken walked in and out.

The worked several hours, close to six p.m. with time out for a couple of breaks, he said. All he recalled her drinking was two cokes.

As she talked, said Satterfield, he would work up notes, then take a page at a time down the hall to be typed.

The statement was then introduced into evidence. The witness identified it and said that in this statement of six pages, the girl related that Almon had nothing to do with the killings and neither did Lovan – "on at least two or three occasions."

On cross examination, Satterfield told Lyne that he hadn't warned Carolyn Brown Hampton about what she was about to say, and that what she said might be held against her. He gave her no admonitions, he said.

"This then is your version?" Lyne asked

"Yes," Satterfield answered.

Pictured left, right and below: Inconsistent statements. It's especially eye-opening that when Kenneth Almon's attorney approached Carolyn Brown Hampton for an interview, she asked if he were Kenneth Almon after she'd accused Almon of being at the crime scene.

Defense Summation

(The Hon. Wm. Scent)

--Summarized--

The Commonwealth's case rests entirely upon the testimony of Carolyn Brown under direct questioning on the witness stand.

If you don't believe her, it is your duty to acquit James Taylor Lovan.

Who is Carolyn Brown?

By her own testimony, she is a 15-year-old accomplice. . . a mental defective with a sociopathic personality, according to the Commonwealth's own psychoanalyst and the psychologist called by the defense.

What is her reputation?

She has a horrible reputation as a woman and as a witness you couldn't believe. The Commonwealth called no witness to rebut what was said about her character.

Compare her testimony on the witness stand with what she said in an interview by Det. LeRoy Poole on April 30, 1970.

TO POOLE: She drove the white Cadillac to Lewisburg. TRIAL: Almon drove the Cadillac. Harvey and Carolyn were in the Mustang.

TO POOLE: Lovan and Harvey went into the restaurant and drank coffee. TRIAL: Almon and Jimmy D. got the coffee.

TRIAL: Harvey, Lovan, and Almon were in the store. POOLE: No mention of the store, a grocery.

POOLE: And at the restaurant a lady gave her pins to hold up her Levis. TRIAL: This happened at the grocery.

POOLE: No mention of a policeman's house. TRIAL: After leaving the grocery they went to a policeman's house.

POOLE: Almon had a .25 caliber pistol. TRIAL: Lovan had a .25 caliber pistol.

Headline Misleads On Harper Story

In the July 2 News-Democrat the headline on the continuation of a story from Page 1 about the Harper-Givens case was misleading. The story dealt with sworn testimony by County Attorney Jesse L. Riley, Jr. on how a convict, Alfred Finley Harvey, allegedly told him details about the Harper case. The erroneous heading read: "Convict Told How Killings Took Place." It was originally written to read: "Riley Says Convict Told How Killings Took Place" and the words "Riley Says" were dropped off in making up the page. Harvey has subsequently denied Riley's version of the story.

December 10
Both Sides Agree: Harvey Was Freed From Jail

On Wednesday, Dec. 16, the 12th day of the trial, attorney W. Currie Milliken of Bowling Green, Counsel for Kenneth D. Almon, was recalled to the stand by defense attorney William Scent. Milliken, attending the trial as an observer, had been placed under oath and first questioned, by Scent, on Tuesday.

His testimony Tuesday was interrupted by a conference for attorneys and the judge, outside of the courtroom.

Scent showed to Milliken an FBI record of arrests for Alfred Finley Harvey, 26, one of the three men indicted in the killings of Edgar C. Harper and Ella Maria Harper Givens.

Milliken, who reportedly obtained the record, read from the document a history of arrests of an Alfred Finley Harvey that dated back to 1963. They included Nov. 23-24, 1965 at Fresno, Calif.; May 26, 1965, Modesto, Calif.; Dec. 18, 1964, Fresno; Oct. 24, 1964, Crescent City, Calif.; May 20, 1964, San Jose; Feb. 18, 1963, Fresno, and Feb. 2, 1963, Long Beach.

The violations were mostly traffic, Milliken said.

Milliken then noted that on Dec. 9, 1965, according to the record, Harvey was arrested in Raytown, Mo., on a warrant from California.

Scent then read into the record a stipulation that the defense and State had previously agreed that the records of Raytown police and Jackson County, Mo., Jail show that Harvey was arrested there Dec. 9, 1965, 5:10 p.m. and he was released the following day, Dec. 10, 1965 (which would have been on a Friday, the day before the Saturday, Dec. 11, 1965 when Harper and Mrs. Givens were abducted and slain.)

MRS. KENNETH ALMON

At 11 a.m., Mrs. Nina Lovan Almon was called as a defense witness. She said she lives in Earlington, is the mother of four children, is a sister of the defendant and wife of Kenneth D. Almon, also a defendant in the Harper case.

Although she has been a spectator in the courtroom during the trial, she has heard no testimony about the phone calls, she said.

In 1965 and 1966 she and her family lived at 307 West Main, Earlington, she said, and she wrote the checks for the family bills, including phone bills for December, 1965 and January, 1966.

Mrs. Almon said she paid a telephone bill dated Jan. 23, 1966 which covered calls made in December, 1965, including a long distance call made to her residence, collect, on Dec. 11, 1965 from California, Mo. (A town in Missouri.) The bill and a toll slip were introduced into evidence by Scent after the papers were first examined by Commonwealth's Attorney Lyne.

Lyne noted the perforations on the bill and asked Mrs. Almon if she had the records for phone bills in December 1965, November, 1965, and February, 1966.

"I couldn't be sure, I would have to look," she replied.

"Please do so when you return home and bring them back to court," Lyne asked. "Do you have a cancelled check for these bills?"

"I may," she said.

"Please bring that, also," Lyne asked. "Where was this bill found?" In a box where she kept cancelled checks, records of a household nature. Mrs. Almon said she found the records during a search of the house after May 5, 1970, the day after her husband was arrested—he has not been brought to trial, as yet.

CALLED AS a defense witness was W. Currie Milliken, an attorney, who told how he and defense attorney William Scent interviewed Carolyn Brown Hampton and got a different story from the one she gave the jury.

WILLIAM G. FUQUA

THE HARPER CASE . . . Sheriff Jim Johnson, left, with Det. Lt. Wm. Smith, had promised an arrest in killings. Photos by Ron McIntosh

The Grand Jury listens to the indictments.

Jury Deliberation Begin in James Lovan Murder Trial

A Christian County jury began deliberations Monday Dec. 17 in the James Taylor Lovan murder trial after final address and instructions to the jury.

The instructions explained that Lovan was charged with conspiracy for murder. "If you shall believe from the evidence beyond a reasonable doubt that the defendant, James Taylor Lovan, and Alfred Finley Harvey, and Kenneth Almon, or any two or more of them, including the defendant, conspired and agreed to and with each other to rob and (or) kill and murder Edgar Harper and Ella Maria Harper Givens—then you ought to find the defendant guilty of willful murder as charged and fix his punishment at confinement in the state penitentiary for life or death, in your discretion, according to proof," read part of the instruction.

"The law presumes the defendant innocent until proved guilty beyond doubt, and if you have reasonable doubt as to the defendant being proved guilty, then you shall find him not guilty," the instructions said.

THE ★ LOGAN ★ LEADER

VOLUME 3 NUMBER 51

RUSSELLVILLE, LOGAN COUNTY, KENTUCKY, MONDAY AFTERNOON, DECEMBER 21, 1970

PRICE 10¢

Jury Clears Lovan In Harper Murder

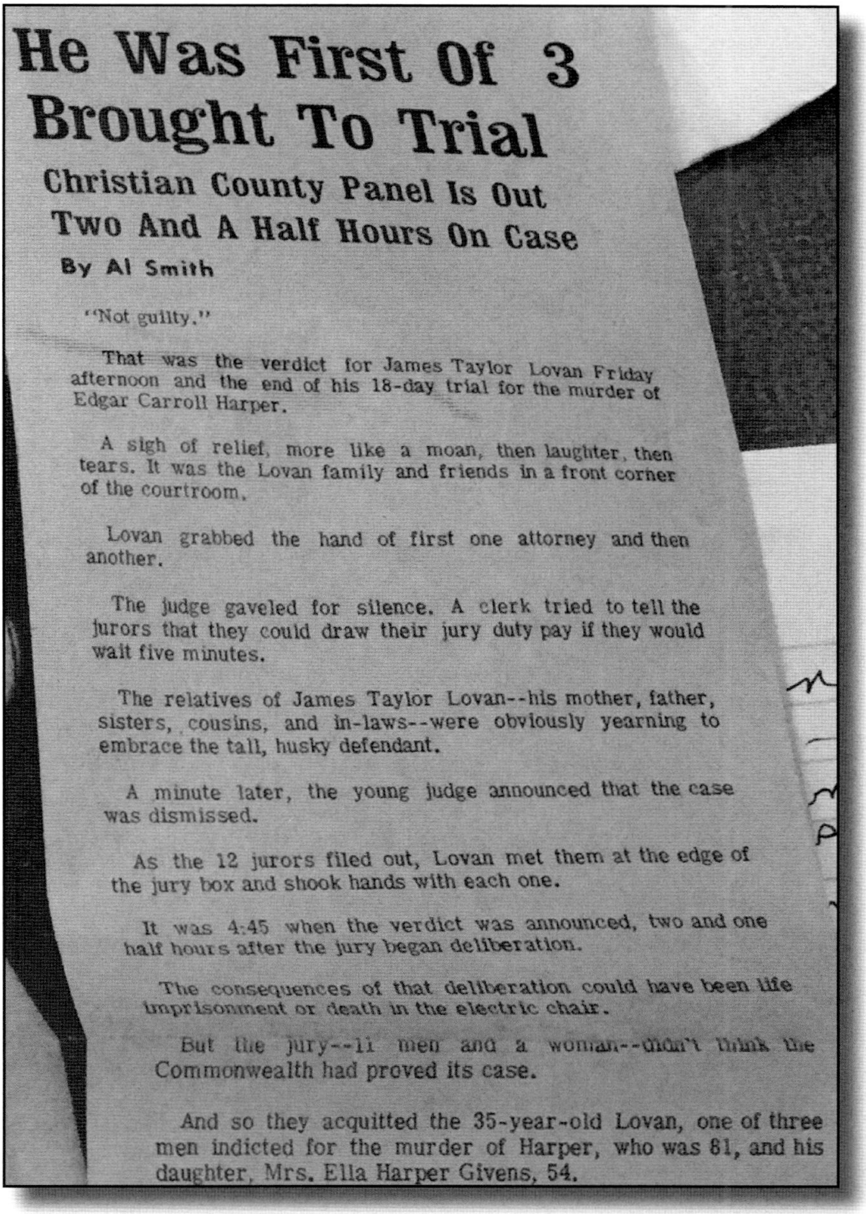

He Was First Of 3 Brought To Trial

Christian County Panel Is Out Two And A Half Hours On Case

By Al Smith

"Not guilty."

That was the verdict for James Taylor Lovan Friday afternoon and the end of his 18-day trial for the murder of Edgar Carroll Harper.

A sigh of relief, more like a moan, then laughter, then tears. It was the Lovan family and friends in a front corner of the courtroom.

Lovan grabbed the hand of first one attorney and then another.

The judge gaveled for silence. A clerk tried to tell the jurors that they could draw their jury duty pay if they would wait five minutes.

The relatives of James Taylor Lovan--his mother, father, sisters, cousins, and in-laws--were obviously yearning to embrace the tall, husky defendant.

A minute later, the young judge announced that the case was dismissed.

As the 12 jurors filed out, Lovan met them at the edge of the jury box and shook hands with each one.

It was 4:45 when the verdict was announced, two and one half hours after the jury began deliberation.

The consequences of that deliberation could have been life imprisonment or death in the electric chair.

But the jury--11 men and a woman--didn't think the Commonwealth had proved its case.

And so they acquitted the 35-year-old Lovan, one of three men indicted for the murder of Harper, who was 81, and his daughter, Mrs. Ella Harper Givens, 54.

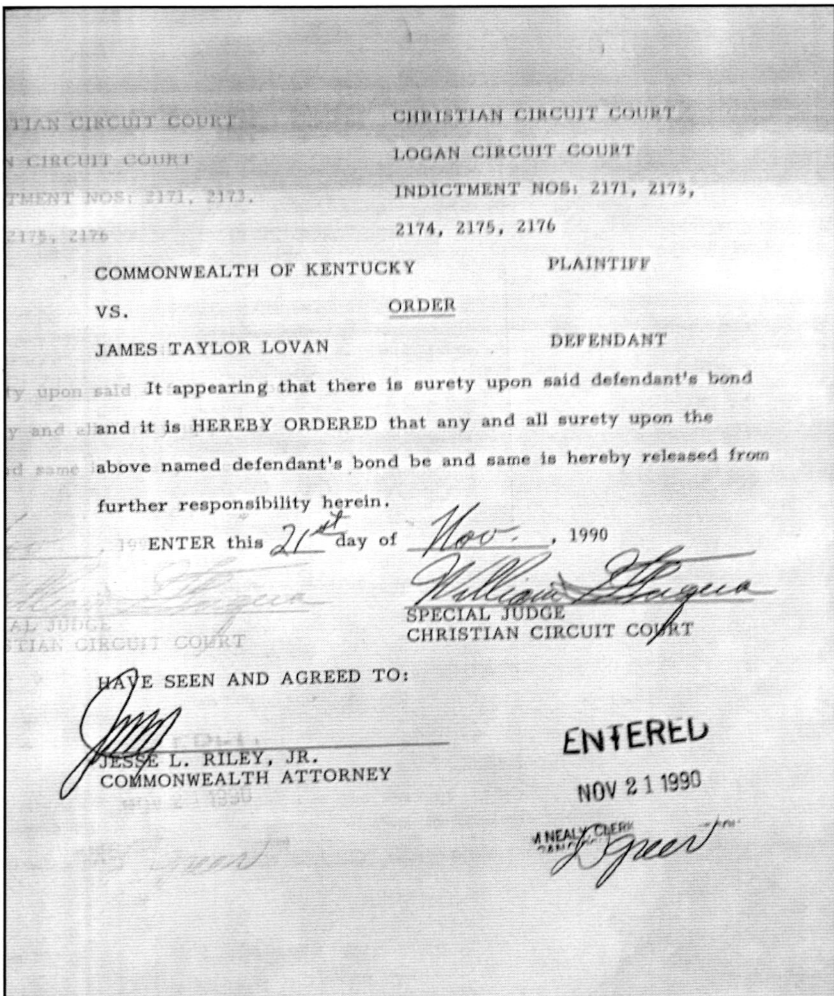

CHRISTIAN CIRCUIT COURT
LOGAN CIRCUIT COURT
INDICTMENT NOS: 2171, 2173,
2174, 2175, 2176

COMMONWEALTH OF KENTUCKY PLAINTIFF

VS. ORDER

JAMES TAYLOR LOVAN DEFENDANT

It appearing that there is surety upon said defendant's bond and it is HEREBY ORDERED that any and all surety upon the above named defendant's bond be and same is hereby released from further responsibility herein.

ENTER this 21st day of Nov., 1990

William L. Fuqua
SPECIAL JUDGE
CHRISTIAN CIRCUIT COURT

HAVE SEEN AND AGREED TO:

JESSE L. RILEY, JR.
COMMONWEALTH ATTORNEY

ENTERED
NOV 21 1990

Lovan was acquitted of murder, but could still have been tried on kidnapping and/or assault with intent to rob charges. Almon was never brought to trial. While already serving a life sentence for armed robberies, Harvey was allowed to plead guilty to two charges of robbery in connection with the case after he had been indicted on charges of armed assault with intent to rob both Harper and Givens. He was eventually released. On November 21, 1990, Lovan's bond money was released back to him, almost 25 years after the murders occurred. No one was ever convicted of murder in the case of Edgar Harper and Ella Harper Givens.

Chapter 11

May 21, 1966

"Oh my," Ida placed both hands to her cheeks. "Jane, what have you done to yourself?"

"Do you like it?" Jane smoothed her newly darkened hair. "I tired of the blond bombshell look, so I thought I'd try for Audrey Hepburn from 'Breakfast at Tiffany's'."

"Well," Ida commented. "You are a little thin to capture the bombshell look. Not nearly enough up top."

"Yes, well everyone wasn't blessed with your ample figure."

"Ladies," Minnie chided. "Stop being catty. You both weigh the same. Go ahead, Ida, finish the article."

"'The body found in a sinkhole in Warren County was identified as Robert Crouse, husband of the slain woman,'" Ida read aloud. "'Crouse, whose wife Barbara Smith Crouse, was found murdered in Butler County on April 20th, was identified through his fingerprints. He is believed to have been killed on the same day as his wife.'" Ida sighed deeply. "Another double murder so close to us and only a few months after the Harpers' deaths."

The newspaper crackled as Minnie tapped it with her fingers. "It says right there he's an ex-convict. He may have been involved in something illegal and that's what got him killed. His wife was probably in the wrong place when the killer showed up."

"But Minnie, it's only one county over," pointed out Jane. "The news said Mrs. Crouse was shot in the head and heart. That's exactly what happened to Ella. Do you think that's a coincidence? I don't know about you, but I think we should ask around Butler County, see if we can find a connection."

"Oh, I'm not so sure about that," Ida hesitated and rubbed the spot between her eyebrows. "Asking around about the Harpers is one thing; we knew them personally. Trying to find out about the Crouse's could be dangerous."

"Oh, stop being so scared," Jane snapped.

"Hush, Jane," Minnie interrupted. She picked up her delicate teacup and took a sip. "Go ahead, Ida. Why do you think that?"

"We'd have to insert ourselves into stranger's lives, put ourselves out there. We don't know these people. They have been in trouble with the law."

Jane touched her forefinger to her bottom lip. "We don't have to talk to those types of people. We could speak with people working in public places like gas stations and restaurants. Employees there deal with a lot of people, hear a lot of stories. They have so many customers, and if we don't give them our names, there's no way they will remember us."

"Yes," Ida stood knocking over her chair. "And some have great memories and share everything. I can just hear some gossipy waitress: 'Three ladies from over in Lewisburg were here asking about the Crouse murders.' It's going to get us in trouble. I won't participate."

Jane walked over and set the wooden chair upright, then hugged her sister. "I understand, Ida. I really do. But it scares me not to know what happened, and who did this. We could already be in danger from someone we know."

"Yes, but..."

Jane hugged her tighter and stepped back. "We have to see this through. Our friends deserve justice. You know the police don't have anything. Frank told us they have to wait for something to happen before they can investigate further."

Ida sighed heavily. "You're right. Of course, you're right. Where do we start?"

"Let's go over to that little diner in Morgantown and see what we can find," Minnie suggested.

"But Minnie," Ida argued. "I already have a roast on for supper."

"Turn it down very low. We can come back and have that later. We'll just have a piece of pie or something."

A knock at the door drew their attention. Frank waved through the curtained window of the front door.

"Oh, come in Frank," Jane gushed. "Why are you here?"

Frank gave her a blank look. "Did you have a hard day at school? It's Tuesday; our bingo night."

"Oh, of course. I can't make it tonight."

"What," Minnie blurted. "We can run errands without you, Jane. You go ahead."

"But..."

Minnie grabbed Jane's sheer yellow scarf from the coat rack and pushed her out the door into Frank's arms. "I won't hear of it. You go to your game. Ida and I will take care of everything."

"Will you wait for me in the car, honey?" Jane asked. She turned back to her sisters. "Why did you do that? I want to go to Morgantown."

"We might have to go back a few times," Minnie said.

"So?" Jane challenged.

"I get it," said Ida. "We don't want to raise suspicions by the three of us going back too often. We might need you to go alone next time and find out more info."

Jane looked from Minnie to Ida. "Okay," she hissed. "But make sure to take lots of notes. I don't want to miss anything." They both nodded obediently. Jane banged the door shut. "Sorry," she called out lightly.

"Okay," Minnie said. "Let's go."

They settled into the car and Ida turned the key with shaky hands. How had she let Jane talk her into this?

She eased the nose of the sturdy Buick onto Henry Street and pointed it in the direction of Morgantown. "What's the plan, Minnie? How do we decide who to talk to? What do we say?"

"Let me think a minute."

Ida stopped the car. "You don't know what we're going to do?"

"We have about forty minutes to discuss that while we're driving. We're smart enough to come up with a plan by then."

"I don't know." Ida edged off the brake; the car crawled forward. "If we don't have anything, I'm not stopping. I'll head right back here. You hear me?"

Minnie watched the countryside slip by for a few moments. "How about we find out who has worked at the diner the longest?"

"Okay, why?"

"I would think that person would know the most people in town. The regulars, their habits, temperaments, things important to figure out who might be capable of something as serious as murder."

"That sounds pretty good, but how are we going to find out? We can't just barge in there and demand 'who's been here the longest?' We must be subtle. We need some type of feasible cover story."

"Cover story. That's it. The *The Daily News* has been asking me to write a few articles about the history of this area, Mammoth Cave and some of the others, plus how counties and cities were established. We could use that for our cover."

"That might work."

"Yes, and it will give me the perfect opportunity to get out and ask some questions so I can get this assignment done."

"Alright, let's figure out what we want to ask," Ida said. "Get that shorthand notebook out of my purse. Write questions down so we don't forget anything."

"Great idea."

A half-hour later, they swung the old Buick into a space right by the door of the packed diner. Purple neon lights outlined the small white building, spelling out "McGill's."

"I want to go home," Ida stated, her knuckles gripping the steering wheel. "With all of these people, someone's bound to overhear us."

"With so many people in there talking, no one will be able to hear anything we say. We'd have a harder time if the place was empty. Now come on. We've figured out how to do this. It'll be as easy as lemon meringue pie, which is what I'm going to order."

Ida reluctantly pulled herself out of the car and lagged behind Minnie who cradled the notebook in one arm and pulled the door open with the other.

"Hello," a young waitress with blond curls greeted jovially. Her arms were piled with dirty plates and silverware. "There's a seat coming open right over there in the corner." She pointed with her chin toward a two-person booth that an older man wiped. He finished with a flourish.

"Have a seat, ladies." He extended his arm in invitation.

"Thank you." They settled into the booth and the blond waitress bounced up to them. "Hello, I'm Katie and I'll be your waitress today. Would you like a drink, ladies?"

"Wow, do you wait on all these tables by yourself?" Minnie asked.

"Oh, it's no big deal. Stella is behind the counter over there and takes care of those seats. Charlie helps me clean all the tables. Mike and Harry are in the back cooking. I mostly just have to take orders and deliver drinks and food. Are you ready to order?"

"Yes," said Ida. "I'll have the bread pudding and a cup of coffee."

"And I'll have a slice of lemon meringue pie and a glass of water," Minnie added.

"I'm sorry," Katie apologized. "We're out of lemon meringue. They just pulled a cherry pie out of the oven."

"Do you have vanilla ice cream?"

"Well of course. How could we call ourselves a diner if we didn't have ice cream for warm pie?"

"That has my name all over it," Minnie laughed.

"Sure thing," Katie turned to go.

"Wait, please," Minnie said. "Can you tell me who's worked here the longest?" She held up the notebook. "I'm doing a short article or two on some local history for the *Bowling Green Daily News* and I'm trying to interview a few people."

"That would be Charlie, the man in the blue jeans and white shirt who was cleaning this table when you arrived. He's the owner."

"The owner cleans the tables?" asked Ida.

"Yes, he's a great boss. There isn't anything around here he wouldn't do. I'll tell him you want to speak to him and get your orders started."

She hurried off and Minnie leaned toward Ida. "This is good, very good."

"What do you mean?"

"If he's that involved, then he's probably here all the time. The diner seems successful and the owner has everything to do with that. If people didn't like the owner they wouldn't visit."

"You're so smart, Minnie." Ida said. "Maybe you should pursue becoming a detective."

"No," Minnie twirled the heart locket at her throat. "I'll leave that to Jane."

"Hello again, young ladies." The man who cleaned the table beamed at them. "I heard a rumor you might want to interview me for a newspaper story." He grabbed an empty chair from a nearby table and settled into it at the end of their two-person booth.

"Yes, yes," Minnie nodded her head. "I'm writing a few 'history of the town pieces' for the *Daily News*. First things first, could you give me your name?"

"Charlie McGill."

"Well that explains McGill's Diner," Ida laughed nervously.

"And how long have you lived around here?" Minnie asked.

"My whole life, seventy-two years."

"Wow, you're seventy-two?" gushed Ida.

Ida jumped as Minnie kicked her under the table. "What the..." Minnie's look stopped her and she nodded. "You look way too young to be seventy-two. Must be all the hard work and clean country air. Are you married?"

"Yes, to the love of my life. Beth and I will be married 48 years this coming September."

"Oh, congratulations," Ida said. "It's hard to find someone you want to spend the rest of your life with. I, myself..."

"Tell me about some of the other people you know here in town," Minnie interrupted. "Some of the history of the buildings. Do you know why it's called Morgantown?"

"Now that is kind of a funny story."

"Really?" Minnie jotted in her notebook.

"Yes. A man named Funkhouser donated a lot of land to make the county seat. He probably hoped the city would be named after him, but it didn't happen that way at all." Charlie laughed. "There are actually two theories about the Morgantown name. There was a hunter named Morgan around these parts and there was a child born with the name Daniel Morgan Smith, one of the first children born after the county seat was formed. Either way, it was dubbed Morgantown in 1813."

"That's so interesting," said Minnie. She looked pointedly at Ida.

"Yes, interesting," Ida echoed. "So, do you know everyone in town?"

"Well, most of them. I mean, I have the only eating establishment for miles around, so when people want a break from cooking, they come here."

"Here we go," the waitress placed Minnie's and Ida's orders in front of them. "Anything else right now?"

"No, we're fine," Ida said. "Thank you."

"Okay, I'll check on you in a little bit," Katie rushed off to another table.

"Back to what I was saying," Minnie mused. "Any interesting characters that come in regularly?"

Charlie frowned. "Interesting characters?"

"What my sister means," Ida explained, "is it takes all kinds to make up a community. Anyone who makes you laugh with corny jokes or is especially quiet, but kind? Anyone who makes you wonder if they're up to something?"

"Up to something," Charlie repeated. He looked around the packed diner. "Well, as a matter of fact, there are a few who I like to keep an eye on when they come in here. They've sneaked off a time or two without paying."

"Really," Minnie sympathized.

"Didn't call the police or confront them the next time they came in, because I'm afraid they'll come back later and vandalize the place."

"Vandalize?" said Ida.

"Yes, splash paint on the walls, throw bricks through windows. I figured it was cheaper to let them have the food then to pay a glazier and scrape off paint." Charlie rubbed his chin. He leaned in a little and lowered his voice. "I wouldn't be a bit surprised if they were involved in that theft in the Crouse's house back in November."

Minnie leaned toward the man and knitted her brows. "The Crouse's? Oh," she widened her eyes. "Isn't that the couple who was killed recently?"

Charlie nodded.

Minnie should have taken up acting. "So, you're saying," Ida added, "you might know who broke into the Crouse's home in November?"

He moved in even closer and whispered. "Off the record?"

"Yes, of course," Minnie crossed her heart and raised her hand as if swearing on the Bible.

"They're brothers, last name Miller." He glanced around the entire diner again before meeting Minnie's gaze. "And they're sitting in the booth catty-corner across from us on the other side of the room."

Ida gasped and they both turned in that direction, bringing the men's attention to them. The sisters went back to their desserts. The bell over the door jangled once again and Charlie looked around. "Hey, Jerry. Where ya been? Excuse me ladies. I'll be back in a few minutes."

"Oh, that's okay," Minnie said. "I'm planning a trip to the library and interviewing a few others. Thank you, you've been most helpful." He saluted and went to talk to the new arrival.

"Minnie, I'm scared. They looked right at us, like they knew we were talking about them. Do you think we could be in danger?"

"How Ida? I've never seen them before in my life."

"They might know me from the hospital. "They could have come in to visit someone and I just don't remember."

"Well, there's only one way to find out."

"How's that?"

"Go over and ask them."

"What? No." Ida shrunk back in her seat. "I expect Jane to get me into these things but not you, Minnie."

"It's simple really, you're a nurse. You see a lot of people at the hospital. Just tell them they look awfully familiar and ask them if they've been to the Russellville hospital lately to visit a patient."

"Minnie, I don't want them to know I work at the hospital. They'll come looking for me."

"Then just say you work for a doctor. They'll never figure it out that way.

"I-I can't. I'll stumble all over myself. They'll know something's going on."

"Come on then." Minnie rose and grasped Ida's hand.

"What are you doing?"

"Hush, they'll hear you. I'll do all the talking. You just stand there. Smile, maybe wave."

"Okay, but then we leave. I don't want my roast to burn." Minnie led Ida over to the table where the two men sat in overalls and white T-shirts. One had a pack of Marlboros rolled into his sleeve. A blue fog of cigarette smoke hung over the table.

"Hello, my sister here thinks she recognizes you two from somewhere, could you have possibly met before?"

The men looked them up and down. "No ma'am," one said, "I don't think so."

"Where do you work?" demanded Minnie.

"We're farmers," said the other one. "Unless you've come to the farm, I don't think we know you. What's your names?"

Minnie pushed Ida in front of her. "She works for a doctor. Have you visited one any time lately? She's sure she knows you from somewhere."

"Look, ladies. I think you've mistaken us for someone else. We were just leaving." The men pushed their way out of the booth and stood. One grabbed a straw hat off the table and plopped it on his head. "Ladies." He tipped the hat and they headed for the door.

"Minnie," Ida exclaimed. "They left the check again."

Minnie picked up the check and waved it. "Yoo-hoo, fellas."

"What are you doing?" Ida hissed.

"They don't know us," Minnie said. "We can help out Charlie a bit." The men turned toward them. "I think you forgot this."

The biggest Miller brother glared at them. The diner grew quiet. He blew out his breath and smiled, showing cigarette stained teeth. "Yes, I did. It was my turn to pay. Thank you." He took the check to the cash register as Minnie and Ida returned to their seats.

"Was that really necessary?" Ida asked. "The more attention we draw to us the more danger we put ourselves in."

"We'll be fine. We didn't give them any clues and they'll forget us soon enough."

The waitress placed their check on the table. "You certainly put those guys in their place," she said. "Don't see many willing to challenge them."

"It was nothing," Minnie said. "Sometimes people don't get enough discipline as kids and just need a push in the right direction."

"Minnie," Ida shrieked near hysteria.

"Shh," Minnie calmed. "People are staring. What?"

"They're staring at our car, at our license plate." The men looked at them through the glass and the one with the hat touched it again with a slight nod of the head before they got into a truck that was more rust than metal and roared away.

"Don't worry about them," said the waitress. "They won't do anything to make the police notice them. Next time they get in trouble, they could be looking at some serious jail time. Need anything else?"

"No," they said in unison.

"Let's get out of here, Minnie, while it's still light and we can make sure they don't follow us home."

"Don't be in such a rush. Let me ask a few more questions and then we'll go." Minnie made her way to a few tables as Ida sat and picked at her bread pudding. Finally, Minnie returned. "Alright, let's go."

Ida picked up her purse and rushed for the diner entrance. She quickly got in the driver's side and slammed the door, locking it. She reached across and locked the other door, then watched Minnie waving and talking as she slowly came to the passenger side door.

Ida rolled down the window a crack. "Are you sure you're ready now, Queen Minnie?"

"Yes, I guess," Minnie laughed. "Unlock the door."

They settled in for the drive home. "My roast is going to be ruined, just ruined. Wouldn't be surprised if all the water's gone and it started a fire. I'm sure the house is filled with smoke." Ida glanced over at Minnie. "Why are you sitting there smiling like that? Our house could be burning down."

"I was just thinking how wonderful it is to find something new you want to do at my age. I'm so excited about this writing thing."

"You've had a column for three years now. This isn't anything new."

"Yes, but history and research excite me more than I thought they would. I can't wait to get started. How does this sound for the beginning of the next article?

> 'Murder, a familiar, but unwelcome, guest visits Logan County, Kentucky.
>
> The police are confused by the murders of banker Edgar Harper and his daughter Ella Harper Givens. While these murders have garnered national attention because of the mystery surrounding the crime and so many unanswered questions, the murders of a husband and wife in a nearby county has awakened new interest in the case. Could they be connected?
>
> The city of Lewisburg, Kentucky, population 600 or thereabouts is no different than most rural towns. But in this close-knit community of unlocked doors and people who know everything about everyone, no one saw what really happened on that dark, rainy night of December 11, 1965.'

'What do you think, Ida?"

"Sounds good. Don't get too caught up in this story. Once it's solved, your special column may be over." Ida pulled the Buick into their one car garage.

"It's okay if it's just one time, as long as we find out what happened. I welcome the new experience. What do you think? Did we find out anything new that might lead us to who killed the Harpers?"

"No, we only managed to stir up something we shouldn't have put our noses in."

"Stop worrying. This isn't a TV show. We're not going to be chased by the one-armed man. What's this?" Minnie pulled an envelope stuck into the screen door. "It has your name on it."

Ida took the envelope and tore it open. Her pearl pin glittered from inside. She reached for the spot on her jacket where it usually sat. "I didn't know I lost that."

"What does the note say?"

"I found this while you were sneaking around with secrets to hide, but I know what you're doing. Be careful not to lose anything else. I'll be watching."

"Oh," Ida shouted. "I knew we shouldn't do this. Someone is after me. Someone is after me."

Chapter 12

June 12, 1966

"Francis Beauregard Carter!" Jane exclaimed. "I can't believe you said that. What do you mean I can't keep a secret? The only people I've ever told anything to are my sisters and you know they won't say a word."

"Jane, people are looking at us. Lower your voice."

The waitress waited until Jane quieted before she slowly walked to the table and poured their coffee.

"I'll have my usual drink please, Dinah."

"Sure, I'll bring a cup of cocoa and an extra cup. Be right back to get your order."

"Do you have to do that?" Frank questioned.

"Do what?"

"Order coffee and hot cocoa then pour them together into a cup."

"Why Frank. I've been drinking my coffee like that since I read the article about different types of European coffees a year ago."

"Yes, I know."

"What's that supposed to mean?"

"Nothing."

The coldness of Jane's voice banged off the window. "It's not nothing if you have to mention you've noticed it for a year. What are you saying?"

"Fine, you want to know? You read all these things and..."

"So, I shouldn't read?"

"That's not what I'm saying. You read all of this and try to copy it then start to put on airs like you're the Queen of England or something."

Jane stomped her foot on the gray tile floor and grabbed her purse. She made for the exit. "Stay and have your breakfast. I'll walk back home." She marched through the door.

By the time Frank paid their bill and followed, she was down the road a half-mile. He pulled up beside her and rolled down the window. "Aw, come on, Baby."

"No, Frank."

"You know I didn't mean anything by it."

"I thought you liked me the way I am. Isn't that what couples are supposed to do? Overlook the little things and only argue about the big ones?"

"Well sometimes, it's just..."

"There's no 'sometimes' about it. You either accept me the way I am, or you don't."

"I do, I do."

"Then why would you say such hurtful things?"

"I'm sorry."

"It's about time you said that. How about we take a drive and talk."

"I'm truly sorry," he said taking her hand once she slid into the seat beside him. "Work has been so crazy, and it's put me in such a foul mood. I shouldn't have taken it out on you. Two double murders in the area. Neither one of them is close to being solved yet. I'm so sorry. Can you forgive me?"

"I'm sorry, too. I've been so worried about Ida. She's buried herself in that house for almost a month now. Rennie couldn't even lure her out last night."

"We'll figure it out, Honey. We'll figure out something to get her out of the house."

They rode in silence for a while before Jane spoke again. "Frank, do you think the cases are connected?"

"What? You mean the Harper's case and the Crouse's? No. I don't think so."

Jane glanced at the countryside. Maybe if she encouraged him to talk about the case, he would feel better. "You know the body of Mr. Crouse was found the day Minnie and Ida went to that restaurant in Morgantown. That's when Ida got that stupid note from those two guys.

"Yeah, so?"

"I'm just thinking out loud. May 20th, exactly one month after his wife was found shot and killed. They thought he had done it, you know, until they found his body and realized he'd been killed about the same time."

"What are you getting at?"

I don't know. I read in the paper Crouse was an ex-convict and died of a gunshot wound to the back of the head, similar to Mr. Harper."

"Not exactly similar. He was shot in the neck. Jane, we've decided the cases are unrelated."

Jane's heart accelerated. Frank was so by the book. What if she could give him another perspective? "And didn't Mrs. Crouse die like Ella? Two gunshots, one to the heart and the other to the head."

"Yep, but they weren't found together. He was hidden in a sinkhole in Warren County covered with rocks and they found her near Richelieu in a ditch."

"The cases have to be connected, Frank. I mean, what are the odds both women would be shot in the heart. Maybe it's a scorned lover or something. Why else would they shoot them in the heart? I wish we knew if the Crouse's were beaten. The coroner's report said Edgar and Ella were severely hit many times, especially on the head."

Frank stared at her. "They weren't beaten. We're pretty sure the Crouse's case dealt with drugs. They also found Polaroids of the woman half naked in hotel rooms with men who weren't her husband. They were into some shady stuff."

"Exactly."

"Exactly what?"

"If you get into trouble with drug people and such, what do you need to get out of trouble? Money!"

Frank laughed. "Jane Clack, you're going to be a detective yet."

Jane beamed under the compliment and then brought up Ida once again.

"That day at the restaurant Ida said those guys headed toward Richelieu. McGill said he thought they robbed the Crouses. Do you think they live there? Could they be the ones who killed them? Because if that's what happened, Ida could really be in trouble."

"I don't know. We'll have to keep an eye on her." Frank stated. "I have an idea. The drive-in opened up last month and we haven't been yet. Do you think your sisters would want to go? Surely Ida would go with all of us. I mean, I am a cop."

"That's true." Jane gave Frank a quick hug. "It might just work."

Frank pulled over on the side of the road. His eyes darkened as he moved in for a deep kiss. "Not that I wouldn't rather spend the night alone with you, but it might help relieve some of your worry."

Jane giggled. "Let's get going."

Frank took the quickest route back, pulled into the drive and parked. Jane ran ahead, excited to ask Ida about the drive-in. If this didn't work, she didn't know what would. Once up the steps. She turned the knob and ran smack dab into the door.

Frank roared with laughter.

Jane rattled the doorknob and banged on the window. "Ida! Grrr. Ida, unlock this door! Geez, it's me, Jane."

The curtain moved a couple of inches and Ida's eyes appeared through the crack.

"Oh, for goodness sake, Ida. It's me. You're being ridiculous."

The lock clicked, and the door opened. "I have to be careful, Jane. The Miller brothers are stalking me."

"Oh, poo. You don't know that." Jane threw her purse on the table. "And even if they are, you can't quit living. Burying yourself in this house isn't healthy. Minnie and I can't drive you back and forth to work forever, that is, when you don't call in. You need to get back to your normal routine. You've got to quit taking time off or you're going to lose your job."

Ida lowered her gaze. "I know."

Jane grabbed Ida's hand and pulled her into the living room. "Where's Minnie?"

"I'm right here." Minnie entered from the kitchen. "What's going on?"

"They opened the Russellville drive-in last month. Frank wants us all to go tonight."

"What's playing?" Minnie asked. "I'm not going to see some old western."

"I don't think I can make it," announced Ida. "I have so much to do to get the lesson ready for Sunday school tomorrow." She turned to go up the stairs.

"You'll be safer there than here alone. I'll be with you." Frank prompted. "I'll protect you."

"No, I'm fine. I'll just lock everything, and if I hear something, I'll call the police."

"It'll take them at least fifteen minutes to get here. Come on, Ida? You haven't been out since you received that second note last month" Jane turned to Frank, her eyes pleaded for a solution.

"They're showing Gone with the Wind." Frank added.

Ida stilled.

"On the biggest screen for fifty miles around."

Ida swallowed hard and turned around. "Well, I guess I know the lesson well enough. We will lock all the car doors, won't we?"

"Yes, if we have to," Jane sighed. She would do anything to get Ida out of the house.

***

Excitement mounted in Ida's chest. She couldn't believe she'd agreed to go to see the movie with the others. Being out of the house felt good. Maybe her sisters were right. She was being childish hiding from the world.

When they arrived, previews showed on the screen. Maybe she had time to run to the restroom. She'd forgotten to go before they left the house. Ida looked around. The facilities weren't that far away. She hated to bother Frank to escort her. Maybe she was being a big baby about this. She'd just run over there and come right back.

"Get the speaker, Ida." Frank pointed toward the pole next to the car.

"I will. I need to go to the restroom first." Ida climbed out of the car but hesitated. Taking a deep breath, she made herself put one leg in front of the other until she reached the small building. After relieving herself, she started back.

Someone grabbed her arm from behind. "I thought I saw you."

Ida screamed. The gripped tightened. "Frank! Help!" She yelled as she swung at her predator. "Let me go, you no good..."

The man let her arm drop. "Ida, it's me, Bruce."

Frank grabbed the man firmly by the arm. "What's going on here?"

Ida looked from Frank to Bruce. How would she explain she'd overreacted?

"Uhm, can you give us a moment, Frank? I'm sorry I screamed. I'm okay. Bruce just scared me."

Frank stepped over to the concession stand, but the taut muscles in his shoulders showed he would be ready to pounce if Bruce tried anything. Ida smiled. Frank said he'd protect her.

"Bruce, what were you thinking giving me such a fright?"

"I'm sorry, Ida. I didn't mean to startle you. Haven't seen you at the store for a while and was just happy to see you again. Are you busy next Saturday? The VFW is having a dance."

"I'm sorry. I don't want to be mean but I met another man a few months back."

Bruce turned to stare at Frank. "Is that him?

When she didn't answer Bruce turned and walked away.

Jane gawked at her when she returned to the car. "Who in the world is that? I know everybody you know, but I don't know him."

Ida lowered her head. "Oh, just someone from the hospital."

Jane stared at her. You're lying. Ida...?"

"Shh. The movie's starting." Ida slid into the car. The others followed.

Jane and Frank scooted toward the middle of the back seat so they could see the screen better. Jane laid her head on his shoulder and snuggled closer, still thinking about Ida. She sighed deeply. Did Ida have a boyfriend they didn't know about? How could she?

"Are you okay?" Frank pulled away so he could see her face.

"What? Oh, yeah, I'm fine. Just thinking."

"About what?"

"Would you two be quiet?" Ida whispered. "I thought we came to see the movie."

Frank looked at Jane. "I want to know," he mouthed to her.

Jane nodded. "Later," she mouthed back. Settling in his arms, she relaxed and enjoyed the movie.

During intermission, Jane and Frank got out to stretch their legs. Frank jumped at the chance to be able to talk. "Now, what were you thinking about in the car? That was an awful deep sigh."

"I'm really worried about Ida. She lied about that guy being from the hospital."

"How do you know?"

"She's my sister. How could I not know?" Confusion crossed Frank's face.

"She always lowers her head when she's lying or afraid."

"She didn't seem afraid." Frank said.

"Exactly. Why wouldn't she tell the truth?"

"I don't know."

"Why don't you ask her to help get some Cokes. Maybe you can find out what's going on."

"Jane, that's none of my business. I can't ask her about men."

"Please. Ida doesn't tell untruths very often. Something's wrong. I can feel it."

Frank stared at her for a second.

"For me?" She fluttered her eyelashes.

"Okay, I'll do it, but if she gets mad at me, you owe me another trip to the drive-in, alone."

Jane walked around to Ida's window. "Hey, will you go with Frank to the concession stand and help him carry our Cokes back? I'm going to the little girl's room." She walked away without waiting for an answer.

Fear crawled up Ida's spine. "Sure. I guess I'm safe enough with a cop." Ida opened her door.

Minnie put down the flyer she was reading and rubbed her finger down her cheek. "I'm really proud of you for coming out tonight, Ida."

"Thanks, Minnie. We'll be right back. Ida relaxed for the first time in weeks as she walked with Frank to the concession stand. Her sisters were right. She needed to quit hiding and start living. Maybe tomorrow she would call Rennie.

"Honey."

Jane jumped, almost knocking the drink from Frank's hand when he returned. "Oh Frank, I'm sorry. I didn't hear you coming. Minnie and I were deep in conversation."

"Evidently." Frank waited until Ida slid into the car before he spoke. "I think she's going to be just fine, ladies."

***

Frank pulled the Buick into the drive as Jane woke her sisters. "Come on sleepy heads. We're home. Get on up to bed. I'll be there in a minute."

Minnie and Ida pulled themselves out of the car and trudged toward the house.

"Don't lock the door." Jane yelled after them. "I don't have my key."

Frank put his arm around her once Ida and Minnie disappeared inside. I thought I'd never get you alone. Come on." They walked to his truck hidden in the darkness. "Next time we go alone."

Bending down he nibbled at her lips. Jane's spine tingled as her arms encircled his waist and let him deepen the kiss. Man, she loved this guy.

His moist lips moved down to her neck, and Jane let her head fall back. She groaned as he spread sweet kisses there. Her insides melted from the heat he aroused in her.

"You know that groan drives me crazy." He whispered pulling her closer and capturing her lips again.

Jane pulled away and took a deep breath. We need to cool it. My sisters might come looking for me if I stay out too long."

Frank moaned but let her go. "Your sisters are killing me. Can't even have ten minutes alone with the woman I love. This is ridiculous."

The woman he loves. She hugged her torso. He loved her.

Frank gave her a final kiss and waited until she was inside the house before starting his truck and backing down the drive.

The door clicked with a twist of her wrist. She headed up the stairs, hoping she could stay awake until Frank called to let her know he got home okay.

"Did you lock the door?" Ida called out as she passed.

"Yes, Ida. I locked it. Good night."

"Night, Jane."

The phone rang shortly after she reached her room and closed the door. She grabbed the receiver, thankful she had paid to put an extra line in her room. "Hello."

"I'm home. I sure hated leaving you."

Franks voice soothed her. She crawled under the blankets and closed her eyes as she lowered her head to the pillow. "I miss you."

"I miss you, too. It's late. I better let you get some sleep. We've got church in the morning."

"We're not going to get much sleep. Are we?"

"Nope. But I love you."

"I love you, too."

"Good night, Doll face."

Jane smiled. “Sleep tight, Honey. Oh, wait. You didn’t tell me what Ida said during intermission.”

“Oh, yeah.” Frank cleared his throat. “She ran into Bruce again.”

“Bruce?”

“Yes, that’s the guy’s name. She talked to him while I stood in line. He said he’d missed her the last few Wednesdays.”

“Wednesdays? Maybe he does work with her. But she’s never mentioned him.”

“No, I didn’t get the idea that they worked together. He talked about produce. Said he had some great produce for her.”

Jane bolted up in bed. “Produce? What the hay? Wait a minute. She goes to the grocery on Wednesdays. I know he doesn’t work at the one here in town. Why would she go to another store when ours is so convenient?”

“Hmm, I don’t know, but I did ask her about him after he left. She held to her story. Said she worked with him.”

“What is she up to?”

“Oh yeah, he said something about fixing the parking lot.”

“Fixing the parking lot?”

“‘I got the lot repaved.’ Those were his exact words, I swear.”

“I believe you. I just can’t figure it out. I haven’t seen any newly paved lots here in town. Maybe it’s by the hospital somewhere. Want to do some investigating tomorrow?” Jane asked.

“Sure, we can go after church. But now we need to get some sleep. I’ll see you in the morning, okay?”

“Perfect. I hope we can at least figure out this mystery. By the way, thanks for the information.”

“Anything for you,” Frank said.

After they’d hung up, Jane lay awake going over and over what Frank had told her. I don’t know what you’ve been up to, Ida, but I’m going to find out tomorrow.

Chapter 13

Jane's gaze never left the window. She would figure out Ida's secret if it took her all day. Why in the world would she lie anyway? That was not Ida's style.

Frank drove slowly past the hospital once more. "Jane, there aren't any newly paved lots in Russellville. We need to go farther out."

"Okay, I just wanted to make sure. I can't see Ida going beyond the hospital when she leaves. It doesn't make sense. I'd be tired and want to get home after a long day. Wouldn't you?"

"Yeah, I guess so." Frank rubbed his stomach. "How about we get something to eat? I'm starved. There's a little eatery about twenty minutes away that my parents really like. Want to try it?"

"Sure." Jane pulled her eyes from the scenery they passed and looked at Frank. "What kind of food do they serve?"

"Good home cookin'." Frank threw her a big smile. "The best you've ever had, according to Mom." He straightened in his seat and whipped the truck into the turning lane.

Jane's tummy rumbled. She hadn't even known she was hungry until Frank mentioned food. A home cooked meal sounded good, but she'd already gained a couple pounds. Frank sure did love to eat.

The truck rattled along while they talked. When there was a lull in the conversation, Jane glanced out the window. Her eyes grew big.

"Stop!" Jane's scream filled the truck as the brakes squealed, and the vehicle slid sideways.

"What's wrong? Are you alright?"

"Back there." Jane pointed the way they came. "Look back there."

Frank turned and looked out the window, expecting to find a dead body in the ditch. He saw nothing.

"What is it? I don't see anything."

"New pavement, at that grocery store back there. I think we found Ida's secret."

Frank groaned. "Don't ever do that to me again. I thought you were hurt."

Jane looked at Frank's stricken face and started to giggle. "I'm so sorry. I didn't mean to scare you."

He sat up and put the truck back in gear. "Well, you did." He made a u-turn and headed back to the store.

Jane climbed out of the truck before Frank turned off the key.

"I'm so excited." Jane squealed. "I can't believe we found it. This must be what it feels like to be undercover."

Frank rolled his eyes and shook his head. "This is nothing like going undercover. We are just checking out a lead. There's no danger. It doesn't matter if someone comes along and knows who we are. We're definitely not undercover."

"Oh, poo." Jane's gaze traveled the length of the parking lot. Heat rippled, making it shimmer. "This has to be it."

"We'll see. Now take my hand. Remember, we're just a happy couple who need a few things at the grocery. Got it?"

"Of course, I got it. I'm good at this stuff."

They walked in when the door slid open. Jane turned to the left and gasped. "Look. It's produce. Lots of wonderful produce." Jane danced in a circle. "This has to be it."

Frank snickered. ""Yeah, I can tell you're really good at this."

Jane turned toward Frank, her cheeks hot. All the cashiers were looking at her. She returned to Frank's side." Sorry, guess that wasn't very subtle."

"Nope. Don't guess it was. And you wonder why I don't let you help me with police work."

Jane punched him on the arm. "Don't be mean. You have to admit we're two for two. The lot's been repaved, and they have a lot of fresh fruits and vegetables."

Frank nodded. "Let's walk around. Maybe we'll see Bruce."

"I can guarantee it." Bruce rose from behind a display, tomatoes in each hand. He placed the tomatoes in a box in the cart beside him, wiped his hands on his apron, and came around to face them.

Frank accepted the hand he extended.

"What can I do for you?" Bruce asked.

"I—uh—"Jane stuttered. How had they not seen him standing there? Now they were busted.

Frank cut in smoothly. "I'm Ida's friend. We met at the drive-in."

"Oh, yes, Ida." Bruce's eyes brightened. "Is she with you?" He looked around them as if expecting her to walk through the door.

"No, she said be sure to check out your store if we got out this way. It's really nice" He looked around and nodded as if to emphasize the point. "And you've done a great job with the parking lot."

"Thanks." Bruce's voice cracked as if his comment meant a lot. "You guys have a look around. Let me know if you need anything."

They wandered through the little grocery hand in hand. Frank sure was good at his job. While she stuttered, Frank had talked smoothly, making his lie seem like the truth. How many times had he lied to her in the same way?

"You lie very well." Jane turned her head to look at him.

"Thank you, I think…" Frank squeezed her hand and kept walking.

"How many times have you lied to me?"

He let his head fall back as he released a sigh. "Now Jane, let's not do this here."

"How many?"

Frank fidgeted beneath her stare. "It's just that you get so inquisitive when you're interested in a case. You know I'm not supposed to tell you things, but you keep asking. You have to admit the few times I did tell you, things didn't go well."

"What didn't go well?" Jane huffed.

"The bus station, for one." He eyed her wearily. "Jane, you know I love you. And I love your excitement, but I could have lost my job over that. I'm just glad your sisters didn't show up, too."

Jane walked along in silence. He spoke the truth, but she didn't want to admit it out loud. She did get overly excited when it came to detective work, one of the reasons she'd failed the officer's exam when she applied years ago. What had they said? She had a great eye for detail but she'd jumped the gun with every scenario she wrote for the pretend assignments they had to assess.

"Are you mad at me?" Frank shook her hand, his brown eyes probing hers.

"No. What you said was true. Maybe you can help me do better." Jane squealed as they rounded the corner. "Books! This has to be the reason Ida comes here. She loves books. What a great selection. Jane noticed a naughty book and pointed. "Look, they even sell books that are a little risqué."

Bruce walked toward them and handed Jane a small package. A card with Ida's name rested on top. "Can you give this to Ida for me?"

"Aaaaa." Jane looked at Frank. There was no way she could give the gift to Ida. She wasn't supposed to know about Bruce.

"We'd be glad to." Frank smiled. "I'm sure she'll love it."

Frank complimented Bruce on his store and quickly excused himself, saying they were meeting someone for lunch.

Once in the truck, Jane fell silent. Her gaze traveled over the package. She flipped it over and then back.

Frank started the vehicle and headed for the café, his stomach rumbling loudly. He looked toward Jane. "What's wrong? You haven't said a word since we left."

"It's the package." She turned it so he could see it.

"What's wrong with it? It's just a gift from Bruce. I think he's sweet on her. A lot of guys send gifts to their girl. She hasn't been out of the house since she got that first note and he's probably missing her."

"That's it! The first note." She'd known something was strangely familiar about the package. "Look at the handwriting. It's the same. I'm sure of it. Look at the way he made the "I". It's the exact same as the notes she received at the house. I know, because I studied them. What should we do?"

Frank rubbed the whiskers on his chin. "What exactly did the notes say? Could we have misinterpreted them?"

Jane thought for a second. "Well, the last one said something like, 'I'm waiting, and watching.'"

"Now that we know Bruce is interested, it makes perfect sense. I mean, she hasn't been out of the house except for the drive-in. He's probably waiting and watching for her."

"I guess so. And that first one, well, he was just returning the pin he found. I wonder where he found it." Jane giggled. "In the back room?"

Frank shook his head. "Jane, you're terrible."

"I'm just teasing. Do you mind if we go back? I want to explain what happened. You know, tell him why Ida hasn't been to see him. I believe he's really worried about her."

Frank rubbed his stomach and sighed. "The things I do for you." He turned and headed back the way he came.

They both grinned as they climbed out of the truck. "I'm sure Bruce will get a good laugh at our mistake. Don't you think?"

"Yeah, it is kind of funny. Frank grabbed her hand and they headed for the door.

When they entered the cashier looked up and grinned at Frank. "Can I help you?"

"We're looking for Bruce." Jane said.

"He's not here. Is there something I can do for you?" Again, the cashier looked to Frank for an answer.

"We were just here." Jane snapped. "And he was here."

Frank winked and stepped in front of Jane. "Do you happen to know where he went? I really need to talk to him." He gave her a big smile.

A second later he groaned as Jane's elbow entered his side. How dare he push her out of the way? And to flirt with that imbecile to boot.

"Sorry." Her voice thick with sweetness grated on Jane's nerves. "All he said was he'd be back later, he was tired of waiting." The girl gave a little laugh and flipped her hair. "I have no idea what he's been waiting for."

"Okay, thanks for the info. Have a good afternoon."

Jane half-pulled Frank out the front door. "What in the heck was that all about?"

"Have to keep my options open. Never know when you might decide to dump me." Frank's tummy shook with laughter.

"You're so funny. Don't talk to me." Jane climbed into the truck. How dare he embarrass her like that? Was he punishing her for making him miss his lunch? Well, he would miss it now for sure."

Jane folded her arms across her chest and stared out the window.

"Oh come on, Jane. I was kidding. I only flirted to get the information we needed. We sure weren't going to get it with you snapping at her."

"Where do you think he's going?" Jane asked.

"Well, detective, let's put some clues together. We have a note that said, 'I'm waiting and watching,' and now the man who wrote that said he's tired of waiting."

Jane's eyes grew wide. "We need to go to the house. Ida will be scared to death. When Bruce shows up, she'll think he is the guy that's after her."

"Surely she'll look out and see that's its Bruce. She'll be fine. I thought we were going to get something to eat."

"That was before you pushed me aside to flirt with another woman."

Frank huffed and the truck roared to life. "This is ridiculous. The last thing Ida or Bruce want is us barging in on them. They're sweet on each other."

"I thought she liked Rennie. Either way, she'll just hide and won't even look out to see who's knocking."

Frank slammed the truck into gear and headed out of the parking lot way too fast, but Jane didn't say a word. He was right. If Ida and Bruce were interested in each other, the lovebirds wouldn't want them there, but she was still stinging from being pushed aside while Frank flirted. He'd pay for that.

***

Ida knew her sisters were right, but making herself leave the house took all the strength she could muster. She strolled down the street, relieved to be out in the sunshine and fresh air. Going to the drive-in helped, but still her stomach twisted with anxiety. She straightened her shoulders and took a deep breath. She'd hidden out long enough.

Working in the garden earlier, she'd enjoyed the hot sun on her back and then sipped tea on the patio. Her sisters would be proud watching her stroll down the sidewalk all alone.

The first terrifying note filled her with fear while the second unsettled her more. The man actually admitted he watched her, even though she saw no one watching the house. She peeked out the windows enough to know if someone was there.

It was time to toughen up. Ida looked up at the fluffy clouds floating in the sky above. "Lord, will you help me be brave? I'm tired of hiding."

Their neighbor, Goldie Watson, wearing her nurse's uniform, carried a basket to the clothesline. She hung a pair of curtains to dry in the warm sunshine before heading to her car and starting it up. Ida waved as Goldie passed by on her way to work.

Nearing their neat rust-colored house, new buds on the trees waved at her and she smiled. A few birds flitted between the branches and took off again.

Another movement caught her attention. She froze in place. The figure of a person disappeared behind the back of the house. Her house.

Ida struggled to hang onto her dwindling courage. She hid behind a tree and strained to make out the intruder, but couldn't see him. What should she do? Goldie Watson had left and no other neighbors appeared to be home.

She edged closer, slipping from one tree to the next. Well, Lord, I did say I needed to be braver, but I didn't know you would test me so soon. Of all afternoons for me to take a walk! Ida's hands shook. Where was Minnie when she needed her? Everything in her wanted to run, but she stood her ground. This was her chance to see who'd been leaving the notes. To find out who was after her.

They wouldn't see her if she stayed hidden, but she could see them when they left.

"Oh, this is ridiculous." Her gaze traveled to a somewhat familiar blue car parked on the street. Where had she seen it before? She took a deep breath and started for the back of the house, refusing to live in fear anymore. She quickened her step and rounded the house. Hands came out to grab her as she slammed into the body coming her way.

"Oomph!" The hood fell from his face.

Ida gasped. "You? You're the one who's been leaving me threatening notes?"

"Threatening notes? I'm not leaving threatening notes." Bruce turned different shades of red. "I left you mysterious and seductive notes." He ran his fingers across his eyes and pinched the bridge of his nose. "When I saw you steal those naughty books…."

"I did not steal anything."

"Okay, when you took the books and secretly left the money," Bruce grinned. "I knew you were my kind of woman. I like 'em naughty."

"Naughty?" Humiliation washed over her. "I have never been called naughty in my life."

"That's because no one knows," Bruce winked and chuckled. "Do they?"

Ida straightened her shoulders and swallowed hard. "If you saw me take the book, why didn't you stop me?" Ida slid her hands in her pockets, thankful he hadn't called her out in public.

"You paid for the book. I didn't need to." Bruce ran his finger down her arm. "Don't worry. I like those books, too. Your secret is safe with me."

Ida stepped backwards as a chill traveled up her spine. "Look, Bruce, I'm sorry, but ...I'm not like that. You got the wrong idea about me."

"Oh, come on. You travel all the way to my store to get 'produce' and you always have the girls call me to help you out. Admit it. You wanted me to catch you stealing. You probably wanted me to frisk you."

Bruce backed her up against the wall, blocking her in. "Didn't you?"

The remains of her breakfast roiled. "No, I didn't. I'm sorry if I gave you that impression. Now let me go."

"I don't think so. I've invested a lot of time into wooing you." He tangled his fingers in her hair and pulled her closer. She heaved at the stench of his bourbon breath. She pushed against him and tried to get away, but he tightened his grip on her hair and held her in place. She screamed.

He pulled her into the shadow of the ivy-covered trellis. "How about we try some of those scenes from the last book you bought?"

Ida shut her eyes and screamed again.

"Let her go." A man's voice came from behind Bruce. Had someone come to save her? Or were the Miller brothers here to kill her? Either would be better than what was about to happen. Bruce looked toward the voice. Ida didn't hesitate. She took aim and kneed him in the groin. Bruce went down.

Footsteps pounded toward her. Ida collapsed into a man's strong arms. "Ida. Ida, honey." Rennie helped her on the stoop and chased after the man scurrying hunched over, hands covering where Ida kicked him.

Bruce disappeared around the house.

"Help, somebody help!" Ida screamed

"Halt! Police!" Frank yelled as he chased the man running away from Ida. "Halt, I say!" Frank pulled his gun and pointed it in the air.

A gunshot resonated from the corner of the house, enveloping Ida in fear. Panic greater than Bruce's assault gripped her. "No! No!" she screamed. "Don't shoot! That's not him. Please, Frank, don't shoot Rennie."

Jane dropped to the stoop beside Ida, and put her arms around her," It's alright. Frank knows what he's doing.

"Don't let him shoot Rennie. He saved me from Bruce."

"What are you talking about?" Who was that? Bruce? Rennie? Who?" Jane asked.

"Rennie's chasing Bruce. Bruce attacked me."

"Attacked you? I thought he loved you. Are you hurt?" She searched Ida for bruises. "My goodness, Ida, your love life is more complicated than mine."

"I don't have a love life, and I never will if that boyfriend of yours kills him. Now go stop him. Don't let him shoot." She waved both arms frantically, shooing Jane after Frank.

Frank marched back around the house, one hand locked onto Rennie's shirt collar and the other digging into his back with a Smith and Wesson. "What's going on?" Frank yanked Rennie around to face Ida.

Rennie glowered. "Let me go! He's gettin' away. Come on. Let's catch 'em!" He tried to run, but Frank tightened his grip.

Ida ran toward them, shouting for Frank to take his hands and gun off her boyfriend.

"Will someone let me in on what's going on here? Who's getting away?" Frank lowered the revolver.

"Bruce!" Jane yelled. "He attacked Ida. Go after him, hurry!" She stomped her foot.

The two men took off in a run, but it was too late. Bruce was nowhere in sight.

Ida, Rennie, Frank, and Jane stood in a huddle, each repeating his or her version of what had just happened when Minnie and Tom entered the back driveway. Minnie hopped out of the car, demanding to know what was going on and why were the neighbors standing on their front lawns peering in all directions. Jane and Ida explained simultaneously until Minnie, gathering the gist of the situation, examined Ida.

Ida turned her eyes to Tom, and Jane followed suit. Minnie blushed and gave an explanation that her car failed to start, and Tom drove her home from choir practice.

Frank turned a piece of gravel over with his toe. "I, for one am hungry. How about we all go inside and order pizza? I'll file the report when we're through. We know where he works. He isn't going anywhere. I'll call the station and have a couple of deputies case the store and bring him in."

What would happen when they all began asking her questions? Ida wondered. "Wait, Frank. Before you make that call, I need to tell Rennie something. I'll explain to you guys later."

"You two take your time. We'll be inside." He gave her shoulders a gentle squeeze.

"I have a pot roast cooking as we speak," Minnie interjected. "Come on in everyone. I'll fix a skillet of cornbread."

Frank bounded toward the back door rubbing his belly. "Come on ya'll, Minnie's pot roast is better than pizza any day."

"Yes," Jane agreed, "it will be ready by the time Frank gets through apologizing to Rennie, and Ida tells us exactly what happened. And did I hear something about a boyfriend?"

Five pairs of eyes stared at Ida, and heat crept up her cheeks. Rennie saved her again. "I'm hoping she was referring to me. I care a lot for your sister. And Frank owes me no apologies. He was merely doing his job. And doing it well." He rubbed his neck where Frank had held him by the collar.

Everyone laughed and followed Frank inside.

Taking Ida's arm, Rennie escorted her to the swing in the backyard. "Tell me if you want to. Or don't if you're uncomfortable. I know you, Ida, I love you."

"I-I want you to know." She told him everything, the erotic novels and how Bruce caught her. Him asking her out and she never said no. Bruce's assumption that she was naughty. Everything. Then she covered her face with her palms. "I guess you hate me now."

"Ida, honey, you've done nothing wrong." He closed his arms around her. "Did I hear you say something about a boyfriend?" He kissed her right there in the yard in front of all the eyes peering from the kitchen window.

Hand in hand, they joined the others for dinner.

Ida turned to Frank. "I did something which led Bruce to think I was someone I'm not. He could and would exaggerate my misconduct to all of Lewisburg. I'm not sure if I could cope with the embarrassment. So, unless he continues with the notes and the assaults, I won't press charges."

"Of course, Ida. I'll leave it up to you. Let me know if anything changes."

The conversation lulled and Jane felt the need to fill the silence. "Frank said the Harper murders may have hit a wall. There's no new information coming in and until something happens, they don't know where to go next."

"Oh that's terrible," Minnie said. "Those poor families."

Rennie mentioned hearing a couple of hospital orderlies say the Martin Cemetery, where the Harpers were found, was haunted by a mysterious lady. Tidbits of conversation about Tom's hobby of being an amateur ghost hunter floated around the kitchen.

Ida sat and held Rennie's hand. She wasn't interested in ghosts. Rennie understood about the books, and he still loved her.

***

July 1967

Jane jolted as an odd noise stole through the open window. Her eyes not adjusted to the darkness of the moonless night, she crept toward the sound; the light flipped on.

"Ida, turn off that light. There's something going on at the Harper place." Jane squinted to peek at the house across the street. "Somebody's up to something. I thought the new tenants had already settled in."

Ida joined Jane on her bedroom floor as they peered through the thick night.

"I can't see what they're doing, but there's definitely something happening. Looks like someone's carrying a flashlight or candle in the downstairs front room." Ida agreed.

"We should do something, but what? I'd hate to call the State Police this late only to learn the renters were cleaning up and blew a fuse. That would be embarrassing"

Minnie tiptoed up behind them, pushed lightly on the backs of their heads, and laughed as Jane's and Ida's noggins thudded into the window screen. "Is it too hot for you gals to sleep, too?"

"Jane spotted something over at the Harper House. Someone's moving around and we're trying to figure out if it's the renters or not."

"If you must know what's happening across the way, go over and look around like you're searching for a cat. If anyone asks, just say one of Mrs. Schneider's cats has wandered off and you're looking for it. No one would question that. I'd think, by now, you nosey neighbors would've learned how to snoop."

"Good idea, Minnie." Jane stood and grabbed a robe. "I'm not even going to dress; it'll seem more real." Jane paused. "But what if it's not the new neighbors?"

"The cat story will work with anyone and don't think you're going without me." Minnie rushed out and met them by the door with her robe and scarf.

Ida raced down the front steps but skidded to a stop and pointed at the Harpers home. "Right there, evil culprits committed a kidnapping and only the Lord knows what else." She waggled her pointing finger in the air. "Right there. What if they've come back? You know they're still on the loose. Nobody was ever convicted." Ida's head shook back and forth.

Jane perked up. "Oh my, Ida, you could be right. Come on let's go see. Quick, maybe we can catch them." Minnie grabbed the bottom of her robe and Jane slapped at Minnie's hand. "Stop holding me back. Turn my robe loose. Time is of the essence."

Minnie didn't let go. "In the first place," Minnie stated, "I doubt the criminals are back, but if they are, remember they've killed once and probably wouldn't hesitate to kill again."

"Oh..." Ida fidgeted with her handkerchief. "I think I'm going to stay here." She handed Jane the flashlight, and retreated to a dark corner of the porch.

"That's a good idea, Ida," Jane said. "You watch us for a signal. If I blink this light, call the police." Jane commanded Minnie to walk slowly and quietly. The Harper house's porch light was off. She flicked off the flashlight and looked up at the inky, starless sky. Jane didn't believe they would be spotted, but no need announcing their presence to the entire neighborhood.

The two sisters crept across the darkened street and entered the front yard. They hunkered below an open window, staying out of sight. From where they were, they could see nothing but heard furniture scooting across a wooden floor. Jane trembled with excitement. Frank would be so proud of her if she captured a real criminal.

"Jane," Minnie whispered.

"Shhh!" Jane put her finger to her pursed lips.

"Jane," Minnie whispered again. "Listen. Girls. Giggling."

Jane stopped solving crimes in her head long enough to concentrate. Giggles floated from the window above. That would not be kidnappers." Minnie, hunch down and lace your fingers together."

"What? What are you talking about?"

"I want to peek in the window to see what's happening, but I need a boost."

"Alright," Minnie hissed, "but next time, you get to hold me up."

Jane nudged her eyes just above the bottom of the windowsill and gazed silently for a moment before signaling to Minnie to lower her back to the ground. She was glad Frank couldn't see her at that moment, crouched below the window of a bunch of silly teenage girls.

"What's going on?" Minnie asked.

She motioned Minnie away from the screened window so they could talk. "Over here under this tree, where we can discuss the situation."

"Not much to discuss, Jane. The girls are having a pajama party or something."

"Or something, alright. The Forgy girl, the new neighbor kid, McHendricks, I believe, and a bunch of girls are sitting cross-legged in the floor holding hands in a circle around candles. Looks like they're having a séance. Minnie, those kids are out way past their bedtimes, and they're trying to solve our mystery."

"For goodness sake, Jane, it's summer and they're just having fun; an innocent pajama party gone rogue. Besides, the mystery doesn't belong to us. I wish someone would solve it." Minnie pointed toward the side door where a group of boys stood spying on the girls. "Look at that. We should get a good laugh soon. Oh, Jane, I can't believe we're snooping on kids and their games. But I could use a good laugh. What about you?"

"Might as well. Think I'd have time to fetch Ida? She's probably still watching from the front porch."

"Yes, just hurry and stay out of sight."

Jane ran over and pulled Ida toward Minnie. They discovered a lower window and waited. One of the girls around the candle commanded everyone to turn off their flashlights. The Clack sisters took this opportunity to peek in the window. Shadowy forms and flickers of candles shifted around the darkened room. One girl pressed her hand into the girls beside her and whispered, "I'm shaking all over."

"Why?"

"Well, what will we do if the spirits come this time? We've been calling them for days."

"I don't know."

"Should we be scared?" another girl asked.

"Maybe. I have my escape route all planned out. You gonna run if something happens?"

"Yes. Don't want no haint taking over my body. Shh, time to chant now."

The words floated to where the snoopy sisters hid, but they could barely see inside the window standing on their tiptoes. Voices unevenly mingled into a chant. "Spirits of Edgar and Ella, we call you from death unto life. Be guided by the candlelight. Spirits of Edgar and Ella, we call you from death unto life. Be guided by the candlelight."

"As they mouthed the words, from "death unto life" a third time, a flash soared through an open back window toward the circle of candles. Flashes of red, green, and orange lights spewed upward, popped, danced around the candles and popped more, before fizzling out.

Screaming girls tore out the front door, the back door, and jumped through windows, vacating the house. All except one little girl. The window slammed down on a child's rear, capturing the young Forgy girl, with her head sticking through the opening. The Clack women raced to her aid, but someone or some-thing yanked her to freedom, leaving her red cotton shorts hanging on a broken windowpane.

Ida, Jane, and Minnie barely scampered home before the front porch lights snapped on. One after the other, neighborhood moms and dads swarmed Henry Street to investigate the commotion. One mother pulled a boy down the street by his ear. A dad broke a branch from a peach tree and switched another in the opposite direction. A scared-witless mother picked up her daughter and shook her until her curls bounced, then hugged her so tightly she burped. Family by family, the Henry street neighbors absconded. The porch lights went out.

Ida flopped across her chair laughing, and Minnie and Jane did a quick high-five. "Well, sisters, we actually solved a mystery tonight." They shared a big belly laugh. "What caused those weird sparks of fire?" Ida asked. "I nearly swallowed my gum. Thought maybe the spirits really were there."

Jane scratched her head. "Well, it's almost the Fourth of July. I'd say those sparks were fireworks. Jumping Jacks if I'm not mistaken."

"Yes, of course," Ida responded. I should have recognized them from the Thompson boys playing with them in the street every day for a month last July. We might as well go back to bed. We solved one mystery, but no one got any closer to what happened to Ella and Edgar."

"Yes," Minnie said. "Let's hit the hay."

They plodded up the steps to their beds. Even though the night air heaved with the humidity of a Kentucky July, Ida shivered as one of her eerie feelings enveloped her. Maybe Ella and Edgar were there tonight.

Chapter 14

Five Years Later
May 1, 1970

Minnie found a place to park on the street and looked around for Tom. His car needed servicing and the garage couldn't get to it until later in the afternoon, so she'd agreed to pick him up. A Kentucky spring day, not too hot nor too cold, made residents want to skip down the sidewalk to a bluegrass song. Minnie turned her face to the sun as she rounded the corner of the courthouse and almost bumped right into Tom and Sheriff Jim Johnson in serious conversation.

"Hello Tom, Sheriff."

They nodded at her and continued talking. "Arrested them last night. All three. Thought we were going to have trouble with the one big guy, but he calmed down when I put my hand on my gun.

"Oh my," Minnie gasped. "Did some cattle rustlers give you trouble?"

Tom put his arm firmly around Minnie. "No, the sheriff was just telling me they made an arrest in the Harper murders late last night."

Minnie's world seemed to tilt slightly and Tom squeezed even tighter. "Who? Was it someone we know?"

"Sheriff Johnson here said he'd get them if he were elected, and that he did."

"Remember that come next election now, Mrs. Pryor."

"But you didn't tell me who."

"If you'll excuse me, Sheriff, I've promised Miss Minnie some lunch and then an afternoon drive." He then turned and said, "We'll discuss this over lunch." He led her to the car and settled her in the passenger's seat before sliding into the driver's side. They sat silently for a moment as Minnie's world slowly slid back to slightly normal again. She then turned to him with a puzzled look.

"Car keys?" Tom asked, gently.

She opened her purse and rooted around without looking until the cold metal ring slipped over her finger. She lifted them toward Tom.

As they drove, tears finally started to slide down her cheeks.

"Oh honey, why are you crying?"

"I'm not sure. Maybe that it took so long. How could Sheriff Johnson do something so quickly when even the FBI couldn't figure it out?"

"I don't know. Maybe he just got lucky or maybe he's just that good. There's just something about that man. Either way, someone's been arrested."

Minnie wiped tears from her face and looked up at Tom. "I'm so glad you were with me when I found out. I don't think I could have heard it from someone else without fainting. Thank you for being there for me."

"Always. Instead of tears, I thought you'd be happy."

"Oh, I am. It's just...just that...you know, I never thought any one would be arrested. It's been what...almost...five years? With no new leads."

"Well, Jim Johnson must have found something new to solve the case." Tom slowed the car to navigate one of the sharp curves so common to this area of Western Kentucky. "According to Sheriff Johnson, if the Grand Jury decides they're guilty, he'll have them arrested within an hour and will charge them with all kinds of things."

"What other charges would there be except murder?"

"There's that," Tom said as he pulled the car into their favorite diner. "But they could also be charged with intent to rob, kidnapping, and armed assault."

"Oh my. I hope they put them away for a long time. They did awful things to my friends. By the way, do you know their names? Are they from our community?"

Tom took her hand. "Not that I know of. I think they're from Earlington. I wrote their names down." He pulled out a small notebook. "James Lovan, Alfred Harvey, and Kenneth Almon. I heard one's a teacher. I can't believe a teacher would be involved."

Minnie squinted her eyes closed and rubbed her temples. "Nope, none of the names ring a bell. It makes you wonder what they wanted with the Harpers."

"Yes, it does. Let's go have lunch and I'll split a piece of pie with you."

"Okay." Minnie reached for the door handle, but Tom held firm to her hand.

"Before we go in, I need to talk to you about something."

A troubled feeling came over Minnie. Tom had seemed different in the last few weeks, distant. Was he sick? Did he want to move on?

"I've been thinking about this for a while. To me, you and I seem to walk in the same rhythm, but I'm not sure if you feel the same way."

Minnie smiled and nodded.

"I don't have any fancy five-dollar words, so I'll just say it. I...well, I really. Would you be interested in being my wife? I mean, dating is great, but my feelings for you have grown way past that."

Minnie blushed. It was about time he made his move. She was no youngster. "Oh Tom, I'd love to. I feel the same way." Minnie sat smiling as her heart thumped against her chest. She'd thought God would never bring her another man after losing Curtis, but now she had Tom.

Tom squeezed her hand. "Thanks, Minnie. You just made me the happiest man in these parts."

Amiable banter punctuated their lunch with Tom teasing about a big church wedding and Minnie suggesting Jane for a flower girl, just like in her first wedding.

"Finish your coffee and we'll pay a visit to Jane. She'll want to hear all the news that's come about today."

"That's true. She's been so down since Frank passed away. I've tried to get her to move back home, but she won't come. She used to laugh a lot, and I haven't heard that in I don't know how long. She won't even argue with Ida. Once she always had an adventure planned, even got us to go to the Grand Ole Opry, now she rarely leaves her apartment. I don't know what to do to get her out of her funk."

"Let's go see if she wants to go for a drive. It's such a nice day and it'll be good for her to get some fresh air.

As they reached the car, Tom took her in his arms, hugged her, and kissed her on the lips.

"Tom, right here out in the open? What will the neighbors think?"

"They'll think we're in love."

He opened the door and Minnie settled in the seat, a smile playing across her tingling lips.

He climbed in, leaned over and kissed her again. "That little one just won't do. I can't wait to spend the rest of our lives together. Let's get started now. Let's go back to the courthouse and have Judge Fuqua marry us right now."

Minnie giggled. "I can't do that. My sisters wouldn't speak to me again if they didn't come to the wedding. Besides, I want to tell Jane before anyone else does. It might be the kick in the pants she needs to get excited about her work at the detective agency again. She's only been going through the motions."

Tom took her hand and kissed it. "Alright, but we're getting married as soon as possible."

"Agreed."

They drove the short distance to Jane's apartment. Tom knocked several times before Minnie took over.

"Jane. You open this door right now. Your car's in its usual spot so I know you're in there. Open up!"

The lock clicked and the barrier between them slid away. "Come on in," Jane said, before plopping down on the couch that seemed to have a Jane shaped spot melted into the fabric.

Minnie settled down beside her and studied her sister. Jane's hair was a mess. No makeup, dark circles showed under her eyes. "I have some news."

"Minnie's agreed to be my wife," Tom piped up.

Minnie blushed. "That wasn't the news I was talking about, but it's true."

Jane gave an "I knew it" look and swatted Minnie's leg. "That's wonderful. I'm so happy for you both." She jumped up and hugged Tom before remembering her manners. "Oh, I'm sorry. Do you want something? Some coffee or I have those lemon shortbread cookies you like so much, Minnie."

"No, no. We ate before we came."

"Oh, I ask her to marry me, and suddenly she's the boss."

Minnie glanced at Tom, a big grin stretched across his face. She blushed again.

"Oh, I'm just teasing. I don't want anything, thank you."

"So, what's the other news?" Jane asked.

"Oh, yes. They arrested three people in the Harper case."

Jane stiffened. "They what? I thought...I thought. I didn't think that would ever be solved."

"Me either. Sheriff Johnson told him they have warrants for three men. What were their names, dear?" Minnie asked.

"Aww, you called me dear." Tom came up to her and touched her cheek. "I love when you talk sweet to me."

Minnie swatted at him but missed as he jumped away.

Jane laughed out loud. "Minnie doesn't like the mush in public. But wait until you get home and wham! I used to catch her and Curtis kissing behind the shed, in the garage, and by the side of the house."

"Jane! Stop that." Heat crept up her body. "Tom, do you remember those names?"

"Alfred Harvey, James Lovan, and Kenneth Almon."

"Who are they?" Jane demanded.

"We were hoping you would know. Neither of us did. I think they are from Earlington."

"Alfred Harvey, Alfred Harvey. Something about that is familiar. Maybe Frank mentioned him in passing or something. Never heard of the other two at all, but I'm glad they finally got them."

They talked for a while about the case, and then Minnie asked Jane to go for a drive with them.

"No," Jane shook her head. "I've got so much to do around here."

They glanced around the spotless apartment. This was the perfect opening for Minnie to bring up the subject dear to her heart. "Jane, you look terrible. Please consider moving back home, I would love to have you. Spending time around family will help you move on from Frank's death."

"I can't."

"And why in the world not? Frank wouldn't want you locked up here all alone. He would want you to be out and about. Building up the business you two started together. He'd want you to be happy."

"Yes," Tom nodded in agreement. "Honor his memory, you're not going to forget him, but get out there and start living again. This place is like a morgue."

"How do you know he wants me to be happy?"

"It's simple." Minnie exclaimed. "Would you want Frank to bury himself in here if you passed?" Minnie waited for an answer but didn't get one. "Well, would you?"

Jane looked up with tears in her eyes. "No. I wouldn't want that. I would want him to finish the investigation and bring the killers to justice. Not to give up on life like I have." Once Jane started she couldn't seem to stop. "I would want him to find someone to love him again. I wouldn't want him to go through life by himself. That wouldn't be fair. I would want him to be successful and proud of who he is."

Minnie put an arm around her. "And I'm sure he would want the same for you."

"Do you really think so?"

"I know so. Will you at least think about moving back home? If you don't want to move into the big house you can live in the apartment over the garage. The one Dad built for me and Curtis when we first married."

"I'll think about it. But first I need to finish a few things."

Minnie hugged her once more and turned to Tom. "Are you ready to go? I think it's time to leave. Jane has things to do."

"Sure am." Tom turned to Jane. "Behind the shed, you say?" Jane laughed and shooed the two lovebirds out the door.

A week later, Jane felt almost back to herself. She took a walk around the neighborhood, stopped to talk to a few people and even watched for signs of any activity that signaled an investigator might be needed soon. As she returned to her apartment, an envelope sticking out of her mailbox caught Jane's eye. "What's this?" She ripped it open and read the contents. She hopped from one foot to the other, energy seizing her body. Jane let out a small shriek and ran inside to call Ida. "A letter…in my mailbox…I can't believe it."

"Jane, what are you babbling on about?"

"I just got a letter asking me to come to the courthouse in Russellville next Monday morning. I'm going to sit on the grand jury."

Chapter 15

May 11, 1970

Jane pulled together the flaps of her new suit jacket over her bright pink blouse. Her matching grey skirt reached her knees and black heels completed the ensemble. She sure had changed over the past five years. Gone were those awful hairdos she used to love and choking through clouds of hairspray to get them to stay in place. The ones that took hours to produce, hours she didn't have any more since she and Frank had opened their own detective agency.

Shaking her head, she ran fingers through the layered shag she now sported. Easy to take care of and professional. That's exactly what she needed. She dabbed a splash of blush and a touch of mascara and voila, finished in less than ten minutes.

The coffee pot gurgled its last hideous growl. Jane hurried to the kitchen of her two-bedroom apartment and grabbed a cup. She'd have to hurry to be on time for the Grand Jury hearing at the Logan County Courthouse in Russellville.

Four years ago, she would've been ecstatic to be involved. She was excited, but her heart wasn't into it. Paying clients expected results quickly. Her detective agency, "Effective Detectives" was doing well. It kept her busy during the sleepless nights since Frank had died helping someone change a tire on the side of the road. She took one last glance in the mirror, finally happy to be leaving the house again.

Her Volkswagen bug sat in the drive waiting for her. She should get a more professional car, but she couldn't seem to part with this one…a gift Frank helped her acquire.

Jane put the car in gear and backed out of the drive before she let herself dwell on the loss of her fiancé. They had lived together for a while, before he died, something that brought frowns whenever they went out together, but no one had said anything. They planned to get married, but that stupid drunk driver. When would people learn drinking and driving don't mix? It just didn't seem fair. How was she supposed to go on without him? Nobody seemed to know, so she buried herself in the detective agency they opened together. He would be proud. She was fulfilling their dream.

She parked, shivered, and took in a deep breath. How in the world had she been chosen to sit on the Grand Jury for the Harper case?

There were just too many memories. She lowered her head to the steering wheel and remembered Frank letting her come as they dragged Wolfe Creek after finding Edgar Harper's hat. It was that very day she'd decided he was the one.

Purse and notebook in hand, she forced herself out of the car. The double doors creaked as she struggled with their weight. She wandered the hall until finally pulling the envelope out and reading the contents again.

Please report to the grand jury in courtroom B at the Russellville Courthouse. The proceedings will begin promptly at nine o'clock a.m.

Jane found Courtroom B on the second floor, why didn't the letter say that? She smoothed her skirt, wanting to look her best in case photographers and newspaper interviewers showed up. Image was everything if a woman wanted to make it in a man's world. She'd spent the last three years trying to develop a reputation as a competent private detective, but for some reason, men didn't want women competing in certain fields. Women were to do the trivial work, the tedious work. She shook her head to chase away those thoughts. Thanks to Frank she was now a detective—a good one.

Shortly after she was seated, Judge Fuqua took the bench and addressed the jurors.

"Today you're going to hear the testimony surrounding three men, Alfred Finley Harvey, James Taylor Lovan, and Kenneth Delaney Almon. Your job is to determine if there is sufficient evidence to believe that these three men on the night of December 11, 1965, did kidnap Mr. Edgar Harper and Mrs. Eustace Harper Givens from the Harper house and subsequently caused their deaths. You will listen to all the testimony with an open mind and not make a determination until you are ensconced in the jury quarters together. You are not to talk about this with each other or with anyone else outside of the courthouse. With that understanding, let's begin testimony. Bailiff, will you call the first witness, please?"

G. C. McMillen was sworn in and Commonwealth's Attorney James Lyne started his questioning. Jane struggled to focus on what was being said.

Lyne cleared his voice. "Your name is G.C. McMillen?"

"Yes, sir."

"And at the time of December 11, 1965 you were, and to this day are, a detective with the Kentucky State Police."

"That's right."

"Could you tell the court what happened on the morning of December 12, 1965?"

McMillen tugged at his tie, moving it back and forth before he answered. "At approximately 9:10, I received a call at the Russellville Police Station about two people missing in Lewisburg."

"That would be Edgar Carol Harper and his daughter Mrs. Ella Harper Givens?" Lynn's brow raised just a notch.

"Yes, correct."

"What did you do next?"

McMillen thought a moment. "I called Deputy Sheriff Elect Gene Sweat and asked him to accompany me. He came right away, and we arrived at the house at approximately 9:30."

"Did your father, Logan County Sheriff Guy McMillan, accompany you?" Jane waited for an answer pencil poised over her notebook. If both McMillen's were involved, this could get confusing.

"No, he was in Louisville that morning, but came back after I called him. He arrived in the afternoon."

"Could you tell if it looked like the house had been entered forcefully?" Again, Lyne's brow inched upward.

"I didn't find any evidence of forced entry. The doors and windows seemed undisturbed."

Lyne stood tall, his dark suit emphasizing his good posture as he continued his questions. "Do you recall if it rained the night before?"

"Yes, it was still raining lightly when we arrived."

"Did you find any muddy footprints or anything in disarray in the house?"

"No. From a housekeeping standpoint, the house was extremely neat and clean. Almost everything seemed in place."

"When you say almost everything, what do you mean?"

"There were two suitcases in the bedroom that Ella slept in. One was on the bed and one on the floor. Both of them were open. The door hit the one on the floor when we entered the room. There was a box of clothes on a chair that seemed to be summer clothes." Jane squirmed in her seat and smiled as a memory of that day surfaced. Sneaking into Ella's room to search for clues, what had she been thinking? How bold she'd been.

"What about Mr. Harper's room?" Lyne's voice broke into Jane's thoughts.

"The only thing I noticed is that the bed was turned down. This was strange considering everything else in the house seemed to be in place. His medicines were on his bedside table and his teeth were in a glass on the table as well. There seemed to be an imprint where someone had sat on the bed."

"Was there anything under the bed?"

"Yes. A lockbox was under there, but it didn't seem to be disturbed."

"Was there any money found in the house?"

"Yes. A cup in the kitchen contained $4.50 and Mrs. Given's purse, which was lying on her bed, contained $8, if I remember correctly."

G.C. McMillen stated the facts and nothing else. Jane admired that. She wasn't one for chit chat.

"After they did not return that day, what did you do?"

"We alerted the FBI it might be a possible kidnapping. Police departments from several surrounding counties pitched in to help. We went door to door to determine if neighbors saw anything, and organized search parties. When those didn't produce much, we invited the public to walk the county. Once the hat and hose were found, we drug lakes and ponds, plus a strip mine, with no results."

Sadness crept back into Jane's heart as she recalled the announcement asking everyone to search their property for any sign of Edgar and Ella. She and Frank had done that, of course, but they had gone a lot farther, searching behind local businesses, in strange, out of the way places, even around Lake Malone, but nothing had materialized.

"On what date were the bodies found?"

"March 26th, 1966. The bodies were found in a cemetery off of Peach Orchard Road. Martin Cemetery."

"How were the bodies found?"

McMillen straightened in his seat. "On Sunday March 20st, a local man, Randall Adler, was taking his son out to get some air, he had an illness, the measles, I believe. While walking in the cemetery, he found half a pair of glasses. It didn't occur to him until the following Thursday that they might be related to the missing father and daughter. Mrs. Given's optician examined them and determined they were the same frames and prescription as hers. A search party was set up for the next day, and that's when they were found."

"Where were the bodies found?"

"Over a barbed wire fence at the cemetery, through some brush and briars, small cedar and pine trees. A burned-out house with a garage that was still standing stood nearby, and a barn that was dilapidated and could not be used stood next to the shallow creek they were found in. It's been torn down since."

"When the bodies were found, was anything covering them?"

"Yes, some boards from the barn and some pine boughs torn from nearby trees."

McMillen sat straighter in his seat. "The branches were still green, as if they'd been torn off recently. We even sent them to Forestry Department to see if they could determine how long they'd been removed, but with the cool weather slowing down the process, they couldn't tell how old the branches were."

"What condition were the bodies in when they were found. Could you determine a cause of death?"

"They had been beaten. It wasn't until the coroner did the autopsies that it was discovered they had been shot as well."

"How long after the bodies were discovered did you first hear of Alfred Harvey?"

"I already knew about him. I first talked to him about a possible connection to the case in February 1966, before the bodies were found."

Jane straightened coming to attention. G.C. knew of Alfred Harvey before they found the bodies? Why had it taken so long to arrest him? There was so much Frank hadn't told her.

"How did you hear about a possible connection?"

"State Police Detective Leroy Poole from over in Madisonville requested that I and others who were investigating the case come there, that he had someone he would like for us to talk to. Harvey was in jail on an armed robbery charge and Detective Poole thought he might be connected in some way."

Jane scribbled in her notebook. New information. It might be important.

"Did you get any information from him?" Lyne stared at G.C. as he waited for an answer.

"Some. We're talking about a boy who's pretty smart, intelligent and street smart. He admitted to the armed robberies—he knew there were witnesses. He implicated James Lovan and Kenneth Almon in the robberies too. We didn't bring up the Harper case, he did."

What? Jane's mouth fell open. Who would do that?

Lyne folded his arms across his chest. "In what manner did he bring it up?"

"He said, 'It looks like you're going to clear up all the other crimes in the county, why don't you ask me about the Harper case?' A detective asked, 'Well, do you know anything about the Harper case?' He replied, 'No, I do not. I have never been to Lewisburg.' When questioned further about the routes taken to commit armed robberies with, Lovan and Almon, he described a route that brought them right through Lewisburg."

"Would you describe Harvey as someone with a conscience?"

"No, not at all. He carried a gun at all times and sometimes committed robberies on a whim. At other times, he planned them out. If it crossed his mind not to rob a man because he liked him, or liked something about him, Harvey wouldn't rob him. He went into the Holiday Inn in Madisonville, pulled out his gun and told the night clerk it was a stickup. The man said, 'Go to hell; I'm not going to give you any money.' Harvey put his gun back in his pocket and walked out saying, 'I don't blame you. I wouldn't give it to nobody neither.'

He was just as likely to go into a grocery store, eat a candy bar in the checkout line and say, 'Give me all your money or I'll pull my gun and kill you.' He's probably never told us the complete story, but we know he, Lovan, and Almon came to Lewisburg in two vehicles; a stolen red mustang and Almon's White Cadillac. What happened after that is still a mystery."

Chapter 16

Eustice Givens raised his right hand and swore to tell the truth, then took his seat in the witness box.

Jesse L. Riley approached the box and spoke in a firm tone.

"Ella Harper Givens was your wife, correct?"

"That's right."

"And Edgar Carol Harper was your father-in-law?"

"Yes."

Riley glanced at Eustice before continuing. "Sometime in the late fall of 1965, a Sunday, the date you are unable to remember, did you observe a large white car you were unfamiliar with in the immediate area of the Harper's home?"

"I did."

"How many people were in this car?"

"Three males, not too old. I'd say twenty-five to thirty."

"Mr. Givens, I'll exhibit to you a photograph of Kenneth D. Almon, James Taylor Lovan, and of Alfred Finley Harvey and ask you if you can identify those photographs, sir?"

Eustice stared at the pictures, even picking them up and laying them back down. "Well now, these pictures resemble what I thought I seen in the car." His gaze left the pictures and focused on Riley. "There was one kind of blond headed, one heavy and one big looking fellow."

"So, to the best of your knowledge and recollection, the three photographs I exhibited to you were the three individuals in the large white car?"

"That's what I'm thinking now, and especially Almon and Harvey."

"No more questions, Your Honor."

Eustice stepped down and Leon Brown was called to the stand.

Jane's head popped up. Brown? That was the name of the brothers who the FBI first considered suspects. Could he be related? The bailiff opened the door to the courtroom, and she waited for the man. When he appeared, she lowered her head and wrote in her notebook. "Cannot be related. They aren't the same race."

James Lyne stood taking his position in front of the witness. "Your name is Leon Brown and you live in Earlington, Kentucky and have lived there since prior to December 11, 1965?"

"Yes."

"Do you know James Taylor Lovan, Kenneth Almon, and Alfred Harvey?"

"Yes, all three. Leon crinkled his face. "But I only know Harvey as Harvey. Didn't know that wasn't his first name."

"How did you know them?"

"They would go hunting or fishing and bring the game to my house. I'd clean it for half of it. Sometimes I cooked it, too."

"I'm going to show you three photographs. Could you identify each, please?"

Lyne laid out three photographs and Brown touched each as he named them. "Harvey, Lovan, and Almon."

"And you know all of them well, Mr. Brown?"

"I don't know Harvey what you call 'well', but I know him when I see him. I know Lovan and Almon mighty well. We all live in Earlington."

Lyne returned the pictures to a nearby table before continuing, "Do you recall reading about the kidnapping and murder of Mr. Edgar Harper and Mrs. Ella Harper Givens in Lewisburg in December of 1965?"

"Yes, sir."

Attorney Lyne paced in front of the judge's bench.

"Sometime prior to that date, did any of the three in the photographs discus with you going somewhere else for a similar type job?"

"Yes, sir. Kenneth Almon and Jimmy Lovan." Guilt crept across his face as if ratting out his friends left a bad taste in his mouth. "They wanted me to go to Horton's Gap and take a fellow who works at the bank and get him to open the vault."

"Did you agree to go?"

"No, sir."

"Did they mention the possibility of killing somebody?"

Leon hesitated and Jane wondered if he would continue. What could be so bad that he couldn't bring himself to say it. At last he blurted out the answer.

"No, not right then but a little later on, I don't know how much time was in between, but Almon and Lovan, while I was out of work, just doing odd jobs, asked me did I want to make any money. I asked them how; Almon told me to kill Harvey."

Harvey! Jane sat back in her chair stunned. These guys were ruthless.

"I told him 'No,' that I didn't want to make any money like that, Leon said, Almon told me he was afraid Harvey talked too much."

"This was after the Lewisburg murders?" Lyne held Leon's gaze,

Leon didn't look away. "Couldn't swear to it, but I think it was."

Mr. Lyne pointed at Leon Brown and shook his finger. "So sometime before Harvey went to the penitentiary at Eddyville on March 9th, 1966, Almon wanted to pay you a sum of money to kill him?"

"Yes, sir."

"How did he want you to do it?"

"He and Lovan were going to give me a sawed off 12-gauge shotgun. Said Harvey was talking too much, and they wanted him gone. I didn't agree to do it."

"Did you hear anything more about the shotgun after the Lewisburg murders?"

"Yes, Almon and Lovan said they were going to throw it in Earlington Lake because Harvey didn't have sense enough to act with it or something. The way they talked they were scared somebody would see him with it."

"Did they ever discuss any of their other crimes with you, Mr. Brown?"

"No, sir."

Jane relaxed back in her seat as Lyne retreated and Riley came forward. The guy had to be lying. People wouldn't tell you things like these unless you had built a type of mutual trust. These men probably discussed everything.

Jesse Riley cleared his throat before starting.

"Do you know anything about any other guns that Kenneth Almon, Harvey, or Lovan had?"

"I saw Harvey with a .38. I don't know what brand it was. Said it belonged to Almon. This was sometime around 1965."

"Do you know what happened to this gun?"

"He told me that he pawned it in Hopkinsville and Kenneth, I believe he said, went and got it out of pawn."

"Do you know what happened to it after Kenneth Almon got it out of pawn? Did anyone ever tell you where it went?"

"No, sir."

Mr. Riley walked to the witness box and stared straight into Mr. Brown's eyes. "Now remember, you are under oath, Mr. Brown. Do you know anything at all regarding the kidnapping and murder of Edgar Harper and his daughter, Mrs. Eustice Givens?"

"No, sir."

The next witness claimed not to know anything, so Attorney Lyne called Jesse Riley himself to the stand.

"Mr. Riley, in the preceding week, did you have chance to speak by telephone to former Lewisburg resident Joan Harlow?"

"Yes."

"Did she disclose that she was working in a place of business, a grocery store, in Lewisburg on the night of December 11, 1965?"

"Yes, she did."

"Did you mail her copies of the photos of the three defendants that were seen here in court today?"

"Yes. I called her at the noon recess to ascertain if she had received them and could identify the suspects."

"Please tell the Grand Jury what she told you with respect to whether or not she recognized the three defendants?"

"She positively identified the photographs as the people who were in the grocery store in Lewisburg early in the evening on December 11, 1965."

"Now Mr. Riley, there was no mistaking the fact that she positively identified them, she didn't say it looked like them, she didn't say I think they were, but she positively identified them. Is that right?"

"She positively identified each photograph and so stated on the telephone to me and also to Detective G.C. McMillen."

"Thank you. That is all, Your Honor."

County of Lyon
State of Kentucky SS Affidavit

I, James F. McKinney, the Affiant, first being duly sworn on oath, do hereby state that the following statement by me subscribed, is the absolute truth, so help me God.

As a Christian I feel it is my duty to inform this court that I am well acquainted with a Mr. Leon Brown (a witness in a kidnap murder case). Brown is undoubtedly the most perverted and unscrupulous character I have ever come in contact with. During his confinement in the penitentiary he would resort to any technique to curry favor with the prison officials as it is common practice in prisons to use informers they must be given special privilege such as being allowed to indulge in sexual perversion and since they weren't trusted by their fellow inmates they never have any information to pass on to the prison officials they are force to lie and frame other prisoners. It is simple logic to say a man that is not above being an informer is not above telling a lie.

I further state that I make and tender this affidavit in of my own free will, without the promise of reward, consideration, fear, threat, abuse, duress, or any undue influence. I further state that I make, and tender said affidavit in the sole interest of whom it concerns.

Affiant further saith not.

/S/ ____________________

Affiant

Subscribed and sworn to before me, a Notary Public, this 18 day of June 1970.

____

Notary Public

My commission expires 1-20-1974

Chapter 17

October 1970

Ida pasted the rest of the green stamps in the book and shoved them into the kitchen drawer. "Just two more books and I'll have those nice blue cushions for the summer porch."

Rennie smiled and took her hand. How about we ride over to the Logan County Tobacco festival. You know Jane's in the parade.

"Yes, I remembered. And I'm glad she's finally back to herself again. A parade is perfect—she's always liked to be the center of attention. Let me grab my purse and I'll meet you at the car."

They parked in a field behind the town square and walked to the festivities. The parade was in full swing when they reached the main road. Rennie found them a spot along the way where they could see the floats go by.

Pulling her in front of him, he put his arms around her. She sighed in contentment. Marrying him was the best thing she'd ever done.

Soon shrieks of laughter sounded as candy flew their way. Ida scrambled to get a piece.

Coming up with her prize, she opened the butterscotch and popped it in her mouth.

"There she is!" Rennie pointed to where Jane stood on a float with a huge magnifying glass. She was examining every inch of the float for clues. Effective Detective Agency read a banner along the edge of the float. Ida laughed. Leave it to Jane.

Ida hollered and Jane threw candy at her. Once again, she scrambled to grab a piece, this time giving it to Rennie.

Once the parade passed Ida took in the town. Main Street had been blocked off and festive banners hung from the buildings. Kids ran and played as the adults visited the different booths or stood in clusters and talked. A big Ferris wheel went around and people screamed down at the crowd from above. Food peddlers sold their wares and a sack race was in progress. Rennie took her hand and wandered over to the game booths set up around the town square.

"Well, look who it is." Ida started as someone tapped her on the shoulder.

"Well, hello there." Ida turned to Rennie. This is Monroe and Thurston. They've lived in Quality since they were born."

Rennie shook hands. "Nice to meet you. Are you farmers?"

"Well I am," Thurston answered. "Monroe here has the easy life of owning a hardware store."

"Easy life? You should be there at planting season or when the first snow is predicted. Can't keep enough stuff on the shelves so people won't think I'm going out of business."

"Thurston lives across the road from Eustice Given's farm," Ida interjected.

"Really?" Rennie turned to the man. "Did you know Mr. Harper?"

"Sure did. He and I helped each other on our farms from time to time. Such an upstanding person."

Rennie nodded. "So I've heard."

"It's so sad what happened. It's been almost five years and they're still unsure if they have the people responsible."

"That's true," Monroe agreed. "But I think the guys they arrested are the right ones, don't you?" He looked toward Ida. "I know your sister sat in on the Grand Jury twice in May. All the indictments from that should put those guys behind bars before you know it."

"Well, I hear that Harvey guy might even plead guilty," Thurston added. "They may have worked out a deal where he testifies against the others, but that might just be a rumor. You know how gossip can travel faster than the truth."

"It looks like he might do that, depending on how the first trial turns out," Ida clarified. "All three were indicted on the kidnapping, murder, and armed assault with intent to rob."

"And I heard the trial got moved to Christian County" Rennie added. "Something about a fair trial."

"Well," Monroe sighed. "Yes, it did. But I don't think that's going to help them. This case was widely publicized. I mean, even the Cincinnati paper posted the story."

"That it did." Rennie said as music started to play. "If you'll excuse us, I would like to dance with my wife."

The men laughed as the couple joined others dancing in the square.

Huffing, they finally wandered over to the competition tent, where Ida found a shiny blue first place ribbon on her tomato plant, which spouted two giant tomatoes.

"I can't believe I won."

"And I won second on my corn. Wonder how I'll come out in the tobacco judging event." Rennie's brown eyes turned golden with pride as he talked to a man about his land. How he planted seeds and they burst through the ground like tiny blades of grass, continued on into stalks of corn or tobacco plants.

"I'm so glad you agreed to live with me on the farm, Ida. I love it there."

She kissed him on the cheek. Mortified, she turned her head and tucked her chin. Had she done that in public? Ida drew her fingers through a wayward strand of hair. "I do, too." She said taking his hand in hers. "Let's check Minnie's canned beans."

Ida squealed when she saw her sister had also gotten a first place in the canning division.

"The Clack sisters have outdone themselves this year," Rennie said, squeezing her waist.

"I'm a Pryor, thank you very much." Minnie stepped up beside them and Ida immediately hugged her.

"Tom and I are getting ready to go watch the pie eating contest. Do you two want to come along?"

"Do we ever." Rennie grabbed Ida's arm and led her away from the food displays. "I might even want to enter that."

Ida laughed as they put the bib on Rennie. Why hadn't she remembered to bring her new camera? The newfangled thing spit out instant memories.

The whistle blew. Pie flew as the contestants gobbled blueberry, apple and pumpkin pies. Rennie came in second.

"Tell Rennie not to fret. Buddy wins every year," said a gruff voice from behind her. "That man can put away some pie."

Ida turned to find Mr. Porter, the postmaster, standing there. "Thanks, that might save his ego."

They all laughed.

"Rennie doesn't need to save any ego. He's a good man." Tom said.

"Speaking of good men." Mr. Porter straightened. "Have you guys heard anything about the Harper case?"

"Not much." Ida gave a weak smile. "I think they're getting close to setting the trial date." Why did everyone insist on talking about the Harpers? "They've filed the indictments, denied bail to Lovan, and as far as I know, Fuqua is staying on as special Judge in the case. You know they tried to have him removed, don't you?"

"Fuqua? Yes. I voted for him myself. He's got a great career ahead of him. Why don't they want him as Judge?"

"Something about his neighbor, Mrs. Alban Day." Minnie interjected. "I heard she's related to Edgar Harper somehow. They talk all the time and it's felt like she might have swayed his opinion of Lovan. They don't think he can be impartial."

"Doesn't Judge Faqua's family also own substantial interest in two newspapers?" Mr. Porter asked.

"Yes. And those papers have printed stories that show bias against the defendant, too." Tom blurted. "I've read some of their editorials."

"Well, it turned out it was too late." Ida put in. "You have to file that before pleading to the indictments or moving bail and all that."

Ida caught Rennie's gaze upon her and stumbled over her words. "And..a...well you know Almon is out on $10,000 bond."

"You should have studied law," Rennie beamed proudly.

"I think it's strange that they're trying them one at a time." Tom said. "I heard it's going to start sometime next month, but I'm not sure. You know how slow the court systems are."

Rennie slid his arms around Ida's waist. "If you'll excuse us fellas, we need to go home. I think I'm going to be sick."

Ida laughed. "Oh, you poor thing. You ate too much pie."

"Yes, do you think we could sneak out of here without anyone seeing us?"

"Go on, Ida, take him home. We'll cover for you if anyone asks." Minnie gave her a wink.

"But we'll miss the biggest event of the whole week. I always enjoy the reenactment of Jesse James robbing that bank right across the street." Ida pointed to the old Russellville Bank."

Rennie grimaced and rubbed his stomach.

"Well," Ida relented. "We've seen it dozens of times. I guess I can miss it this once since I'm needed elsewhere." She gazed lovingly into her husband's eyes.

Ida and Rennie walked back to the car. "I hoped I could get you away from the crowd. Is it bad I wanted you all to myself?

Her heart did a little flip. A teen on her first date wouldn't feel this giddy. Her husband was flirting with her. He wasn't sick at all.

Chapter 18

The Trial, December 1970

Jane tucked her multicolored skirt under shaky legs. Who would have thought years ago, she would be sitting here in the courtroom listening to testimony on the Harper case? And why did she feel so uneasy? She'd been waiting to hear Carolyn's testimony, and now she wasn't sure she actually wanted to know what happened. She remembered how badly beaten her friends had been. Things like that happened. She was a real live detective, after all. She knew how cruel people could be.

Unable to believe she would be part of Lewisburg history just by being here, she shook her head and tapped her pencil against her notepad. Her neighbor's justice depended on this trial, the reason her case files had been cleared so she could attend. But not only that, she needed closure on the death of her friends, and the part of her life she and Frank had shared all those years before while searching for clues.

Her gaze swept the area, anxiety mounting as she took in the familiar faces that decorated the crowded courtroom. Faces of friends and family determined to see this through to the end no matter what it brought in its wake. Would fairness prevail or would pain and fear inch its way back into the hearts of the community?

The door opened and Jane's sisters finally made their way into the courtroom. She used to always be the late one, now she was first to arrive. Jane lifted her coat and purse so they could sit beside her. As soon as they were seated, the Judge entered, and silence settled over the jam-packed room.

"The state calls Carolyn Brown Hampton to the stand."

Jane squeezed her hands together and took a deep breath, readying herself for a lengthy trial. She inched forward on her seat, eyeing the woman in the green and gold jumper who stood. So, this was the famous Carolyn Brown. The person who claimed she'd been there when Edgar and Ella were murdered. Carolyn raised her right hand and put her left hand on the Bible the bailiff held out, but before anything could be said, William Scent stood.

"May I request a conference in the judge's chambers?"

When the judge complied, Minnie's face crumbled in disappointment. Poor Minnie. With her arthritis flaring up, it would be a really long day for her.

As time dragged on, Jane rested her head on the back of the bench and sighed. The rumors, of course, had made their rounds, but she refused to believe them until she heard the girl's story. She would listen carefully, watch her face and body movements, and weigh the evidence before she made a decision. Innocent until proven guilty, right?

Maybe Carolyn's story would help put things into perspective. Maybe even eliminate many of the theories she and her sisters had come up with over the years.

When at last Carolyn returned to the stand, Jane pulled a small notebook and pen from her bag and wrote what Carolyn said as she told the court about herself. "Age 20. Lived in Madisonville the last six years. Married to Prentiss Hampton. Husband in hospital..."

Jane stopped. This woman's life hadn't been easy by any means. Only 20 and married three times, her third husband now a patient at a hospital in New Orleans. Going on two years? Jane silently thanked the Lord that her life had turned out differently. She and Frank had thoroughly enjoyed their time together.

Jesse Riley, the Logan county attorney approached the witness stand. "Mrs. Hampton." Riley's voice boomed across the quiet room. "Do you know all three men indicted for the killing of Edgar C. Harper and his daughter Ella Harper Givens?"

"I do." Carolyn wiped her mouth and blew out a heavy breath.

"Can you tell the court how you know them and how you met?"

"Well, I met Alfred Harvey in 1964 at Leon Brown's house in Earlington." Carolyn picked at the fuzz on the white sweater she'd laid across her knees before she continued. "I met James Lovan, and Kenneth Almon in 1965. The four of us traveled to Lewisburg three times that year."

Of course, the infamous Leon Brown. She remembered him from the Grand Jury and still wasn't convinced he was innocent.

"Can you tell us why you and these three men traveled to Lewisburg?"

Carolyn looked down guiltily, then looked up at Riley. "To rob them."

"To rob who?"

"Mr. Harper and his daughter. That's what we went for."

Jane held her breath. This girl didn't just know who did it. She was with them. How unbelievable was that?

"So, you made three trips?" Mr. Riley asked eyeing the girl suspiciously.

"Yes."

"Can you tell us what happened on your first trip to Lewisburg?"

"We cased the home of Mr. Harper. The purpose was to figure

out how to get Mr. Harper and Mrs. Givens to the car without being seen." Carolyn glanced toward the jury and then quickly looked away.

Mr. Riley lifted a photo from a nearby table and handed it to Carolyn. "Can you tell the court what this is a photo of?" He waited while she studied the picture.

"Mr. Harper's house in Lewisburg."

"And this is the same house you were casing?"

"Yes."

Jane glanced quickly at her sisters. Minnie and Ida were absorbed in every word and no doubt, like her, were taking in every action and reaction to the testimony given; the attorney's body language as well as Carolyn's.

"Okay, what about the second trip?" Riley's taut shoulders rippled beneath his jacket as he leaned against the stand.

"Well, we came back a week or two later," She said. "We drove around town a bit and then ended up at a little house. I didn't get the guy's name and wouldn't know him if he walked in the courtroom."

Jane stiffened. So, someone in town was in on the kidnapping. She scribbled a couple notes at the top of her tablet.

"Where was the little house?"

Carolyn scratched at her forearm. "I, I just can't remember."

"What happened while you were there?"

"Well on that trip, Jimmy T. Lovan..."

"I think you mean James Taylor Lovan?"

"I call him Jimmy T." Carolyn's scared eyes darted to Riley's and then back to the hands curled in her lap.

Riley nodded.

"Anyway, he walked into the house and a couple with a little kid walked out. That's all I know."

Jane's heart accelerated. Could the couple with the kid be the Crouse's? Maybe the murders were connected after all.

"And the third trip?" Riley crossed his arms and waited.

"On December 11, 1965, we set out from Leon Brown's house in Earlington and headed to Lewisburg," she replied.

"Go on."

"We took both cars. It was nasty out." She went on to explain how the wind blew so hard the rain pelted against their faces.

Riley interrupted. "Who rode with who?"

"I rode with Alfred Harvey in the red mustang. The other two took Almon's white Cadillac."

Riley walked over to the jury then turned to face Carolyn. "Tell us what happened when you got to Lewisburg?"

Carolyn's leg bounced at a rapid rate. Riley waited.

"We parked behind the bank Edgar was President of—The Lewisburg Banking Company."

Jane gasped. So, they had planned to rob the bank. Why else would they park there? Carolyn said they'd cased the house to see how to get them out without anyone seeing them, so they hadn't planned to rob the house. They were probably planning to take him back to the bank. She jotted down a few notes then refocused on Carolyn's story.

"We all got in the Cadillac and went to get something to eat, but only Harvey and I ate. The other two drank coffee. After that we went back to the little house.

"What happened then?" Riley asked.

"We went to Will's grocery. I remember because my pants were too big, and a woman there offered me a safety pin."

Riley leaned an elbow on the stand and strummed his fingers on the polished wood. "What kind of food did you buy?"

"Sandwich meat, bread and stuff."

"Did all four of you go into the grocery?"

"Yes."

"After that, where did you go?"

Carolyn's forehead crinkled as she thought back. "I believe it was a policeman's house."

Minnie grabbed Jane's arm. "Those were the people who knocked on the door that night asking for an officer," she whispered.

Luckily, Riley's voice covered hers. "A policeman's house? That's a little odd, isn't it? Why go to an officer's house if you're planning on committing a crime? Why take that risk?"

"We wanted to see what he had going on. Make sure he wouldn't get in our way."

"Where was this house?" Riley asked.

Carolyn looked at him sheepishly and stated that she didn't know. "Somewhere before we got to the Harpers, for sure."

Jane rolled her eyes and mentally placed the location Carolyn was talking about—Marvine Pogue's House. Marvine had already testified earlier in the week that a man had come to her door looking for a policeman that night.

Riley's voice grew hard. "Okay, Ms. Hampton, what happened next?"

Carolyn paled. Beads of sweat hovering on her forehead.

"We drove around for about thirty minutes and then went to the Harper house. We drove there in Almon's white Cadillac and parked in the back of the house by a little shack. It looked like a sawmill." She hesitated and then went on. "Jimmy T. went in first. He kicked the door open, making the porch light flicker."

Jane scribbled a reminder in her notes. Kicked the door in? The police said there were no signs of forced entry.

"Did James shoot Mr. Harper right after entering?"

"I object your honor." Scent stood and looked at Riley. "Leading the witness."

"Overruled."

Riley sighed and continued. "Did any of you have a weapon?"

"The men were wearing gloves and carrying weapons."

"Can you describe them? The weapons, I mean? Do you know what they were?"

"Alfred Harvey told me what they were. They had two .38s, and I think the tiny gun was a .25."

Riley rose to his full height. "Who carried which gun?"

She rubbed her temples as if willing the information to appear and thought a minute before answering. "Alfred had the .38s, and Jimmy T. held the little gun."

Jane leaned forward not wanting to miss a word. She couldn't believe they were going to finally find out what happened on that rainy night back in 1965.

Riley handed Carolyn another photograph. "Can you tell the jury what this is a photo of?"

She took the photo and stared at it for mere seconds before responding. "It's the back porch of the Harper house."

Riley pursed his lips and hesitated. Jane gave an internal groan. She could see this going on for hours. Mr. Riley had the knack for drawing out his questions to add suspense. Why couldn't he just get to the point?

"Where were Mr. Harper and Mrs. Givens when you went into the house?"

"Mr. Harper was in his bedroom." Carolyn's voice cracked.

"And Mrs. Givens?"

"She was also in her bedroom."

"How were they dressed?"

Carolyn looked up, a bit surprised at the question. "Well," she said. "Mr. Harper had on a shirt, pants, and brown boots." She looked down at her hands, as she thought. "Mrs. Givens wore a dark house dress. I remember, the hem was torn out. She also had on a white sweater and tennis shoes.

Riley rubbed his chin. "So, they were getting ready for bed?"

"No."

"What did Mr. Harper and Mrs. Givens say when you came in?"

"Mr. Harper said, "What in the world is going on?"

Mr. Riley slid his fingers together and stared at the lady before him. The pause seemed to drag on. When Jane could stand it no more, Mr. Riley finally spoke.

"What exactly did you know about Edgar Carroll Harper at the time of this crime?"

"The guys told me he was a banker and supposedly very wealthy."

"So, it was a simple robbery?"

Jane wanted to jump out of her seat. There was no way it was a simple robbery. They cased the house to see how to get them out without being seen. They planned a kidnapping. There was no doubt in her mind.

"Yes." Carolyn answered. "Alfred Harvey searched Mr. Harper's bedroom, and I rummaged through Mrs. Given's. Jimmy T. and Kenneth Almon stayed with Mr. Harper." Drops of sweat beaded on her brow and started to roll down her face. She wiped them away.

"How long did you stay at the house?" Riley's gazed probed Carolyn as he waited for an answer.

She shrugged her shoulders. "I guess about fifteen minutes."

"Who gave the indication it was time to leave?" Riley now shot his questions quickly and Jane wondered why the change.

"Jimmy T. did."

"And by Jimmy T., are you still referring to James Lovan?"

"Yes."

"Did you move anything?"

"I dumped suitcases on the bed, ransacked some drawers, and left them."

Jane eyed Carolyn. She was lying. She might have taken out the suitcases and looked through them, but nothing was trashed. She'd witnessed that herself.

Riley rushed on as if he didn't want to give her time to think. "What was taken from the home?"

"When we left, Mrs. Givens took, um...I would call it a crochet bag. Alfred took canned goods and ham."

"Once outside, what happened?"

"We all got in the Cadillac. Almon drove, and I sat in the passenger seat. Mr. Harper and his daughter were put in the back with Lovan and Harvey. "

Jane growled a low growl. Who would take their crochet bag if they were being kidnapped? She has to be making parts of this up, but why?

Riley rushed on. "Was the porch light on when you left?"

"No."

"When you left, was anyone out? Did anyone see you leave?"

"An old lady looked out the window. Her house was caddy corner to the Harper's."

"And where did you take your captives?"

"We picked up Harvey's red mustang from behind the bank and then drove to Martin Cemetery on Peach Orchard Road."

Hmm, Jane relaxed back in her seat and crossed her legs. So, they went back to the bank but didn't go in? Didn't even try? Yet she kept stating their intent was to rob. Maybe Mr. Harper had already told them about the time lock and that he couldn't get in. But why head directly to the cemetery? And such a remote cemetery. How had they known it was there? Only locals knew about it.

Riley walked back to the jury and leaned against the railing slowing his pursuit. "Who drove the red mustang?"

"I did." Carolyn's voice quivered, and a flush stole over her face.

Pushing himself away from the rail, Riley returned to the stand. "Earlier, when they were all together in the Cadillac was anything done to Mr. Harper or Mrs. Givens?"

"They were cut and slapped a few times."

"Did you all get any money?"

"About sixty dollars. It came from Harper's billfold. I then threw it out, under a culvert on some road that led away from where we were going. I don't have any idea where it led."

Letting out a deep breath, Riley continued. "Carolyn, how did you get to the cemetery?"

She tugged at the bottom of her jumper before answering. "We went up a big hill and around a real sharp curve. As we got to the graveyard, there was an old shack about torn down. It was about eight miles from Lewisburg." Carolyn gaze wandered the room.

Jane fumed. What? You know exactly how you got to the cemetery but not where you threw the wallet? Or where the little house was that you'd been to at least twice. She jotted something in her notes. When she looked up, Minnie was staring at her.

"They called a recess. I think we're going on home. I'm really hurting. Are you sure you're okay? A lot of emotion has been going across your face today."

"I'm fine. You guys go on. I'm going to try to find some coffee and hang around for the rest of the day." Jane waved goodbye and then wandered down the hall to a large glass window. Things would be so much easier if Frank were here. He could probably tell her if Carolyn's testimony had any truth in it.

Her gaze rested on the cold blue sky. "Frank, I hope you're watching," she whispered. "We shared so much about this case. I just want us to finish it together."

Chapter 19

Eleven days of trial had passed, or was it twelve? How much longer would this go on? Jane hadn't planned on taking two weeks off. Definitely not three.

Glancing through her notes once again, she yawned. Talk about long days. The last two weeks had been the longest. So many witnesses called to the stand. So much information.

Her unending headache still lingered. The cold can of soda from the vending machine felt good against her forehead, but she wouldn't get anything done sitting here like this. If only the ibuprofen would kick in, she'd be on her way home.

Jane struggled to study her notes while she sipped her drink. One of Carolyn's ex-husbands, Virgil Coakley, had testified against her.

His testimony hadn't helped the prosecution. He'd claimed that he never knew her to tell the truth, along with ten or twelve others who said the same thing. Jane understood why he was bitter. Carolyn had actually cheated on him after their second week of marriage. How could a husband ever trust a wife again after something like that?

Tapping her fingers on the table, she thought about Carolyn. It seemed like everyone knew her well. A liar. Even Dr. George had found her to have a psychopathic personality when she was fifteen. And this latest trick she pulled proved it.

Ms. Ogden, the receptionist with Millikin and Milliken who typed up Carolyn's statement said, "Carolyn had signed the six-page document and even made comments confirming the truth of the remarks."

And yet, when on the stand, Carolyn fabricated an entirely different story that didn't match either of her previous two statements. That had everybody in an uproar and added days to the testimony they'd had to endure.

Jane dropped her can in the garbage on her way out. She'd finish this for Frank, but it was taking its toll. She was sure Lovan was guilty, but for some reason the attorneys were focusing on Carolyn. Tearing apart her character and trashing her reputation. Jane felt sorry for the poor girl, even though she didn't seem like a very nice person. She'd given three different stories and now they had to sift through a ton of information to prove or disprove any given theory. But the part she really didn't understand was why Carolyn's attorney wasn't objecting more to the parts of her testimony that didn't seem relevant to the crime.

Jane walked past the courtroom, backed up and entered. Riley stood collecting his notes, but turned as she walked toward him.

"Miss Clack, did you need a ride back to Lewisburg?"

"Oh no. But thanks. I was really just wondering what happened these past few days?"

"You and me both. Lovan's lawyers are good. Heard they came all the way from New York. They destroyed our key witness. It's a shame, because I know she knows things she wouldn't know unless she was there. We'll just have to wait and see what happens."

Talking about the case was taboo. She knew that. He'd already revealed more that he should've. Her questions would have to wait. "I guess you're right." She said softly. "See you later."

Shadows filled the darkened lot as she made her way alone to her yellow Volkswagen. She dreaded the long drive home. Even though she understood the change in venue, the distance to attend everyday was a pain; and why change the venue and not the attorney and Judge? It didn't seem to make sense. She shook her head, sure, she'd read the story in the paper about Almon's attorney trying to get Fuqua to step down, but he had hung on saying he could be impartial.

Jane struggled up the steps to her apartment. Her notebook fell to the concrete landing as Jane wrestled to retrieve her key from her apartment door. I really need to get that fixed. She kicked off her black pumps and they landed on the floor with a thump. She didn't bother to pick them up, but instead headed to the kitchen to get something to eat. Nothing looked good, so she backtracked to the living room and picked up the remote. The newsman blurted the coming story.

"Carolyn Brown Trashed as a Witness."

Jane groaned and turned off the TV. She couldn't take anymore today. Covering her head with a pillow, she laid there sorting through this week's testimony. Who was telling the truth? Could a store clerk really remember someone they saw for only a few minutes five years ago? And one car could easily be mistaken for another. Other people in Lewisburg and its surrounding counties had to have white Cadillac's. It wasn't like Lovan owned the only one. Was it?

And she called him Jimmy T. That sounded a lot like Jimmy Seay. Hadn't Lovan's attorney testified that Carolyn had asked if he was James Lovan when he went to question her? Did Carolyn really know who Lovan was, or were she and Alfred Harvey trying to frame him?

A knock at the door brought another groan as Jane pulled herself from the couch and stumbled over her shoes to open it.

Minnie and Ida stood there holding dishes of food that smelled heavenly. "Come in."

"You look terrible, Jane." Minnie said as she brushed past her to set the hot roast on the table.

"I'm so sorry we couldn't make it to the trial this week. I had to work," Ida said, and Minnie is having trouble with her arthritis. You know how this cold weather affects her. How did it go?"

Ida followed Minnie and sat a big bowl of potatoes, and carrots next to the roast.

"Long." Jane replied as she gathered plates and silverware before taking the seat next to Ida. "They must have called thirty people to the stand yesterday. And today they called a lot of the defense witnesses. You know, attorneys and such. I could have laughed when they called Riley. I mean he's the big prosecutor, right? And he gets called to take the stand."

The sister's laughed good-naturedly and pledged to tease him about it the next time they saw him.

"Why on earth did they call him to the stand anyway?" Minnie's forehead wrinkled with concern.

"Something about taping a conversation with Mrs. Harlow without her consent. They're really cracking down on stuff like that nowadays. I think Milliken and Milliken did the same to Carolyn. I guess everyone has rights."

The ladies settled down to say grace, and then Jane started talking again, stopping only to stuff more food into her mouth. She told them everything, her exhaustion disappearing as the wonderful dinner filled her, and the stress of the week faded away in her sisters' company. She hadn't known how much she missed them.

Finishing the dishes, they retired to the living room. "That was so wonderful." Jane rubbed her belly and sighed. "I think I ate too much, though."

Ida laughed. "I think we all did, but I agree it was good."

They continued to talk, Jane waiting until the perfect time to broach her subject. "Minnie, did you mean what you said about me moving home? Because I'm ready."

Minnie raised her hands into the air. "Yes, yes, and double yes. I am so lonely in that big old house by myself."

"Then you wouldn't mind me moving in the house and not the apartment over the garage?"

"Of course not. I will love having you there. I miss you both so much."

"What about Tom?"

"Tom's not there yet, but he won't mind at all. He worries about you just as much as I do. Once we marry, I think we'll move into the first-floor bedroom. I may move there before that. I just can't do the steps anymore. Do you think we could talk Ida and Rennie into living over the garage?"

They both looked toward their sister with hope on their faces.

"Sorry guys, you know Rennie loves the farm. We're planning on buying more land, but we'll have to wait until someone around us sells."

Minnie thought a minute. "Why couldn't he farm dad's land? It's a given we're not going to need it. We could give the land to you and him. You could build your dream house there. Please ask him."

Ida smiled. "It would be so great to live close to you guys again. I promise I'll ask, but don't get your hopes up yet. I want Rennie to be happy. If he agrees, we'll do it, but if he doesn't, I'm going to do what he wants. Okay?"

"Okay," the sisters said in unison as they all hugged before heading their separate ways.

Later, after her sisters left, Jane was surprised at the happiness she felt. Could she be healing? She smiled to herself as she crawled under the nice warm blankets on her bed. "Thank you, Lord, for my sisters. I don't know what I'd do without them."

Chapter 20

Ida quickened her pace as she neared the 118-year-old courthouse. She'd promised Jane she'd be on time, but how could she know the closest parking space would be a block away? She definitely would have left earlier if Jane had said something. To be fair though, her sister talked about all the witnesses they called to the stand last night at dinner. "I guess I should've figured it would be crowded," Ida muttered as she slowed to catch her breath. "I mean, you have jurors, attorneys, judges, and even other staff besides."

A movement from across the back alley made her head turn; a half dozen officers emerged from the police station, Lovan in the midst of them.

All six halted when they saw her, hands going to their guns. Ida hesitated only a second before darting around the two-story, red brick building. Surely, they didn't think she wanted to hurt Lovan, or help him escape.

She slid into the seat next to her sister, nodding at Eustice as he turned to see who entered. Poor man. Dark circles hung low beneath his eyes, a testimony of many sleepless nights. Jane had said he came every day. She couldn't imagine how brutal that would be; to listen to every detail of your wife's death. Such a grueling death, at that.

Her gaze slowly switched to Lovan, who now sat at the defense attorney's table having come in the back door, while she had circled the building and come in the front. Tension broadcasted itself from every pore of his body.

"Oh, I'm so glad you're here." Jane gushed. I was going over my notes, and you won't believe what I found…"

Uninterested in Jane's narrative, Ida only half listened to her revelations. Why hadn't the trial started? After all, she'd almost twisted her ankle running up the road in shoes she shouldn't have worn just so she could be here when Lovan took the stand. What was the hold up?

"Ida, you're not listening," Jane said softly. "This crime shows an organized plan. They knew where, they knew how. They even had a place to dispose of the bodies beforehand. These perpetrators were smart. They planned this kidnapping robbery thing down to the detail. They even made sure they had alibis' even if they were questionable."

Jane continued, warming up to her favorite subject. "A profiler I talked to earlier this week said criminals like these often choose spots to kill and hide the bodies close to their homes. Since none of the accused are from this area, I believe someone else who lives in town or very close to it, planned the murders. Maybe it was the person in the little house."

"Too bad Carolyn couldn't remember where that was."

"Oh, I think she remembered. I mean, she described how to get to the cemetery in great detail. Even described the surroundings once there. She's a liar. She lied about the little house and about not knowing where the road led when she threw out the wallet. I'd bet my life on it."

"Either way, we'll never know where it is. If you ask me, I think Alfred Harvey killed them and then got Carolyn to do what's she's done. With all the different versions of her story, they have to throw her testimony out. And since she's the states key witness, all three will probably go free."

"Oh, Ida. You may be right, but you have to admit it could've been one of Edgar's friends or an associate of his from Quality or from his previous job as Postmaster. We all have enemies. They could have hired Harvey to take him out. Ella just happened to be there." Jane insisted.

"Jane, I don't want to talk about this. I don't want to think about someone in our own town being the culprit. That's scary." Ida pulled her black knitted cardigan together as if she were cold. "I wonder when they're going to start the trial. It's already 9:45. What are they waiting for?"

Jane laughed. "They're probably in the judge's chambers. They've been doing this all week. Asking for conferences and recesses like they were candy. The problem is, they never tell us why? It's kind of frustrating."

Judge Fuqua entered the courtroom a few minutes later. Ida looked over at Lovan, who had been talking to his parents and sisters, but now sat alone. He didn't look like a killer, but then, what did a killer really look like? Bruce's face came to mind, and Ida shuddered glad he hadn't caused any more trouble over the years.

It took forever for initial things to be taken care of, and then some legalities had to be ironed out, but Lovan finally went to the stand. Ida looked at her watch—2:40. She could have worked a half-day.

William Scent stood and squared his shoulders as if ready to do battle. His no nonsense persona gave his baby face a hard look as he walked to the stand with purpose in his step. Jane pulled her notebook and pen from her bag, ready to take down everything the man said.

Ida smiled. It was good to have Jane back to her old self again. It had taken awhile but...

Scent's voice shook Ida from her thoughts. "James, you have been called to the stand in your own defense. Can you tell the court who you are, please?"

"My name is James Taylor Lovan. I was born on Dec. 10th, 1935. I am the son of Mr. and Mrs. Willie Lovan and the father of four children. I am currently serving a term in the Eddyville state prison."

"James, can you tell us about your travels? Is it true you've gone back and forth between California and Earlington numerous times?"

Lovan seemed to sit up a little straighter. His shoulders tightened. "Yes, in the latter part of 1961, August, I think, I went to California and stayed for a little over two years. I returned in January 1963. Ended up staying here for eleven months. Then in 1965 I went back to California."

Ida wondered how much it cost each time Lovan traveled to California. Did he still do that? She struggled to make it through the week on her tank of gas. She had never had the means to travel.

"James, will you tell the court what happened in 1965." Scent crossed his arms and leaned against the railing.

"Me, my wife, and infant son stayed in Earlington for three months. We lived at my dad's house from August until November of that year."

"Then what happened?"

James kept his face clear of emotion. "We returned to California."

"Did you stay there?"

"No, my wife and I ended up getting a divorce, so on November 27th, I left California and came back home."

Scent paced between the stand and the jury. "What can you tell me about your criminal record?"

Heat surfaced in Lovan's face, but quickly disappeared. How embarrassing this must be for him, Ida thought. He shifted in his chair and looked at the audience with weary eyes. When his attorney nodded, he began.

"The police have charges against me for breaking into storehouses, schoolhouses, and auto theft. I also have two charges of forgery, but at no time have I ever gotten convicted of breaking into a private home.

"Have you ever held a job?"

"Yes, in California, I worked for long periods of time. I earned several thousand dollars."

"Scent held up some U.S. tax withholding forms. Are these yours?"

Lovan looked at the forms. "Yes."

"Your honor, I would like to introduce into evidence, Lovan's U.S. Tax Withholding forms. While in California he worked at Senior Citizen Village and Ranchers Cotton Oil."

The forms were taken to be logged into evidence. Scent continued.

"Have you ever worked here in Kentucky?"

"Yes. I worked at Bell and Zollar Coal Company, and King David Coal Company. I also worked at a tie company in Evansville right before I went to prison for a conviction from 1967."

"And what was that charge for?" Lovan took a deep breath and then relaxed. "I met Alfred Harvey's mother through a friendship between Harvey's mother and my older sister. After I got promoted to assistant maintenance manager at Senior Citizens Village in California, Harvey worked under me." Lovan scratched his head behind his ear and hesitated.

"Go on."

"Harvey introduced me to James Floyd Seay at the Cotton Tail Club in Fresno. He went to school with him. Anyway, when Harvey got a parking violation, he suggested we get Seay to drive us back to Kentucky. So, on the 27th of November 1965, the three of us set out in Jimmy's 1948 Plymouth convertible. His car broke down on the way, so we traded it for another one. When it also broke down, we sold it for junk, and got a stolen Mustang in Amarillo, Texas. That was what the charge was for."

Jane's pen flew across the page as Lovan told about Harvey's arrest in Claremore, Oklahoma for driving without a license.

"We ended up not getting to Kentucky until really late on Dec 1st, so I took them to the house of a coal miner, Kenneth Wayne Huddleston, who lived alone.

"Your father testified that you came back on the 4th or 5th of December. Is this true?"

"Yes. We stayed at Huddleston's for a few days. But on Dec. 4th, I went looking for a car. When I couldn't find anything in Madisonville, I went to Hopkinsville and bought a 1953 Plymouth from Morris Motors. Shortly after that, Harvey and Jimmy Seay wanted to go back to California, so I took them to Evansville in my new car. I dropped them off at the bus station there."

"We heard testimony from Carolyn Brown who has called you Jimmy Seay, Jimmy C. and Jimmy T. during her interviews and Court hearings. How many aliases do you use?"

"I don't use aliases. Never have."

"Why did you, Harvey, and Jimmy Seay stay at Mr. Huddleston's place?" Scent asked.

"My friends came in from California. What was I supposed to do? I couldn't put them up at my dad's house." He tightened his grip on the chair.

"Why not?" Scent asked.

"Because they both drank. My mother didn't tolerate drinking in her house."

"Good for her," Ida whispered in Jane's ear.

"And you stayed with your friends at the Huddleston's?"

"Yes."

"And what did the three of you do while you were there?"

"We played cards, watched television. Basically, just sat around."

"You didn't go out?" Scent said in disbelief.

"Well, once we did go out to get beer."

"Where did you go?"

"To a well-known bootlegging joint," Lovan smiled and some of the tension left his body.

"Did you hear Jimmy Seay's testimony?"

Lovan instantly stiffened, and his smile faded. "You know I did."

"In his testimony he stated he stayed with you and Harvey, because he feared for his life. He said the blinds were kept drawn and there were guns there. He finally left when you said he could go."

His hand reached for and rubbed his neck as a touch of anger traveled across his face. "Jimmy was not held captive, if that's what you're implying. He could have left at any time. Yes, the blinds were kept drawn. Huddleston worked the graveyard shift and therefore he slept during the day."

"What about the guns?" Scent stared directly into his eyes. "Why did you have guns in the house?"

Ida leaned forward in her seat. Guns? Were they the same guns Edgar and Ella were killed with?

Lovan released a sigh. "Huddleston keeps a collection of guns in his house. As far as I know, no one bothered them."

"Did you stop anywhere on your way to the Evansville Bus Station?"

"We stopped at the Big K-Mart. Then at Twin Lakes Motel, where I rented a room so we could clean up."

"Did you go to Lewisburg during this time?"

"I did not."

"Have you ever been in Lewisburg?"

"Never at any time in my life."

"Yeah, right," Jane mumbled under her breath.

"Have you ever been on Peach Orchard Road?"

"I never heard of it until this came up."

"What did you do after you dropped your friends off at the bus station?"

"I returned to the hotel, spent the night there alone, and then went back to Earlington to live with my parents. I lived there until July 29, 1966."

"What happened to the stolen mustang?"

"Harvey pawned it for a $100. A miner named Albert Holchauser loaned it in my name because he didn't know Harvey. I had to sign a note that I would repay $125."

"What happened next?" Scent shifted from one foot to the other.

"I read that Harvey had been arrested on another case, so I went to see him. He told me the police were asking around about the stolen car. So, I called and warned Holchauser the FBI was looking for the car."

"Did you ever see Jimmy Seay again?"

"Not until the trial."

"How about Harvey? When did you see him again?"

"I believe he called December 11th. He was at the bus station and needed to be picked up. He'd just come in from California. I took him to a Spur station in Madisonville then went home. Didn't see him much after that."

Ida sat spellbound. She hadn't heard any of this before. The men sounded like good friends. Ida had never had a friend like that. Someone she could call no matter what.

"Did you ever see him with Carolyn Brown?"

"No, sir."

"Did you know her? Were you with her in Lewisburg? At Peach Orchard Road?"

"No, sir."

"Jim, I ask you—did you plan any part or carry out the murder of Edgar Harper or Mrs. Ella Harper Givens?"

Ida watched emotion travel across Eustice's face at the mention of his wife.

"I certainly did not," Lovan insisted.

"Are you innocent of this crime?" Scent's forceful voice threw the words at him.

"I certainly am."

"No further questions your honor."

James C. Lyne rose from his seat and walked to the stand.

"Let's talk a little bit more about your trip from California to Kentucky in late November. How much money did you have on you?"

"Somewhere between $300-$400."

"Who paid the motel bill in Amarillo and Harvey's fine?"

"I did."

Lovan rattled on about other expenses he incurred. Lyne then questioned him about roads he may have traveled around Lewisburg, but Lovan denied ever being in Lewisburg.

"No more questions your honor."

Carolyn was a liar. Ida got that. But just because Carolyn lied, it didn't mean Lovan wasn't one, too. So, why were they trying to paint him as a saint? He wasn't. He'd been in prison himself for breaking into places.

She tossed the empty Pepsi can and gathered her things, but her mind wouldn't rest. It seemed everyone who testified saw Lovan in Lewisburg but, Lovan swore he'd never been there. Did everyone on the stand lie but him? No way. And what in the world was all the testimony on Lovan not being a violent man. That didn't prove he wasn't guilty. He'd already been caught in enough lies to show how dishonest he was. At least a dozen witnesses placed him in town and with Carolyn Brown whom he claimed not to know. And besides that, no one ever believes that their loved ones, friends, and/or neighbors would do the crimes they get caught doing.

Chapter 21

The sun rose over the Christian County courthouse on Friday, December 18, 1970. Town folk gathered on the sidewalk, talking amongst themselves as they waited for the doors to open. Each gave their own opinion of the upcoming verdict, of if they thought the defendant guilty or innocent. Voices rose as friends disagreed. Jane leaned against a huge column and listened, not sure herself what the actual outcome would be or even if it mattered. So much of the testimony became Carolyn against Lovan. And with all the lies and faulty statements Carolyn gave, who knew what really happened that fated December day so long ago.

Lovan's testimony yesterday surprised her. He'd denied everything. Which she expected, but he hadn't tried to hide that he associated with Harvey, and they were friends. He told the court about his criminal record and didn't try to cover up the bad things he'd done. Could Lovan be an innocent person deemed guilty because he hung with the wrong kind of people? Harvey was the son of a family friend. According to testimony, Lovan helped his friend whenever Harvey found himself in trouble with the law. Paid fines. Took him cigarettes in jail.

Jane moved toward the door when it opened. Caught in the middle of a crowd, she baby stepped her way inside.

"I thought for sure those Brown brothers would be on trial, but they never called them." A little old woman rattled on. "Mr. Tabb said the FBI questioned them, and I heard the sister just up and moved away after the Harper kidnapping. Left when the boys finished their Christmas visit. I mean who up and moves right before Christmas?"

"I knew it," Jane muttered under her breath. She'd asked Frank about Mr. Tabb's grandsons, but he had taken a stand and kept the secret. Taken it to his grave. She had let it go not wanting him to lose his job or go to jail for feeding her information. Maybe she should have followed up on her own though. After all, it did sound a little bit suspicious. She shook her head as she stepped inside. What was she thinking? The trial was over now. If the FBI hadn't found anything, there was nothing she could do about it.

Jane plopped down in the back row beside a man from the bank, glad she wouldn't have to stand. The tiered courtroom allowed everyone present a view of the court proceedings. Everybody in town must have come to hear the verdict this morning. When the judge entered, the excitement of the crowd swelled in anticipation after the three-week trial.

The courtroom quieted. William Scent approached the jury for his final argument. His voice rang out in the silent room. "The Commonwealth's case rests entirely upon the testimony of Carolyn Brown under direct questioning on the witness stand," he said. "If you don't believe her, it is your duty to acquit James Taylor Lovan."

Scent went on to point out the inconsistencies in her testimony. How she said one thing to Poole in his interview but something else entirely on the stand. He listed every difference and then when Jane thought he might wind it up, he brought up statements Carolyn made with even more discrepancies.

"We get it!" Jane wanted to yell. She lied.

Jane in no way believed James Lovan to be totally innocent. However, based solely on Carolyn's testimony, she would have to vote to acquit. She didn't think Carolyn the most truthful pebble in the creek.

Jane sighed, glad she wouldn't have to make that decision. This would be a hard one for the jury.

When Scent finally finished, Mr. Lyne stood and took his position in front of the courtroom. Jane sat up straight. How would he rebut an argument with three different testimonies from Carolyn giving such altered views?

Pleasantly surprised, Jane smiled as Lyne listed instead everything Carolyn said that matched with someone else's testimony. Carolyn said this. So and so verified this on the stand. Quite clever. If an overabundance of the witnesses agreed with Carolyn, maybe…"

Judge Fuqua then excused the jury after giving them some final instructions. "Remember, to be convicted of willful murder, one does not have to be the trigger man. Anyone in the group, if there is a conspiracy, is equally guilty. And if there is some doubt, you must have reasonable doubt to clear him, substantial doubt, real doubt."

Jane crossed her legs and waited as one hour stretched into another. How much longer would it take? Not that it mattered. A man's life hung in the balance. It was better if they took their time. Made sure they weren't putting an innocent man behind bars, or worse. It had to be healthier for a guilty man to go free than for an innocent man to go to prison. There were other charges, robbery, assault, and a few others they could get him on later.

When at last the jury filed back into the courtroom, Albert Sisk, the Foreman, handed their verdict to the judge, then read it aloud.

"We the jury, find the defendant not guilty."

Sighs, shrieks of happiness, and laughter filled the front corner where Lovan, his family, and friends gathered. Moans of disappointment were heard from others.

Judge Fuqua gaveled for silence. "This case is dismissed."

Jane let out a breath. In her opinion they had made the right choice. There was no way to be sure, especially with such shaky testimony. She gathered her notes, hoping Eustice and the Harper family would understand. She couldn't imagine what thoughts were circling in their minds. Ones of unfairness, hurt, and sorrow? Who could guess? She prayed they would heal quickly.

Her gaze swept over to where Eustice sat. Poor man had been through so much. Such pain. He'd made the long drive from his farm in Quality to the Christian County Courthouse every day. Waiting for the verdict with his son and daughter-in-law, along with Edgar's remaining children, he'd hoped for the justice that couldn't be found.

So many disappointments. Jane slipped on her coat and walked to her car glad the trial was done. It had been a long three weeks.

Minnie sat at the kitchen table when she entered. Jane grabbed a cup of coffee and sat down across from her.

"Are you going to tell me what happened? Did they find him guilty?"

"No, the jury declared him innocent." Jane took a sip from the steaming cup. "I'm sorry."

Minnie leaned against the kitchen table her spirit depleted. "So, the Harper case is over, and no one has been charged with their kidnapping and murder? That's unbelievable. What am I supposed to tell my readers?" Worry twitched at the side of her face.

"Minnie? You're as white as a ghost. Are you okay?"

"I'm fine." Minnie assured her. "It's just that, well don't you see? Someone got away with murder."

"Minnie." Jane patted her hand. "There are two more people who have been charged with murder. Hopefully both of them will be convicted and the Harper family can get some peace."

Minnie glanced at her sister. "If Lovan didn't get convicted, do you think Almon or Harvey will?"

"No one knows. We'll have to wait until they go to trial."

"My readers aren't going to like this. Not one little bit."

"Your readers will have to understand. You wouldn't want an innocent man to go to prison just so you can tell them what they want to hear. Lovan had his day in court. They found him innocent. So, don't you go starting rumors you can't justify." Jane smiled inwardly. Wasn't this the lecture Minnie used to give her? "They couldn't prove Lovan killed them. And even if he did, there's nothing anyone can do now."

Minnie rose from her chair unconvinced. "This is ridiculous. If Carolyn's testimony was thrown out, then what are they going to use on the other two? Won't it be thrown out again?"

"She probably won't be used at all next time. They wouldn't want to jeopardize the trial."

"I bet they all three go free. It isn't fair. They killed my friends."

A knock at the door brought Jane to her feet. "Hi, Tom. Come on in."

"I saw you in the courtroom. You left too early."

"Too early?"

"Yes, Lovan's attorney asked the judge to drop all the remaining charges against his client. Said it would be double jeopardy if he was tried again on the same thing."

Jane's heart fell to her knees. How could that happen? "You know if he does that, they won't be able to try the other two. Did he agree?"

"They are supposed to meet Monday and talk about it."

"I knew it." A tear made its way down Minnie's cheek.

Tom reached for her and she started to cry. "I'm so sorry, honey. I know you and Ella were close. You've been so brave through all this."

"How can they just let them go?" Minnie sobbed. "It isn't fair. A lot of the witnesses backed up things Carolyn said. Jane told me. All that means nothing?"

"I'm afraid so." Tom held her tight. "The jury didn't feel they proved their case. They had doubt. Serious doubt."

Jane tiptoed out of the room. It had been five years and she didn't realize grief still filled her sister's heart. Jane thought Minnie wanted the case solved for her readers' sakes. Now she knew it wasn't for the readers at all.

Chapter 22

Minnie smiled as she gazed at her children and grandchildren. Having them for Christmas filled her heart with joy. Joy she needed after such a disappointment. The judge had dropped all other charges against Lovan, and now didn't know what to do about Harvey and Almon.

"Mom, I think this is the best jam cake you've ever made," Rachel stated.

"You say that every year, Rachel."

"And I'm right every year." She covered her ears. "Kids, keep it down a little. We can't hear ourselves think."

"Who in the world thinks it's a good idea to give children toys that are so loud?" Ida asked.

Jane grinned sheepishly. "Well, they will be taking them home with them."

"I think Chester may 'accidentally' step through that drum tomorrow," Rachel joked.

"Oh no, Rachel," Minnie chided. "I think David has some real talent. Just move it into the garage. He can find some friends who have instruments and start a band."

"You think all of your grandchildren are gifted," said Chester.

"And what's wrong with that?" Pride shone from Minnie's face.

"Not a thing," Ida said. "Now let's get these dishes done."

All the ladies headed for the kitchen and started putting the food into smaller bowls.

"Looks like we did it again," Minnie laughed. "Forgot the cranberry sauce. I think that makes eight Christmases in a row."

"Does anyone really like the stuff?" Jane asked.

"Oh, I do," Ida said. "It reminds me of Mom standing at the stove and stirring for what seemed like hours. She'd talk about when she was a little girl at Christmas and how sometimes she wouldn't get but a few pieces of candy, some nuts and an orange."

"Is that all, Aunt Ida?" Milo squinted. "That doesn't seem like much."

Ida smiled down at her small great-nephew. "She talked about it like it was everything in the world. She wasn't sad at all. Simple things are often the best."

Rachel grabbed Milo into a big hug. "Why don't you and the other kids go back into the parlor while we get the kitchen cleaned?"

"Okay, Mama."

"You ladies outdid yourselves again this year," Rachel encompassed the sisters in a group hug. "Now, I have to ask, what do you know about the Harper case?"

"Well," Jane began, "they found Lovan not guilty and..."

"Not guilty," Rachel interrupted. "How could he be not guilty?"

"Good lawyers, that's how," said Jane. "They destroyed our main witness and made Lovan look like a saint."

"Are you kidding?" Rachel said. "I thought Riley was good."

"He is. It's just these lawyers were versed in the new updated court system. Our folks aren't. Now that he's been tried, they can't try him again."

"That's not good. So, he just gets to go free?" Rachel asked.

"Yep," Jane nodded. "He can't be tried twice for the same crime."

Minnie interrupted. "Let's get this kitchen cleaned up or it will be midnight before Rachel gets on the road home."

"Now you, Aunt Ida, and Aunt Jane go put your feet up," Rachel ordered. "Sarah, Elizabeth, and I will clean the kitchen."

"You don't have to tell me twice," Jane sighed. "Come on sisters, let's put our feet up." They sat together on the couch with the waning sounds of Christmas swirling around them.

"Pray with me sisters," Minnie said. They clasped hands and bowed heads as Minnie said the words that rested in all their hearts. "Dear Lord, thank you for your many blessings. We pray we always have love for one another. Please ensure that our family has a safe trip home and that we will all be together again soon. Remember all of the sick and those who need your guidance and help our lawmakers bring to justice the people responsible for the deaths of our dear neighbors."

"Amen," they said together.

Chapter 23

October 15, 2017
The Neighborhood
by Jane Clack, Lewisburg, Kentucky

Dear Readers, this is Jane Clack, the younger sister of the originator of this column, Minnie Pryor, who contributed to the *Neighborhood* from 1966 until she passed away in 1987. If my sister was reporting to you, she would have told you by now how much she loved autumn and described the colorful overlay of leaves decorating her lawn. She would give you the local football scores and report the health and news of our Lewisburg neighbors, but this is not a regular *Neighborhood* report.

As most of you are aware, Minnie's weekly column was often dedicated to keeping her readers up to date on the investigation of the Harper/Givens slayings. Minnie had so hoped to inform you the criminals were found guilty and in prison, but that never happened. However, as you probably know from the newspaper stories surrounding the crime, Alfred Finley Harvey, did spend fifteen years in prison in connection with the Harper case. Before the arrests were made, Harvey, who was already serving a life sentence plus twenty years in Eddyville Federal Prison, pled guilty to a lesser charge and named Almon and Lovan as killers and kidnappers. He fingered Carolyn Brown as an eyewitness. Neither Brown nor Harvey was brought to trial. However, when Harvey pled guilty, as was prearranged, fifteen years were added to Harvey's time. He was moved to LaGrange Prison, because court officials believed his life to be in danger from other prisoners at Eddyville who may have been connected to the case.

Kenneth Almon, now deceased, was never tried but was under bail until his bond money was refunded in 1991. James Lovan, also deceased, was acquitted, as Minnie reported in 1970, and Carolyn Hampton Brown was never charged. She is also deceased.

Now, after fifty some years, I have accidentally stumbled on more evidence, and perhaps it is as near a conclusion to this mystery as we shall ever know.

Last week, I attempted to call a friend recovering from a stroke in Creekwood Rehabilitation Center in Russellville. Perhaps the operator accidentally connected me to the wrong room, or maybe providence granted us a long-awaited resolve to our query. A talkative and friendly man answered, and after a few minutes, I regretted to tell him I had the wrong number. He told me he realized that, but he was lonesome and needed to talk. "Sure, gets boring up here in this place," he said.

We both laughed and began to chat. Anyone who knows Jane Clack also knows I never refuse to talk with anyone at any time. We spoke of the weather and the rehab services before I asked him his name and where he lived. Surprisingly, he, James Penrod, lived right here in Lewisburg, on Peach Orchard Road, just past Martin Cemetery. I could not stop my curious self from asking if he remembered the fifty-year-old Harper/Givens murder case.

Of course, he did and related his story.

"Those that were arrested and turned loose would be in prison still, if I'd not been out of the country when the trial took place."

Wide-eyed and almost tongue-tied, I urged him to tell me what he knew.

"I'm the son-in-law of Lewis Forgy and did a lot of things for my living. Delivered lumber to sawmills. Farmed. Drove a semi and took large machinery to a lot of farms. Traveled some with various jobs. About ten in the morning on December 12, 1965, I arrived home with a wide load of farm machinery to put in my barn. As I pulled up and backed it in, a silvery Cadillac and red Mustang came barreling down the narrow, graveled Peach Orchard Road and almost ran into the side of me. I saw Carolyn Brown sitting right in the front between two men. Two other men were driving the Mustang."

I asked how he could be sure it was Carolyn Brown.

Mr. Penrod continued. "Her father had a sawmill down toward Central City—in Greenville. I delivered lumber down there all the time. Recognized that little gal at first glance. She sure looked scared. I've known Carolyn Brown since she was a young 'un. She hadn't changed a lick far as I saw. Just older. Poor kid never had a chance in this world. I reported it to the FBI in Bowling Green as soon as it happened, but I'm guessing they didn't call me to the stand, because I was out of the country in 1970, when the case went to trial. Or maybe I reported what I'd seen after the FBI ceased their investigation. Either way, I never testified in court."

"Oh, my goodness," I clutched my phone. "Did you recognize the men?"

"Sure did. It was the same ones that were accused in the first place. Can't remember the names now, but it was Carolyn Brown for sure. My truck cab sets up high, and I looked right down into the cars. Saw their faces clearly as day because it was light out."

"Are you certain?" I couldn't believe I was hearing this.

"Yeah, I'm certain."

Mr. Penrod could have been on a lot of pain medication for he'd undergone a serious surgery and a stroke. Not that I doubted his integrity, Mr. Penrod appeared to be an honest, law-abiding citizen. However, pain meds can confuse reality with delusion. It's been a lot of years, and I wondered what he'd seen, or how much talk he'd heard since 1965, but his story never wavered.

We chatted for another half-hour and exchanged phone numbers. I liked him, and by now, I believed him, but how could I prove what he said was true? I called him again in three or four days. He reiterated the same story. Only this time, his words struck a bell. The words, "wide load" kept ringing through my head. My private detective years had trained me to listen closely for clues.

I'd hung onto every word of Carolyn Brown's two and one-half-hour testimony, because Mr. Harper and Ella Givens were friends of ours, but fifty years was too long for my memory to retain it all. The Russellville Library let me read their old newspapers, and sure enough, the first paper I found from 1970, *Kentucky New Era*, December 3, 1970, contained a transcript of the trial in Christian County Criminal Court.

Carolyn Hampton, formerly known as Carolyn Brown, told how Lovan, Almon, and Harvey planned to rob Mr. Harper, how they kidnapped him and his daughter, and killed them, leaving the pair near an abandoned cemetery. She related how the men "cussed, slapped, and beat them with an iron pipe" and finally shot them in attempt to force Mr. Harper to tell them how to get into the safe. She also told of fleeing the scene of the crime and meeting a car carrying a "wide load." Wide Load was my ringing bell.

When Mr. Penrod mentioned he was carrying a wide load of farm machinery, I realized why the words stuck in my head. Carolyn's statement varied a little from Penrod's, but they each used the words "carrying a wide load." Plus, both Brown and Penrod said they were traveling Peach Orchard Road, near the old abandoned cemetery that cold dreary morning of December 12, 1965.

The date, the time, the location, and the fact Penrod said he backed into his drive. After they passed the semi, Carolyn said she could see the lights of big truck shining in the rear-view mirror and thought he was following them. This new information James Penrod provided, showed me Carolyn Brown Hampton had told the truth during at least part of her interrogation. Readers, I remind you this girl, Carolyn Brown, was only fifteen at the time of the killing. When the case came to trial, five years later, the defendant's lawyers pled, because of her immoral character and the many discrepancies in her testimony, the now Mrs. Carolyn Brown Hampton's word should not be believed in a court of law. Her testimony was discounted, leaving the prosecution without a case.

I believe if anyone studies the trial records and listens to Penrod's revelation of what happened that morning, they will have to believe the right people were arrested.

As long as one defendant is still alive and living in California, there's still a chance that long-awaited truth might prevail.

The End

Who We Think Did It

From Becky Kelley (aka Jane Clack)

Each of the three writers wanted to present their conclusions about the case after reading all the newspaper accounts, files, transcripts and conducting interviews. The investigators, police, FBI, and prosecutors, did an above average job of trying to solve the crime. The main problem was a lack of evidence. The house was immaculate with no signs of a break in or struggle. Although fingerprints were likely taken in the house, we could find no evidence of them used in the trial. Here are my ideas on the case.

To me, the crime showed an organized plan. They were able to get into the house, get Mr. Harper and Mrs. Givens out, and get away from town very quickly without being seen and positively identified, which leads to the idea that it was someone who would not have aroused suspicion. The killer(s) also seemed to have the disposal place picked out beforehand as the bodies were hidden very well.

Some believed that the bodies lay near the cemetery from December when they were taken and killed, until a funeral was planned for the cemetery in January. I don't believe that to be true. Anyone could have come upon them if they were left out in the open so why would they risk being caught by coming back later to hide the bodies? The spot some believed to be a place where the bodies lay on the ground could have been from deer lying in the brush to get out of the weather.

Perpetrators often choose spots to kill and hide the bodies in places that are familiar to them. Since none of the accused were from the area originally and don't seem to have spent much time there, I believe someone who lived in the town or very close to it, planned the murders.

Coming from today's point of view with the benefit of things like psychological profiling, we can also assume the murderer(s) knew Mr. Harper and Mrs. Givens and that they knew the murderer or they would not have left their house without a struggle. When a person kills someone they know he or she will often cover the person with something. The reasoning is that even though they felt the need to kill them, they also cared for the person and do not want to look at him or her in death. Since the victims were covered up with extra materials; boards, brush, and branches pulled from trees, this could indicate the murderer(s) knew them well.

As for the people indicted, let's take them one by one.

Kenneth D. Almon: Completely innocent. He was in his thirties when the murders took place. People who are going to commit crimes generally start in their teens and the majority have reformed by the age of twenty-five. Mr. Almon had never been in trouble with the law. We couldn't find so much as a traffic ticket. Many times, the paper mentioned he'd never been arrested. I believe he was caught up in the case because of some vendetta Alfred Harvey had against him and his brother-in-law James T. Lovan.

In January of 1966, Harvey had been arrested for robbing a gas station. He accused Lovan and Almon of committing it with him. They were all tried, but only Harvey was found to be guilty.

James T. Lovan: I believe he is not guilty of the murders. Although Mr. Lovan had been arrested and spent time in prison, he'd never committed any crimes against people. He'd broken into storehouses and schoolhouses looking for money and had stolen some hogs to sell, but avoided any type of confrontation when committing crimes. Lovan was also in his thirties at the time of the murders and it would be odd to change the types of crimes he committed. He and Alfred Harvey were in prison together and became friends. It seemed Lovan was trying to remove himself from the friendship and that may be why Lovan ended up accused of the murders.

Lovan's lawyers were able to find the receipt from a business where on December 4th, 1965, Lovan had purchased a 1953 Plymouth for $95. He did not own a Cadillac at the time of the murders.

Alfred Finley Harvey: Not guilty. There is no question he was in jail in Raytown, Missouri and released on December 10, 1965. Phone records showed Harvey called Lovan's home on December 10th. The first time Lovan's father would not accept the collect call, but the second time, Lovan's brother accepted it. Other receipts showed he was still in Missouri on December 11th. He had no car and was trying to get to Kentucky. He asked Lovan to pick him up at the bus station in Evansville, Indiana late on December 11th. Lovan, who is known to be a truthful person, even with his history of robberies, stated he did not go and pick him up.

Harvey mentioned Harper and Givens while being questioned on the gas station robbery in January of 1966. It sounded as if it was an off-hand comment because he thought they were trying to get him to confess to more robberies and other crimes in the area. He said something similar to "If you're going to pin everything on me, why don't you just go ahead and ask me about the Harper disappearance?"

This is all speculation and not to be taken as what did happen, but what could have happened. I believe when Jim Johnson became sheriff, he was looking for any evidence in the files that might point to someone and because Harvey had mentioned the Harper's, Johnson chose to focus on him. By the time of the indictment, Harvey was already in prison for life because of armed robberies and assaults. Johnson could have gone to Harvey and made some type of deal with him. Johnson had some persuasion to make life easier for Harvey in prison by getting him better food, commissary items, or any host of special treatment.

Harvey was eventually released and is still alive at the writing of this book. He lives in California. We found a drunken driving arrest within the past three years, but could find no other arrest records.

There were several accounts of Johnson feeding information about the case to the newspapers and muddying the waters. With so much evidence in the paper, it was much harder to know who was telling the truth.

There is a side story to Jim Johnson that needs to be told. After no one was convicted of the murders, Johnson lost the next election very badly. Harvey pleaded guilty to robbery with intent to harm, which was odd because nothing was taken except some food, but no one was ever charged with murder.

After Johnson left the sheriff's office, he became part owner of a Ford dealership in Elizabethtown, a city south of Louisville, Kentucky. The dealership got into a little financial trouble and there were insurance policies with Johnson and Dusty Rhodes, his partner, collecting money if something happened to the other partner.

Mr. Rhodes had a habit of coming home in the evening and going to the barn to feed horses and spend time there before going to the house. One day in March of 1975, Mr. Rhodes' wife went to the barn to take care of things because Mr. Rhodes could not. There was a bomb attached to the barn door and Mrs. Rhodes was killed. Two men were found who created and planted the bomb and Johnson seemed to be involved. The night before he was going to turn himself in to police, he went into his garage, closed the door, and started the car. He died of carbon monoxide poisoning. It's not much of a stretch to believe a person who would arrange the death of someone they knew, and knew well, would frame someone for the death of someone else.

Carolyn Brown: She was actually a tragic individual, though it doesn't seem like it from newspaper accounts. There's no doubt that she was lying. People did see her close to the place where the bodies were found the day after the disappearance, but does seeing someone in the area mean she was involved in the murder? Could Johnson have fed her information and that's why she was so confused about who did what and when?

According to several sources, she was sexually abused and it was even reported that she was passed around amongst her father's friends. She was married three times by the time she took the stand in 1970 at the age of twenty. Even all of these years later, defense lawyer, Mr. Milliken, said Carolyn Brown was "one of the strangest people I've ever met."

Personally, I don't believe she was involved and only became embroiled in the case because she dated Alfred Harvey. She died at the age of thirty-four.

I spoke to Judge Fuqua, and he went back and forth on who he thought might be involved. He felt Carolyn Brown did have some information that wasn't known to the general public. But he stated: "One thing that always mystified me is why they picked these people. Harvey called from Raytown, Missouri on the night of the murders."

Jesse Riley, assistant prosecutor on the case, believes they had the right people.

So, if it wasn't the three people named, who was it?

Unfortunately, this may never be answered, but I do have a few theories.

Although he'd lived in Quality his entire life, the Mr. Belcher who Mrs. Givens would not let in about three weeks before their disappearance, left town shortly after the bodies were found. He also situated himself in the investigation by suggesting possible suspects, something forensic psychologist have said perpetrators might do. He rented Mr. Harper's farm in Quality after Harper and his wife moved to the house in Lewisburg. Mr. Harper had funded a business venture for Mr. Belcher and Eustice Givens for some cattle, but it didn't work out well. Mr. Harper was angry and vowed he would not put any more money toward similar ventures. Mr. Belcher was known to have a temper and sometimes described acts of violence in which he'd been involved.

I don't believe Eustice Givens was in any way involved. He had three lie detector tests and while the first one was inconclusive, the others showed he was hiding nothing.

The newspaper accounts said other family members were tested and cleared, but they did not say which family members were given the test. About a year before the murders, Ella and her sister Alma had a big fight. Ella felt Alma was not taking proper care of their father and was spending too much money on groceries. Ella kicked out Alma and took over her father's care. Alma's husband said he would never step in the house again and it seemed their relationship was estranged after that. Mr. Harper gave Ella his car and was paying her to take care of him. Anger and greed can be powerful motivators.

One particularly interesting idea that doesn't seem to have been explored much was that maybe the target was not Edgar Harper, but Ella Harper Givens.

Mr. Harper's keys were taken and never found. If he had a key to the bank and someone would have used it to go into the bank that night, they would have found the safe, which was on a timer, left open.

Dewitt Ryan wanted to bring the proceeds from the big basketball game to the bank and put it in the safe rather than leaving it at the school or taking it home with him. He'd left the safe open.

As described in the book, there was a policeman in town, Barney McPherson, who did seem to have a fixation on Ella. He seemed to keep tabs on her and often drove by wherever she happened to be, even turning around in the Harper driveway at night. Stalking was not really recognized back then. If he had a romantic interest in her and she rejected him that could be a reason for killing her. Ella only opened the door for close friends or relatives. What if she opened the door because it was the police?

She was hit about 15 times with enough force that her skull was fractured. She was shot in the heart and the head. It sounds as if she could have been the target.

One last theory has to do with the two Brown brothers who came to town shortly before the murders and left shortly after. Their grandfather, who was represented in the book by the character of Spud at the Christmas party, did tell the FBI that the Brown brothers' father taught them to be criminals. One of them was charged with manslaughter, but wasn't convicted. Another surprising thing about that brother was when he returned to Florida, he reported that all their food was stolen. That is such an odd detail, and it happened at the Harper house too.

The brothers had grown up in Lewisburg, and it was well known that they were criminals. Did someone from the community hire them to kill Harper and Givens?

The car one of them was driving when they came to town was white on the hood, top, and trunk. It was brown on the sides. Could this car have been the one Mr. Forgy saw leaving the Harper house that night? Mr. Forgy told several people he was very scared to testify. Could someone have been threatening him? Mr. Forgy died of a heart attack the night before he was to take the stand.

The $1,000 reward was never claimed. Will it ever be? Do you have information that could help solve this crime?

*****

From Diane Theiler (aka Ida Clack)

It's really hard to pull all the evidence together and sort out exactly what happened in this mystery. In the beginning I really thought the Crouse case was connected and still do, to a certain extent. Leon Brown's place seemed to be the place where riff-raff gathered. He was no angel himself, dealing in moonshine and most likely drugs. He committed his share of crimes, had been in prison, and hung with people who were in trouble with the law.

In Carolyn's testimony, which was not available during the Crouse case, she stated that they went to Leon Browns on the day of the kidnapping and a woman, child, and man were leaving as they came in. She also said later that day they went to the house of the woman, child and man. Could this have been the Crouses? I think it probably was.

We'll never know for sure, but if the Crouse's needed money for drugs, and Harvey needed someone to help with the robbing of the banker, they could have paired up. Maybe they arrived at Leon's to ask him to help. Maybe he didn't want to commit the murder himself so he gave them the name of the couple who owed him a lot of money. That would be a good reason to go see them after they left Leon's. And if they refused, it would be a good reason to kill them because they would know too much.

Police didn't feel the cases were connected. The Crouse's case had to do with drugs. Well, in my world, drugs have to do with money. Criminals rob for the money. They might steal things but usually they sell those things to get money, a lot of times to get drugs. However, as someone else was convicted of that crime, I needed to look elsewhere for my murderer, or did I? Could the people arrested for that murder also be the ones who killed Mr. Harper and his daughter?

I feel if the murderers focused on the Harper's, they needed lots of money. Almon, Harvey, and Lovan were already robbing stores and getting caught. Had already spent time in jail. Why take the risk of going bigger unless they were in trouble? Harvey was, of course. He was wanted in California for Child Support. Maybe the man with the woman and child were in trouble too. Maybe not wanted by law officials but maybe Drug Lords, or blackmailers, or maybe Leon Brown himself. I hear tell there were pictures of Mrs. Crouse with a man at a hotel, but could never find factual proof of that.

I do know the killings were similar to the Harpers, the man shot once and the woman shot in the chest and head. Leon testified that Almon and Lovan asked him to kill Harvey, but he wouldn't. Maybe because he'd known him for a long time, maybe because they were friends, or maybe he just drew the line at murder. However, Leon might've been ok with killing the couple, or having them killed. Harvey being in jail at the time, made him harder to get too and they had more risk of being caught.

My second choice through all of our research was the Brown brothers. We searched high and low for information on the Brown brothers but didn't find much. The story goes like this: Both brothers had been in trouble from an early age and then moved away. They both decided to come back to visit family for Christmas, arriving on December 9, 1965.

Both brothers stopped at the pawn shop on the way because they were broke. The younger brother and his wife pawned some of their belonging. The oldest and his wife took out a loan for $50 against their vehicle.

The oldest brother drove a dark Chevrolet. His brother drove a brown Oldsmobile.

They both worked on their cars Saturday morning and then the oldest disappeared leaving his wife and four children at his sister's house. He claims he spent the afternoon watching movies first at one theater and then at another. This struck me as odd especially since they'd just finished borrowing money. And besides, the sister and his younger brother didn't approve of his Native American wife. Why leave her there to fend for herself?

The other brother and his wife disappeared and weren't seen until the following morning. They claimed they slept in their car somewhere near the house.

The thing that was really odd about this story is that the older brother went home at the end of his visit and then decided to move back to Logan County because his half-brother had broken into their home and stolen all their food. I guess stealing someone's food just sounds weird to me and yet here are two cases where all the food was stolen.

Another strange fact is that the sister and her husband decide to move during this same time: right after the murder. Both quit their jobs and moved with no notice at the end of her brother's visit. The younger brother even helped them move to where her in-laws lived. The FBI interviewed the brothers, but didn't arrest them, so again I went back to the drawing board.

My third and final guess would have to be that the testimony was correct. The testimony of quite a few people matched with Carolyn's story she gave on the stand. Everybody can't be lying, So, I do believe she was there. During Lovan's testimony, I could see where he could have been in the wrong place at the wrong time. They may have seen him as someone who could have been used as a fall guy. I may have stuck with that except he lied too, just like Carolyn had. He claimed he didn't know Carolyn and that they were never together, but other people who knew them both told on the stand how they had been together.

After much deliberation I have to agree that the three arrested were most likely the three that did the crime, but I believe there might have been a fourth. Maybe it was the policeman that followed Ella, Mr. Belcher who moved away, or someone else who knew them well. Someone they would let in the house. Someone they would go with.

Nothing in the house was out of place except the suitcases, which I believe Ella was doing something with (going through her clothes or hiding Christmas presents, etc.). The doors didn't appear to be kicked in. So, I believe they left the house willingly. But how did someone get them to let them in or lure them out? They were such cautious people. Maybe it took the police officer to get them to open the door...maybe Jim Johnson himself.

*****

From Jean Kinsey (aka Minnie Pryor)

As we began to write this book, I placed a notice in the Russellville Forum where I asked for information on the Harper/Givens killings, which led to many responses about hauntings, weird stories, and families defending some of the named suspects, but no real leads until I got a cold, short comeback from a Harvey in California saying, "Alfred Finley Harvey still lives." Earlier, I had traced this man to Fresno, California. It didn't quite feel like a threat, but still gave me chills.

As we were ending the book without a proven closure to the case, I accidentally made the phone call and got a wrong number when James Penrod answered the phone. If you read Jane's column, I conclude everything Penrod said was true, and the three men and Carolyn Brown were guilty. Fictional Jane exposed the real truth. However, it is my belief that one or more people in the Lewisburg area was involved. Whom, we shall probably never know.

Becky Kelley, Author

Becky Kelley has been a freelance writer since 2003 and published in many magazines, newspapers, and anthologies. In addition, she has won several writing competitions and taught English and writing at the college level. *More than Blood Reveals* is her fourth book. She has a self-published children's book *A Tail of Christmas*. Her first non-fiction book, *Wineing Your Way Across Kentucky*, was published by Acclaim Press in April 2015. Her second book with Acclaim, *Wineing Your Way Across Indiana*, was released in 2017.

She'd love to hear any feedback you may have. Contact her at kelleyboo@hotmail.com.

Diane Theiler, Author

Diane Theiler's passion to write gives her hours of pleasure. Whether it be her own books, the articles she creates as content coordinator for the *Bullitt County Neighbors* magazine, web articles, anthologies, or copywriting, she's all in. Imagination is not something she lacks and she enjoys surprising her readers with something different. Check out her books, *Heaven's Bait, A Journey of the Soul*, and *Black Mamba.*

Diane would love to hear from you. She would love to know what you think of her books and what you'd like to see her write about next. You can reach her at: annieban53@gmail.com.

Jean Kinsey, Author

Jean Kinsey lives in Brooks, Kentucky and is known for setting most of her books in Kentucky, her native state. Jean began writing short stories at an early age and began writing inspirational novels as a great-great-grandmother in her seventies. With six published books and one e-book to her credit, Jean has won awards with several stories published in *Chicken Soup for the Soul* and other anthologies, periodicals and newspapers. Two of her novels were finalists in the Inspirational Grace Awards.

Jean serves as Public Relations Director for the Board of Bullitt County Arts Council, plus Chairman of the BCAC Literary Group. She also teaches classes on the basics of novel writing. She writes for the *Bullitt County Neighbors* Magazine.

Jean enjoys hearing from her fans. She can be contact her at kystorywriter@gmail.com

Index

T

W